COVET

Book Two of the Past Life Series

Terri Herman–Ponce

Covet
Copyright 2014 Terri Herman-Ponce
All Rights Reserved

Cover design by Steven Novak

ISBN-13: 978-0-9911017-1-9
eISBN-13: 978-0-9911017-3-3

First Edition: March 2013
Second Edition: May 2014

For Harry and Erik

Acknowledgements

Narelle – you pushed me to write my best and accepted nothing less, and reassured me and buoyed my spirits when I felt ready to give up. There is no one quite like you.

Patti – your encouragement, support, and cheerleading meant everything. Even though what you did may have seemed insignificant to you, it was never insignificant to me.

The Guppies and the wonderful author friends I've made through Sisters in Crime – you are, without a doubt, the smartest and most amazing writers I know. I've learned so much from you and am so lucky to have you on my side.

CR Sisters – you are the support group and lifeline I need, who listened to my venting and who knew how to turn a bad day of writing into a better one.

And last but certainly not least, my dear readers – I do this for you. It brings me no greater joy than to know I've entertained you.

Oh, as a reminder, this is a work of fiction. That means I make stuff up, and sometimes I get things wrong. In the end, however, this is all about enjoyment and I truly hope you enjoy reading this book.

Chapter 1

I'm not a guy who plays games but right now I felt like a knight on a chessboard. Moving strategically but unable to set up for checkmate. It wasn't that my patterns were ineffective. It was that fate had decided to throw an extra playing piece on the board.

"She's going to make a move," Galen said.

I'd seen the woman he was referring to from the corner of my eye, watching me. The problem was, she wasn't my target. I downed my beer and ordered another from the bartender. He was juggling two martinis, some pink girly drink, and a white wine while someone at the other end of the bar whined about being cut off. I momentarily wondered if life as a bartender might be a lot simpler and immediately dismissed the thought. I thrived on excitement. That's why I was here, senses alert, adrenalin pumping, on the edge. Ready. And if it got dangerous…well, I was ready for that, too.

"I'm telling you, Bellotti," Galen said. "She's interested. More than interested."

This was going to be a problem. I took the fresh draft from the bartender, slid him a bunch of Euros, and watched the woman through the reflection in the mirror behind the bar. Not bad but I wasn't interested. I'd already committed to the best. Back home.

"Concentrate on the op," I said, lowering my voice.

The music pounded in the adjoining, jammed dance floor. People boozed it up and snorted stuff I didn't want to know about in dark corners of Istanbul's hottest nightclub.

I buried myself in my beer, keeping true to my cover. "We have a job to do," I told Galen. "No distractions."

We were to surveil a local drug dealer, Zev Sahin. Local for Turkey. Not local for Galen and me. I looked the Italian-American tourist, but Galen—a native Australian—somehow inherited Middle Eastern features. That made moving around the country a little easier. The nightclub was top-grade and the food and drink were covered by PROs, the professional military corporation we worked for, and if everything went as planned, in two days the op would be a wrap and I'd be vacationing back home with the love of my life.

Loud laughter broke out at a nearby table and I used the pulsating lights that illuminated the dance floor to scan the nightclub again. I watched the dealer, careful not to draw attention to myself. He sat on a sofa set back in a dark corner, surrounded by women, beefy bodyguards, and empty bottles of Cristal. And I waited for the lynch pin—the person who was going to set the wheels in motion for the night.

"She's playing with her hair and she's staring at you, Bellotti. I think she's going to make a move soon."

"Wipe that grin off your face or I'll do it for you," I told Galen.

"I'm just waiting for the fireworks." Galen laughed as he picked up his glass. "What line are you going to use this time? You have an arsenal that always seems to piss off women."

"I don't piss them off," I said. "They just aren't used to honesty. Which doesn't say a whole lot for relationships or dating these days, does it?"

Galen shrugged. "I think you're jaded. You walk in with attitude and Armani, turn heads, and then moan about the unwanted attention you get."

I studied the two of us in the mirror, both in designer clothes, both trying to blend in with the upscale crowd. Only Galen didn't have the harshness on his face that I did. People probably looked at me tonight and saw someone who wanted to break a face. In reality, it was exhaustion. I really needed that damned vacation.

"You're making too big a deal out of this," I said.

I was going to say more but stopped when I saw our lynch pin walk into the club. She positioned herself near a granite column off to the side of the dance floor, all long legs, blonde hair, and killer body in a tight blue dress.

Lady in Blue slinked through the crowd, every man's head turning as she moved. Galen stilled and said, "Wow."

"We're a go," I said, setting down the beer. I glanced at Sahin once more through the mirror's reflection.

"Do you think this will work?" Galen asked.

"It has to. If we're to get into Zev Sahin's compound and warehouse, we need that keycard he keeps in his wallet. His weak spot for women will get us that card."

"Poor damned SOB has no idea what's coming," Galen said as Lady in Blue moved in. Then he sighed, had a little more of the vodka he'd been nursing, and shrugged it off. "You realize that this will be the easy part compared to getting him to turn."

"That's not our problem," I reminded him, staring him down. Galen knew it was all about the rest of our team, the

DEA, and the U.S. Government. All we had to do was get the card after the wallet was lifted and make the drop, and then the rest of our guys would get into the warehouse and take it down. After that, we stepped out of the picture.

And my vacation with Lottie began. With brisk walks on the beach, huddling in a warm blanket, and relaxing with a bottle of red. I shook my head. Who the hell was I kidding? I intended to keep Lottie in bed for a whole week.

"Do you think it will be that easy?" Galen asked.

I grinned, knowing Lottie wanted that week in bed, too. "Damned straight."

"I hope you're right."

I realized Galen was talking about the op and that I'd let my mind wander. Not good. In this business, distraction led to death.

"She's moving in, Bellotti," Galen said.

Lady in Blue strode toward Sahin, bending over to adjust the strap on her high-heeled shoe, giving him enough bare leg and bare breast to catch his attention. It worked. Sahin smiled at her and beckoned her over with a bottle of Cristal. She cocked her head, giving him just enough coy to reel him in.

A warm body brushed against my arm. I ignored it, watching the way Lady in Blue moved and keeping Sahin just inside my field of vision. A hand settled on my bicep and squeezed. It was the woman who had been trying to get my interest.

"Hi," she said, a smile on her face and in her voice.

"Hi," I said, not smiling at all.

"My name is Yvette." She was decked out in red hair and red dress, and was now officially baggage. "Mind if I join you?" She pulled up a spare barstool between Galen and me.

Past Yvette, Lady in Blue nuzzled onto Sahin's lap. Sahin snagged a waitress, said something to her, and stuffed a wad of Euros down her cleavage. She strutted away, happy with the fat tip.

Yvette snuggled onto the barstool, blocking my view.

"Yvette," I said firmly, "I'm not looking for company."

"Oh." She seemed put off at first but quickly recovered. I got the feeling I'd just become a challenge and she leaned in closer. C-cups, pressed hard against my arm.

That gave me a clear view of the action again. Lady in Blue slipped her arms around Sahin, slid off his jacket, and ran her hands over his chest and stomach. Good. All she had to do next was distract him the way only a woman like her could, snatch the wallet, and pretend to break outside for a smoke, where I'd meet her to make the exchange.

"You're the hottest guy in here," Yvette said, leaning in and giving me a clear view of a nicely filled red and black bra. "You alone?"

Galen tapped the bar to get my attention and flicked his eyes to a position behind him. His six o'clock.

My gaze slid past Yvette's other shoulder. Another woman, dressed in a black pantsuit, stood at the entrance to the dance floor where Lady in Blue had been earlier. Only this woman's body language said she was ready to kill, and I immediately knew who the victim would be.

It was Sahin's wife. I looked back at Yvette. "I saw you making the moves on that Navy guy over there," and I jerked my head to where he sat with a bunch of his friends.

She looked at him then looked back at me. "I'm not

interested in him."

"Yeah." I grinned. "But I am."

Yvette's mouth opened and stayed that way.

"Should we move in?" Galen asked.

Yvette shoved away, probably thinking Galen was talking about the Navy guy.

I watched Sahin's wife weave through the crowd to her husband, whose head was buried in Lady in Blue's breasts. One of his bodyguards saw the wife coming and tapped Sahin's shoulder. Sahin ignored him.

Sahin's wife stood, hands on hips, staring down at her husband. Then, without warning, she picked up a bottle of Cristal and slammed it on the table and started screaming. She took another and smashed it on the floor, then another. The loud *pops* startled the crowd, someone yelled "she's got a gun!" and the place went berserk. People scrambled to get out, shoving off the dance floor, jamming into the doorways, and screaming for safety. Bouncers pushed against the tide of patrons, yelling for them to calm down, and rounding them up like cattle.

Sahin barked at his wife in Turkish. His wife lunged for Lady in Blue and swung at her with another bottle. Lady in Blue dodged the attack, a foot slid out from under her, and she went down, her head clipping the coffee table. She didn't move.

"Watch my back," I told Galen.

"I'll go after Blue," he said. "You get that wallet."

I nodded and took off.

Sahin argued with his wife, surrounded by the bodyguards. I moved in fast, knowing I had one shot at this. Screw it up and

I blew my cover. Succeed and I still had a career. I strode toward the group of them, eyes on Lady in Blue but my mind on that wallet. One of the bodyguards slammed a hand to my chest, stopping me. He said something in Turkish that I didn't understand, but I got the message. I wasn't getting any closer.

"She's hurt," I said, pointing a finger to our spook on the floor. "She needs help."

I made to move in again but the guy put a gun to my head. I stared at him, calm on the outside, heart pounding within. I held my hands up in surrender. No need to piss him off. Let him think he had me. I just needed another plan.

Galen was one step ahead of me. He muscled his way in to Lady in Blue, distracting the bodyguards. The gun that was on me swung to Galen. I grabbed Sahin's jacket, swiped the wallet, and threw the jacket back on the chair. I kept going, not breaking stride, slipping the wallet into my pocket. I didn't look back.

I was almost at the door when a gun fired, followed by a heavily accented shout. "Stop him! Stop him!"

I blew out the entrance and took off, hustling through the panicked crowd. Another gun fired and police sirens sounded in the distance. I made a left down a small street then a right into an alley, jumping a garbage can, hurtling over a short wall, and disappearing into the neighborhood. If Galen didn't make it to our backup rendezvous point, I had to get to the safe house and that was five miles away. And right now, I had no idea if Galen and Lady in Blue were still alive.

I skidded past a corner, wondering if I should take the chance and call an alert into HQ, when I heard screeching tires. I backed up, pressed myself against a wall, and realized who it was. Galen in a Toyota. He threw open the passenger door and I jumped in, slamming the door shut as Galen jammed the gas pedal.

"You get it?" he asked, swerving through a turn then dropping our speed so we didn't draw attention.

I nodded. "Is Lady in Blue okay?"

Galen hugged another turn. "She will be. She came to when the gunshots were fired."

I blew out a sigh of relief. It wasn't the first time a distraction job had taken a bad turn, but it was still a worry. "And the cops?"

"All at the nightclub. But we will have to lose the car." He used his cell phone and dialed our contact, making arrangements for cleanup.

I pulled out Sahin's wallet and lifted the keycard. "Payday," I said, holding it up.

"Mommie Dearest says we should leave the wallet and card with the car." Galen disconnected the call. "They will pick it all up at the Starbucks near the safe house in ten minutes."

I drew in a breath and held it, forcing my heart and my lungs to calm down. Another close call. I loved this shit.

"You love this shit *way too much*," Galen said, glancing my way.

I had known Galen all of three months, and he was far too good at reading my mind already. I was trying to get my head wrapped around the fact that we were connected in a way that didn't make sense, but that didn't mean I had to like it. Ignoring him, I sank into the seat, letting the adrenalin wear off.

"Let's see what else we've got on this guy." Inside his wallet I found a black American Express, a MasterCard, and over five thousand Euros in the billfold. A picture was tucked in with his identification. I pulled it out and held it up to catch the light from passing street lamps.

It was a photo of the love of my life kissing another man.

Chapter 2

To Dr. Lottie Morgan, hindsight wasn't twenty-twenty. It was a curse.

Sure, she knew to be more positive about recent life lessons that led to her to that conclusion, but that was hard to do when you were sitting in your Jeep in the office parking lot, ready to go into work, while dozens of people stood outside the front door waiting to meet you. Or ask for an autograph.

If it had been a one-time incident it wouldn't have been a big deal, but the crowding turned into a regular occurrence, an expectation even. Every morning Lottie ate breakfast, prepared for work, and hoped the day would turn out differently. It never did. And she only had herself to blame. Well, she could blame fate, too, but her life now was the direct result of a decision made several months ago and as much as she wanted to place blame elsewhere, Lottie couldn't. Her decisions and their consequences belonged to her, and they didn't excuse her from her clients or her job.

With a resigned sigh, she cut the engine, locked the Jeep, and strode toward the door. Halfway to Amrose Counseling Center, the crowd overwhelmed her. Head down, Lottie shoved through the group and plunged through the front door, knowing she'd been rude but also knowing she had no other choice. She wasn't a celebrity, only a psychologist trying to help others find their way through life much like she'd found hers.

Some of the bystanders spilled into the building after her, converging on the reception area like sand pouring from a beach pail. Alicia, Amrose's smart-dressed and middle-aged receptionist, jumped from her desk and rushed to Lottie's side, threatening to call the police if the bystanders didn't vacate the premises. The group hesitated and Alicia barked at them again, and when the last visitor loped back outside into the chilly October air, Lottie turned to Alicia and offered her thanks.

Alicia sent a soft smile and returned to her desk.

Someone coughed and Lottie noticed a full waiting room; people who wanted emotional guidance and mental help and who deserved a safe haven that Lottie once again disrupted. Feeling more than guilty and every bit the troublemaker, she strode toward the hall and her office at the end, hoping to leave the bad energy behind. Once inside, she powered up her computer, opened the window a couple of inches, and checked her watch.

Twelve more hours, she reminded herself. Just twelve more hours until David got home and they started vacation. She closed her eyes and let her mind wander to walks on the beach with a bottle of red and a warm blanket, a much-needed respite from the craziness waiting outside the front door. Oh hell, who was she kidding? She intended to keep David in bed for a whole week.

"Just twelve more hours," she said out loud.

But the mantra wasn't going to make the time pass any faster, and counting minutes would only drive her crazy. To get her mind on other things, she launched her schedule and checked her appointments. The calendar showed a new client in ten minutes followed by two regulars, lunch, and two more new ones in the afternoon. A full day but not an unmanageable one.

A knock on the door disrupted her focus. She looked up and found Stuart Hanley, the director of Amrose Counseling Center, standing at the threshold. He strode in and settled into one of the two chairs facing her desk, his large-framed glasses and plaid shirt reminding Lottie of one of her psych professors back in college. He tipped the glasses up his nose and settled Lottie with an incisive, brown-eyed gaze.

"This is becoming a habit," he said, and Lottie knew better than to ask what he meant. They'd been having the same conversation for more than a month, and each time Stuart resurrected it, she responded with the same answer.

"I'm sorry, Stuart," Lottie said. "If I had known the interview in *Current Psychology* would have caused all of this publicity, I never would have done it."

"Our clients expect refuge, Lottie, not a circus."

"Some of those people outside are potential clients," she reminded him. "They're looking for help they can't get elsewhere."

"Because you took a trip to the dark side and invited them in." Stuart shook his head, his dissatisfaction evident in the firm set of his mouth. "Seriously, Lottie, what were you thinking?"

She stifled a sigh. If she explained this once, she explained it too often, and explaining it again wasn't going to make any difference. Still, she needed to try.

"Past life regression is a fact, Stuart. It happened to me three months ago, just as it's happened to many others over the millennia, and people need to know about it. You know that's why I did the interview with the magazine."

"Past life regression is entertainment for movies and books," he fired back. "It has no basis in reality and no place in this Center."

"Then how do you explain the documented cases in perceptual studies, Stuart?"

"Those cases are rigged for publicity—"

"Many are children," Lottie said. "Five- and six-year olds who remembered facts of previous eras and lives. Details that no one else knew about until people started digging and making connections."

Stuart sent her a long, disbelieving look.

"Did you see the article in *NatGeo*?" Lottie asked. "An archaeologist in Egypt discovered a thirty-five-hundred-year-old burial tomb with a story that corroborated the memories I started remembering back in July."

Stuart held up a hand. "I am not here to discuss the article, Lottie."

His demand didn't stop her. "There are other people who are experiencing what I experienced and who need guidance. The article was my way of letting them know they're not alone and that their situations should be addressed and taken seriously."

"Regression therapy I agree with," Stuart said. "Not some bizarre dissertation about a life you lived in ancient Egypt thousands of years ago. Do you even realize how that sounds?"

"Open minds are more conducive to change," Lottie said, even though she knew the words wouldn't shift his perception. People believed what they wanted to believe, even when what they believed wasn't based on complete knowledge or entire truth.

Taking his silence as encouragement, Lottie went on. "Do you realize that my client roster grew by almost thirty percent in the past month since the piece ran in *Current Psychology*?"

Stuart folded his arms over his chest. "How many of those new clients want regression therapy, Lottie?"

"Almost half."

"How many of them are nutcases?"

"Stuart, please don't call them nutcases—"

"How many?"

Lottie folded her arms over her chest, mirroring his defiance. "I'm not answering that question because it's demeaning. You see the office stats. You can figure out my client representation without my help."

"I asked you to seek therapy of your own. Have you done it yet?"

"Stuart—"

"Have you?"

Lottie suppressed a sigh. "No, because it's not necessary."

Stuart leaned forward, challenging her. "According to who?"

"You think that I'm dealing with issues, and I understand that—"

"I think you're not always operating in reality and that you need help. Go get it." The alarm sounded on Lottie's computer, signaling her first appointment. "I want you to find a reputable psychiatrist who will help you through this or I will choose one for you." Stuart stood up and stared her down. "I also want you to clean out your client list and focus only on those people who need help. *Real* help. It's now mid-October, and I want both accomplished by the end of the month."

"I'm on vacation for two weeks after today."

"Then figure out how to do this while you're on vacation."

Lottie stared back at him, meeting his challenge. "And if that doesn't happen?"

"Consider October thirty-first your last day at Amrose."

"Closed minds won't help this practice, Stuart."

"And quackery will destroy it."

Lottie pressed her lips together, the curse of her decision to do the interview once again rearing its ugly head. This was something that should have been simple. She'd been meeting so many people who craved acceptance because they were being dismissed the way Lottie was being dismissed now. And it gave Lottie a better understanding of why prophets and so-called witches were treated as dangerous and often killed. People were afraid of what they didn't understand.

A young girl in a gray baseball cap, pink and gray shirt, and blue jeans rapped on the door. "Who's Dr. Morgan?" she asked.

Lottie stood and looked past Stuart, erasing the impatience and dissatisfaction from her face. "That would be me," she said.

"Excellent." The girl barreled inside and headed toward Lottie. "Can I have your autograph before we start my therapy?"

Stuart caught Lottie's gaze and gave her a stern look just before he left. "By the end of October," he warned.

The girl shoved a piece of paper and a pen at Lottie. Lottie ignored her, walked to the door and looked down the hall, trying to locate either a mother or father and finding no one.

The girl followed and shoved the paper and pen at Lottie again. "For a psychiatrist, you're not a very good listener."

"I'm a psychologist."

Lottie looked down at the girl, took the paper and pen, and placed them on a nearby bookshelf. When she turned back, the girl was thumbing through an issue of *Current Psychology*.

"And that's precisely the point," Lottie said, watching the girl drop the magazine onto the coffee table and move to the sofa where she flopped down, watching Lottie from beneath her cap's brim. "I'm a psychologist not a psychiatrist, and I'm also not a celebrity. Are you Monica?" Lottie added, trying to find out if the girl was her nine o'clock appointment and if someone had made a mistake when they pulled together her profile. Lottie was expecting someone older.

"No. I am," someone else said.

Lottie turned to a woman standing at the doorway. She was short-haired, square-jawed, and olive skinned, and looked as if she had just walked off a Mediterranean photo shoot in a billowy pink blouse and tight jeans. Her eyes were as striking and as brown as her pixie cut, her body fit and tanned, and if Lottie didn't have a file that specified her as forty-five, she would have pegged her for a dozen years younger instead.

Lottie welcomed Monica inside, and Monica turned on the young girl.

"What have you been up to?" Monica asked with a dark eyebrow arched in warning.

The girl's equally dark brow rose with rebelliousness. "I wanted Dr. Morgan's autograph. Is that a problem?"

"Yes, because it's rude." Monica sent Lottie a sideways

glance. "Sorry about that, Dr. Morgan. Ada's smart for an eleven-year old, but she's also impatient. Ever since she's seen your article in *Current Psychology*, you're all she's been talking about."

Lottie looked from Monica to Ada and couldn't rein in her surprise. "Ada reads *Current Psychology*?"

"I also read about the find in Egypt in *NatGeo*." Ada jumped to her feet, came over, and stared up at Lottie, wide-eyed and eager. "Was that really your mummy that they discovered in that dig they did back in July? Was that really all your gold? And was that man buried with you really your lover?"

"Ada!" Monica snapped.

"I only want to know." Ada rolled her eyes. "Come on, Mom. You're always saying how we gotta find the truth in life, and Dr. Morgan's one of us so it's gotta be okay."

"That's enough already." Monica grasped Ada by the arm and escorted her to the door. "Go to the waiting room. I'll be out when I'm done here."

"But Mom—"

"Go!"

Ada made a face and muttered colorful thoughts that were just loud enough to hear, then followed Monica's pointed finger to the reception area. Once she was gone, Monica looked at Lottie with obvious apology.

"Children," she said with a quirked smile that revealed teeth as white as the whitest paper. "A parent's blessing and curse."

Lottie nodded, having heard that wisdom hundreds of times before, and motioned toward the sofa. "How about taking a seat so we can both be more comfortable when we talk?"

"Oh, I'm not here for the entire session," Monica said. "In fact, I'm here for you not me."

"Pardon?"

Monica dug into her Fendi, pulled out a business card, and handed it to Lottie. Only a phone number appeared on it.

"What is this?" Lottie asked.

Monica rested a warm hand on Lottie's shoulder. "There is a group of us who are just like you," she said. "Those who experienced regressions just like you did, who remembered and relived details of past lives, and who've spoken about it and now face persecution as a result. We meet regularly and we want you to join us."

"Meet for what?"

Monica's smile widened. "Whatever it is you will need."

"I don't understand."

Monica patted Lottie's arm. "You will, once you leave this counseling center behind you and move on to what you're really meant to do with your life."

Chapter 3

I sat in my SUV in my driveway, staring at the ass end of my mom's Mercedes and wondering what I'd done to deserve the penance after a long trip back from Turkey.

Mom was great but we had a strange relationship. It was supportive and open, but it sometimes bordered on the bizarre. Back in the sixties, Mom went to Woodstock. She never returned. Still dressed like she was there, too. And she took a lot of what she experienced that weekend and incorporated it into her subsequent career as a sex therapist, using any opportunity to offer advice. Alone, in front of my friends, near strangers, it didn't matter. That made for lots of awkward moments and too many memories I'd rather repress, and if it weren't for her genuinely good heart, I probably would have gone into therapy a long time ago.

I edged past the Mercedes and pulled into the garage, knowing this would go down one of two ways. Either she and Lottie were deep into a bottle of wine and sharing too much information about me, or they were commiserating about life as therapists and sharing too much information about me.

Either way I was screwed.

I killed the engine, grabbed my duffel bag, and hefted it into the laundry room just off the garage door. I dropped it on the floor, opened the door to the kitchen, and halted, preparing for the onslaught. I heard Lottie laugh, my mother said my name and something I couldn't understand, and Lottie laughed even louder. I sighed.

Yep. Definitely screwed.

I sucked it up, walked past the kitchen, through the foyer, and into the living room, and found Lottie and my mother talking in the adjoining turret. Their conversation died as soon as I entered the small room. Lottie's dark eyes met mine, something decadent stirred in her gaze, and every thought flew out of my head. When she licked the red wine from her lips and stood up, giving me a good look at a black dress that left nothing and everything to my imagination, all the blood left my brain, too. I grabbed Lottie and kissed her in a way that promised a hell of a lot more. Then I looked at my mother, hoping she would leave.

"Welcome home, David," Lottie said.

Here's the thing about Lottie. She knows how to purr and she knows exactly when to do it, and her voice had the purr in it now. She smiled up at me, all daring and innuendo, and I would have kissed her again, but my mother joined in for a group hug, killing the moment and the mood.

I gave Mom a peck on the cheek and pasted on a smile that fell somewhere between *I'm trying to be a good son* and *Please go now*.

"You're not looking too good, David," my mother said, reaching up and squeezing my cheeks. "You look exhausted. Dark circles under your eyes. Unshaven. When was the last time you slept?"

"On the flight and it's nice to see you, too." I tried disengaging from the threesome but my mother grabbed on harder.

"You didn't call, Bubbala, and you always call," she said, scrutinizing me from beneath wild hair that was blonde and white and silver. "Did something happen while you were away?"

"No."

I stepped away, took the wine glass from Lottie's hand, and drank. Lottie licked her lips while she watched, and the temperature in the room jacked up ten degrees.

"Was the op a success? Did your debrief go well?" Mom turned to Lottie and smiled with pride. "See? I'm getting the lingo."

"Yes." Lottie nodded and laughed. "I can see that."

"The op went fine," I told Mom, and I searched for the wine bottle so I could drink more but couldn't find it.

"You don't look fine, David."

"I'm okay. No need to worry about me."

"I worry about you because it's my job." She smiled but I knew it was only to hide the concern. She grabbed my cheeks again and studied me with narrowed eyes. "You're hiding something. I can see it in your aura. What's wrong?"

Thirty years old and she still saw through me. And maybe that was the point. Mom had all those years of experience in being a mother, and she'd once mentioned that when you became a parent you never stopped being one. Every time I returned from an op, I got a reminder of that.

My mind drifted to the wallet in my jeans pocket and the photo of Lottie and the other man. "Nothing's wrong."

Lottie cocked her head, seeing right through the lie.

"Really." Mom frowned. "What happened? From the looks

of it, this one was bad."

I battled the image of the photo and what it meant and tacked on more denial. I hated doing it, but I just wasn't in the mood. "I'm tired. That's all."

She let that stand for a while, maybe thinking I'd change my mind and confess all. I didn't. I wasn't hard-wired that way.

Mom glanced at Lottie. "Don't expect much from him tonight, Jelly Bean. A man's performance can be affected by fatigue, and this one," she said, jerking a finger my way, "still hasn't learned his lessons. Just like his father. Always trying to do too much. I remember when his father came home once after working twenty hours straight at the restaurant. Passed out in bed while trying to untie his shoelaces."

I rolled my eyes, finished the wine, and searched for the bottle again, still unable to find it. Lottie picked it up off the tile floor near her chair. "Rita wanted to be here when you came home," she said, refilling my glass. "Wasn't that nice of her, David?"

"Very."

Mom lifted her glass in salute. "What can I say? I love you guys. Lottie's my Jelly Bean and you're my Bubbala, and I couldn't think of anything better to do tonight than to be here and celebrate your safe return."

"Perhaps stay home with Dad?" I offered with hope.

She waved the idea off with a hand. "Nah. I'm writing a new book, *Thirty-Three Things to Do with a Naked Man*, and tried number twelve with him a couple of hours ago. He fell asleep, but I got my second wind and so I came over."

Lottie leaned in closer, lowered her voice, and peered up at me. "Want to know what number twelve is?"

Her cheeks were flushed and the purr was back, and when her breasts brushed against my arm I lost focus of the conversation.

Mom resurrected it for me. "It's an amazing position," she said. "I think I'm going to bring it up during my couples' therapy class tomorrow. It's where the woman stands behind the man and strokes him like he'd stroke himself but with—"

"I got the picture," I said.

Mom folded her arms over her chest and looked at me with a new level of concern. "You were never like this, David. We used to be able to talk about everything."

"Actually, *you* talk about everything—"

"It's the fatigue, Rita," Lottie said, sending me a chastising look that said I should have known better and kept my mouth shut. "You'll have to forgive David's impatience. He gets cranky when he doesn't get enough sleep."

Put a neon flashing light in front of my mother that says *Stop* and she'd keep going. She didn't do well with subtle. The word wasn't in her vocabulary. But she understood back-door tactics and that made her switch gears now.

"So what kind of op did you command this time?" she asked. "Did you kill anyone?"

"No."

"Did you catch any bad guys?"

"Yeah."

"Did they carry guns?"

"Yeah."

"Did you take pictures? Will I see you on the news?"

"No and no."

Something in her expression looked sad when I answered,

like maybe she shouldn't have asked the questions to begin with. But she was trying to engage with her son, and I appreciated that, but the effort had backfired.

She sighed and shook her head. "Such a dangerous job." She started pacing around the circular room, bothered that her son lived the way he did and that there was nothing she could do to protect him anymore. "I think I need to bake some brownies."

Mom wasn't referring to the kind kids ate as a snack.

"Good idea," I said, putting down my empty glass, picking up Mom's handbag, and taking her by the arm. "Go make brownies because, as much as I'd love to talk about my job, I think it's time to call it a night."

She looked at the wine left in her own glass, nodded, and downed what was left. "You want me to drop off brownies for you tomorrow?"

I shook my head. "Not necessary."

She looked inside her glass as if hoping it would suddenly refill itself. "Then at least promise me you'll be safe and be careful." She looked at me with eyes that saw too much, and my heart ached over how much she worried.

I kissed her cheek and handed over her bag. "I promise."

Mom held on as I escorted her to the foyer and the front door, and I kissed her cheek one more time. "Thanks for spending time with Lottie tonight."

"I know how much you love it," she said with a smile that brightened her face and warmed my heart. "Dinner on Sunday at our house?"

I nodded. "Wouldn't miss it."

"We'll be there at three," Lottie added.

Mom waved at Lottie and blew a kiss. "Take care of him, Jelly Bean. And while you're at it, try number twelve. It'll knock David's socks off." She winked and hesitated again, but whatever was on her mind remained unspoken and left with her the moment she walked outside.

I closed the door behind her and rested my head against the doorframe, wondering what bothered me more. Mom's constant reminders about how I could improve my sex life or her overwhelming need to try and protect me.

"David?"

There was a tease in Lottie's voice that snagged my attention, and I turned to find the black dress crumpled on the stairs and Lottie on the second floor landing wearing only a black lace bra, thong, and heels.

I pulled back and admired the view. "New?"

"Bought it just for you," she said, pursing her mouth into a teasing kiss.

It had been three weeks since I had Lottie. And sex. And I wanted those lips *everywhere*.

Lottie unfastened the bra, gazed at me over her shoulder, and tossed it over the railing. The bra landed on the floor at my feet.

"I'm up for number twelve if you are," she called out as she headed down the hall to our bedroom.

"Leave the shoes on," I said, running up the stairs after her, the photo and my Mom long forgotten.

Chapter 4

A rustling magazine woke me up.

I felt like I'd run a full marathon and blamed jet lag and too many nights with too little sleep in Turkey for my exhaustion—though Lottie had done a solid job of finishing me off last night. If I could have spent another day doing nothing but sleeping I'd have done it, but the magazine rustled again and curiosity got the better of me.

I rolled over, grunting through sore muscles and a foggy brain, and found Lottie propped up against a pillow, reading. Her hair hung loose, making her look like a raven-haired Rapunzel. Her black eyes were narrowed and focused, and her mouth moved every now and then when she read. I remembered the things that mouth did last night, felt all my blood rush south, then remembered the image of that mouth planted on another man.

"Something on your mind?" Lottie asked.

My gaze slid up, met hers, and held.

"You let out a really loud sigh," she said in answer to my unasked question. After placing the magazine on the nightstand, she focused on me. "Sleep well?"

"Not enough."

She ran fingers through my hair and studied me like she was looking for something deeper. Then she frowned and sank into her pillow so we were at eye level.

"What's wrong, David? Your mom was right last night. Something's on your mind. I can tell."

"Later."

I didn't want to spoil the morning after even though I'd already done enough damage. If I had my head on straight, I'd have hit Lottie up about the photo last night and not tumbled into bed with her. But I had my priorities at the time.

Lottie rolled on top and straddled me, misinterpreting my meaning. "I like *later*," she said, pressing her warm lips against mine. A warm, woodsy scent that was distinctively hers and that always made me weak in the knees fired up my blood. "What do you want to do for our first day of vacation? Throw on some sweatshirts and go for a walk on the beach?" Her mouth worked over my chest. "Head up to that bed and breakfast we found in Massachusetts?" Her tongue made its way past my stomach and kept going. "Stay right where we are and see where this bed takes us?" She pushed the sheet from my thighs and moved in on her goal.

I grabbed her by the arm and stopped her.

Her head came up. "What's wrong?"

The damned photo.

This is what happens when you let yourself slide into denial. You always pay the price for it later.

I tapped Lottie's arm, signaling for her to get off, and searched for my jeans. I found them ditched outside the bedroom door and tugged out my wallet and the photo inside it. When I handed the picture to her, Lottie stopped breathing.

"Wow." Her faced worked through a bunch of emotions, none of which stayed put for long. Confusion. Surprise. Anger.

Distress.

"Where did you get this?" she asked.

"I think the more important question is, who's the guy that you're with?"

Lottie looked up at me, all expression now shut down and neatly packed away. The psychologist in her was back in play. "Are you jealous?"

"No."

Her eyebrow rose.

"Okay. Maybe a little." I sat beside her. "So who is he?" I rested my head on her shoulder, peering over so I could examine the picture with her. The warm, woodsy scent intensified and I inhaled, drawing in as much of Lottie as I could.

"Jared. He's a friend of my brother's. Or was, anyway." She traced his features with a finger, like she was conjuring up a memory. "I met him at a party last winter when you were in London, commanding an op. The guys were all pumped up with beer and vodka and they dared Jared into kissing me, and he did. I guess someone snapped a shot and I never knew about it." She handed back the picture. "How did you get your hands on it?"

She sounded detached and I didn't know what to make of it. I studied the image more closely, trying to find details I didn't see before. There wasn't much else to see. "Found it in Istanbul," I said, but I didn't offer more. The op, and Sahin in particular, were details I couldn't share.

"That's an incredible trip for a photo to make from Long Island all the way to Istanbul, don't you think?"

Not to mention into the wallet of a drug lord.

Something about the photo didn't sit well with me. It wasn't so much that Lottie was kissing another guy, though that tugged at my ego some. It was more that it felt off. Just like Lottie's mood.

"You're not telling me something," I said.

Lottie rubbed her hands over her thighs. "I met Jared once, at that party. And even though I haven't thought about him since then, I haven't forgotten about him. He was…an unusual person."

"How?"

She thought about it. "You know how it is when you meet someone and something doesn't feel right about them? Like you're looking at still water, but just beneath the surface you know something else is there? That's what I thought about Jared."

"Did he behave inappropriately?"

"Other than the kiss? No. It was just a sensation I had. Not based on anything clinical. Just…a feeling."

I leaned in and kissed the heart-shaped birthmark on Lottie's shoulder.

"So what are you going to do with the photo?"

I returned to my jeans and stuffed it back inside the wallet. "I'd rather hold on to it for now."

"Why? What happened in Istanbul that you can't give it up?"

"Nothing serious," I said, sitting beside her again.

"But something serious enough," she said, and there was an edge to her voice that made me pause. I'd already said far too much and way too little, and the tension in her shoulders showed that it bothered her more than she was letting on.

"We have two weeks." I slid under the bedding and pulled Lottie in. I'd missed her like hell. The way she felt pressed against me, the way she whispered my name when we were in bed, the way she moaned when I made her climax. And I wanted to make up for all of it. "No talk about work for fourteen days, okay?" I said. "No calls, no reports, no complaining. Deal?"

"Like you'd really honor that deal."

"I always try."

"And always fail." Lottie threw a leg over mine, snuggled in closer, and traced her fingertips over my chest. "I really hate this, David. We talk about everything and work is the one thing you and I don't share."

In her case it was because of privacy issues and client privilege. In mine, it was because of security clearances and confidentiality agreements. "I know. But it's complicated, Lottie."

"Isn't it always?"

Neither of us said anything after that because there was no point. No matter how long we'd been facing this issue, it never sat well between us. Three years ago, Lottie and I separated. It was bad and it was because of lies, and when we reconciled we promised to never withhold anything from each other again. Except for this.

I closed my eyes, shifting my thoughts to the bed and breakfast in Massachusetts. Lottie and I had a really good time when we were there, but I wasn't sure I wanted to make the trip. Twelve hours there and back meant twelve hours less I'd have Lottie naked and next to me. It wasn't a concession I wanted to make.

Lottie's fingers moved to my stomach, caressing me out of my thoughts.

"I know we're not supposed to talk about work," she said, "but you need to know that Stuart's after me again." She told me that she had until the end of the month to clean up her patient roster because he wasn't happy with the caliber of people she'd been bringing into Amrose lately. She seemed annoyed when she spoke, but a part of her seemed relieved, too. We'd talked about her starting up her own practice before, and I wondered if she was reconsidering.

She shifted against me and my tired body stirred. "You seem surprised he asked you to do this," I said. I moved her on top of me and pushed the hair from her face so I could look into those beautiful, dark eyes.

"I know he's the director, but he has no right, David." Lottie straddled me and sat up. "Amrose is booming with new patients, primarily because of me, so he shouldn't complain. He's always kept a close watch on the bottom line, and I don't understand why this is an issue for him."

I had my suspicions. We'd been down this road recently as well. "Have you seen a therapist yet, like he asked?"

Lottie looked away. "No."

"Why?"

"Not this again, David." Lottie pushed off, strode to the dresser, grabbed a tee and sweatpants, and tugged them on. I hitched myself up on my elbows and watched her, disappointed she was getting dressed and hiding the view. "You experienced what I did, David, or at least some of it. You know that past lives are real and that you and I lived one. Together. I don't understand why you keep pushing the psychiatrist angle on me, too."

We'd been having this conversation since July. It was entertaining, in a way, watching Lottie get all fired up over the past life stuff. I thought she'd taken it too far when she did the magazine interview but was happy for her when the *NatGeo* article appeared. Yet there were times, like these, when she stepped over the line because she wanted to take me along for the ride. I wasn't sure why she insisted I'd experienced something I didn't.

Lottie stood by the dresser, hands on hips and frustrated. Seconds later, she shook her head, strode toward her nightstand, and rummaged through it. She sank down next to me with her tablet and launched apps for *NatGeo* and *Current Psychology*.

"Look again, David," she said, opening *NatGeo* to an article I'd seen dozens of times before. "Really look. It's the story about General Bakari and Shemei, who was Pharaoh's sister, and Constance Arroyo who discovered their tomb in July. It's a story about *us*. About the lives we led during ancient Egypt's New Kingdom. We'd known each other since we were children, and we were to be married by my brother. We were deeply in love, David. Born to be together then just like we are now. I saw that life, relived it, and learned from it, and there was a time during my regression in July when you relived it, too. We shared it and talked about it."

I talked about it, yes. But relived it? Definitely not.

She took my hand and squeezed. "Don't you see anything or feel anything when I touch you? When I talk to you about that life? Don't the images come to you anymore?"

No. I only saw Lottie's desperation to be believed.

"I don't understand. You've called me Shemei. When we were together, David, just after my regressions began." She pressed my hand to her heart. It beat in time with mine. "You were inside me and you called me Shemei."

Because I thought that's what she wanted to hear.

"That night we were at the beach."

I said nothing.

"And that time when we were in our pool."

Still nothing.

"Then there was that afternoon we went for a bike ride at the park and pulled off into the woods. You called me Shemei then, too."

I shook my head.

Lottie dropped my hand and her head.

I pushed the hair from her face and tucked it behind an ear. "I'm sorry, Lottie. I don't see this the way you do."

She straightened and squared her shoulders, like she'd come to a decision. "I didn't want to do this. I've been avoiding it actually, but I think it's now time." Lottie looked at me with renewed focus that made me pause. "I've been learning hypnosis as a means to help clients break through their regressions. I want to do that with you."

"Now?"

"No. Next year. Of course now."

"Lottie—"

"Afraid?"

"No."

"Then what's the problem?"

The problem was, I'd been going along with Lottie's conceptions about past lives and regressions, and this was taking it too far. It was one thing to be supportive. It was entirely another to play along just to shut someone up. I didn't play those games and I wasn't going to start now. Lottie deserved better than that.

"What's the worst that will happen, David? The hypnosis doesn't work, we lose maybe fifteen, thirty minutes of our day, and you come out feeling more relaxed than you feel right now. At the very least, that's got to be worth something to you. And, in the meantime, I get more practice with hypnosis as therapy."

Lottie slid a hand between my thighs.

I gave her a look. "I'm not that shallow, Lottie."

"Actually, you are. Sex is the only weapon I have against you."

This was true.

"Fine," I said. "I'll do this if you agree that I get sex for the next three days. Anytime I want it, anywhere I want it, however I want it."

Lottie blew out a long, loud breath. "Thank the gods. I thought you were going to ask for something unreasonable."

Lottie helped me settle into the pillows and get comfortable. As she moved me into position, her breasts brushed against my arm and suddenly I wasn't thinking about hypnosis anymore. "Wrong focus, David," she said, smacking my cheek. "Save that for later. Now, close your eyes, take in deep breaths, and listen to my voice. Focus only on my voice."

I nodded and closed my eyes, and listened as Lottie coaxed me into deep breathing and relaxation. Her voice sounded smooth, like silk, taking on a rhythm I didn't normally hear. Except maybe in the bedroom. I thought about how she sounded last night, the things she'd whispered, the things she did, then her voice floated in again, soft and velvety, taking hold of me and pulling me in further. My breathing deepened, her voice moved through me, encouraging me to relax, breathe in, breathe out, and let my mind empty.

An image of Lottie and me at the beach surfaced. Waves hit the shore. A bottle of red rested on the sand nearby. We were wrapped in a blanket, alone. Lottie's voice encouraged me to keep breathing. Keep relaxing. The waves barreled in again, and I pulled Lottie on top of me. A breeze rushed past, ruffling the blanket and then blowing it off us. We didn't care.

Breathe in. Breathe out.

Lottie's voice sounded distant. I heard her, was still connected to her, but the memory deepened. We sat near a huge fire now, huddled under a blanket to protect us from the cold and snow. The others around the fire sang and danced. She looked at me, whispered in my ear that she wanted to be alone, then eased out of the blanket and sauntered away. Her hips swayed, encouraging me to follow. With the blanket tight around my shoulders, I got up and followed her footsteps, scored into the snow, and then the memory shifted to a cave. As I neared its entrance, a different wind blew past. A sharper, icier one. I shuddered through a chill, and shuddered again. A tree branch snapped. I stopped, frozen. Listening. Another snap.

The wind howled past once more, carrying a voice. Her voice. Pleading. Then screaming.

She kept screaming. And screaming. And screaming—

A cell phone rang.

My eyes flew open. The image jerked away. I was covered in sweat, heart pounding, gulping for air. Lottie was saying something, trying to get me to focus on her.

The phone rang again.

I scrambled from the bed, searching for my cell, still hearing the screams. Goosebumps riddled my body and I shuddered over another swift, sharp chill. I found the phone under the dresser and answered on the third ring.

Lottie grabbed my arm and gasped when she felt my skin. She tugged the blanket off the bed and draped it over my shoulders, rubbing my arms and back to warm me.

My boss, Mommie Dearest—MD to those who worked directly for her—was on the other end of the line. "I need you in the office in thirty, Bellotti. I want to discuss what went down with Sahin."

I bent over, my stomach and leg muscles cramping from the cold, trying to focus on the call and something MD was saying about the op. Lottie kept rubbing my body to generate heat.

I responded, vaguely aware I was talking. It was as if my mind was separated from my body, from reality. The room was a cozy seventy degrees, but I chattered like I was sitting in a Subzero.

"We already had a full team debrief yesterday on the mission," I said. Another chill. Another shudder. I clenched my teeth, working hard to get warm. "Why are we having a second one?"

"I have intel that indicates you took something from the scene," MD was saying. "I want it back."

The damned photo.

Lottie guided me back to the bed. By the time I sat down, I was fully aware of where I was and what I was doing. Another frigid wave rolled over and then the sensation disappeared. I was back to normal. And nicely warm.

"No games on this one, Bellotti," MD said. "Bring it with you or consider yourself fired." She disconnected the call.

"Are you okay?" Lottie swept a hand over my forehead, checking for fever.

"I'm fine," I said, but the words didn't come out right and I had to clear my throat and try again.

She pulled back. "What happened?"

"I have to go into HQ for a bit. I'm sorry, but it shouldn't be long." I ditched the bed and went to my closet, found jeans and a shirt, and headed into the bathroom for a shower.

"No." Lottie raced after me and came to an abrupt stop just as I turned on the jets. "I meant when you were under. What did you remember?"

"Nothing."

I started the shower and checked the temperature, then pressed my hands against the tile wall and leaned in, letting the jets of water pelt my back.

Lottie knocked on the glass door of the enclosure. "That was not nothing, David. You saw something."

I peered at her over an arm. "I remembered a nightmare I used to have as a kid," I told her. "Nothing more than that."

It was a lie and I hated it. I hadn't lied to Lottie for almost two years and I was doing it now. Something sour crawled up from my stomach and into my throat. It tasted like guilt.

"Please don't do this, David. Tell me the truth."

I grabbed the soap and started washing. "That *is* the truth."

Lottie hung around the bathroom for a while longer but didn't ask any more questions. When she left and closed the door after her, nausea rolled around in my stomach.

I had no idea how to tell her I'd just seen her die.

Chapter 5

David had lied.

After reconciling from a difficult breakup two years ago, they'd promised each other to always tell the truth and share what was on their minds. Only David didn't this time. And as Lottie sat on the edge of the bed, she realized David's lie wasn't what bothered her.

He was scared.

Whatever David had seen while hypnotized had terrified him, and he was refusing to acknowledge the emotion. It was denial in its most classic form, and Lottie was going to have to figure out how to help David confront his feelings about it. He was the most passionate man she'd ever known but also the most disciplined. Whatever he'd seen had rattled him so badly, his body had literally turned to ice.

The shower turned off, and Lottie wondered if his reaction was somehow connected to the photo. David seemed very edgy when they discussed it. She thought back to that night of the party, digging for details she had long forgotten because they seemed inconsequential at the time. She had taken the keys from Michael, her brother, and driven him home. Jared wasn't in much better shape. It was strange how that photo surfaced now.

The bathroom door opened and David walked out, fully

dressed, shaved, and smelling way too good. Lottie drew in a breath and held his scent, a mix of sultry sandalwood and warm amber. She smiled as he bent down and kissed her, then his kiss lingered and deepened, like he didn't want to leave.

She didn't want him to.

"I'm really sorry about this." With gentle fingers, he brushed the hair from her face. "You know I wouldn't be going in if I didn't have to."

Lottie nodded because there was no point in arguing about it. This was David, and this was his job.

"How about dinner out later," he said, "and then we'll get in my SUV and take off for someplace tomorrow. Anyplace you want for as long as you want to be there. I don't care where, as long as we do this together. Okay?"

"We have to be at Rita's for dinner on Sunday."

"We can cancel. Mom will understand."

"No." Lottie smiled and it felt uncertain on her lips. "I'll think of something for next week instead."

"Okay." David kissed her one last time, cupping her face with his hands. His touch felt oddly tentative and very protective; a sure sign the hypnosis still bothered him.

They needed to discuss this.

"David—"

"Plan that dinner and our vacation. Anywhere you want to go. I mean it."

And the conversation was over. Lottie watched David gather the clothes he'd ditched in a fit of lust last night, bundle them together, and take them downstairs. Most likely to the laundry room where he'd start up a load. That left her alone with her questions and a good amount of doubt.

She studied the bedroom, remembering the first time they christened the bed, the time David brought her homemade soup when she had strep throat, the nights they spent huddled underneath warm blankets watching television. Now, she felt isolated and abandoned.

And the first stirrings of anger.

She'd been left alone while David was in Turkey, and last night, great as it was, wasn't going to get him off the hook so easily. If he could set off to do his own thing, so could she.

Lottie found her handbag, dug around for the business card Monica gave her, and called. Four rings later, Monica was on the other end of the line. Lottie didn't need to remind her who she was.

"Wow, karma is at work again," Monica said with an enthusiasm that made Lottie smile. "I was just thinking about you and here you are, calling me."

"And I was thinking about what you said yesterday, when you came to my office." Lottie got up, went into her closet, and dug around for an outfit. She settled on a pair of jeans and a canary button down blouse. "I'd like to attend one of your meetings, if there's room."

"Of course there's room, and I'd be thrilled to have you there! Ada, bring the red jacket with you." In the background, Lottie heard Ada complain and Monica repeated her request. "Sorry about that. Ada's spending the day with a friend who's visiting from out of town and she's about as disorganized as they come. Where were we?"

"The meeting."

"Oh. Right. I have one scheduled for today at eleven. Come on over. I think you'll find it enlightening, and I can guarantee that everyone there would love to meet you."

The idea enticed Lottie, but she still felt apprehensive. Up until now, only Galen accepted her newly discovered beliefs about past lives. Everyone else just paid lip service or smiled at her, like she was a child who needed indulging.

Galen.

The name, and his memory, came to Lottie over a sigh. Not a day had gone by since she'd met him in July and learned about their passionate past in ancient Egypt that Lottie hadn't thought about him, or heard his voice, or remembered his touch. That night was as vivid to her now as it was thousands of years ago when she invited him to her chamber. It was a night that changed the fates of her, David, and Galen forever.

Lottie closed her eyes and an evocative, spiced scent consumed her. She inhaled, deep and long, letting its warmth radiate over her skin, inside her body. Her soul. It was their scent—hers and Galen's—of when they were together. During times long ago.

Times that could no longer be repeated.

Lottie became aware that Monica was talking and forced herself to refocus on the here and now.

"Could you repeat the address, please?" Lottie asked, and she jotted it down along with directions.

"I'm looking forward to seeing you again," Monica said, and Lottie assured her that she was looking forward to it, too.

Lottie disconnected and went straight into the shower, thinking about what she might expect at the meeting. Part of her was excited, but part of her was still anxious, too. Though she understood her past life better now than she did in July when she had her first regression, the knowledge didn't lessen the anxiety. The more she learned about her past, the more she realized just how important Galen had been to her in that time, and now. And it was a contrast that defied explanation. Inviting Galen completely into her life would surely destroy her relationship with David just as it did thousands of years ago. Yet keeping Galen away would prevent David and her from strengthening and enriching what they shared.

It was a conflict she felt could never be resolved.

A half hour later, dressed in her jeans and blouse, Lottie took the Jeep for the fifteen-minute drive to the meeting. She found the location in a quiet neighborhood near her childhood one, full of well-tended, older homes that had been renovated over the years. She located her destination quickly, a two-story Victorian in purple and blue that was surrounded by maples turning a brilliant yellow and green holly bushes bursting with vibrant red berries.

Lottie didn't find a bell at the front door and knocked. Monica answered wearing four-inch blue heels, a sheer white blouse, a blue bra, black slacks, and a big, eager smile.

"I'm so glad you came." Monica hugged Lottie like she'd known her forever and ushered her into a living room filled with antique furniture that looked as colorful as the home's exterior. "In fact, we're all glad you came."

A dozen people clustered in the room, some sitting on the floral sofa, others standing in corners, all chatting like it was old times. Lit, scented candles accented the space, an exotic blend of cedarwood and clove in an inviting room painted the color of light suede. New age music filtered through the background, the combination of flute and synthesizer setting a comforting mood. The shades had been drawn, and in the darkened space Lottie noticed a haze that hung like a thin veil. A middle-aged man walked by, the haze swirling and coiling as he passed, and beneath the earthy cedar Lottie smelled something pungent and sweet and very familiar. Another glance around the room confirmed her suspicions. Several people were smoking blunts.

Monica tugged Lottie in further, making introductions. A stay-at-home mom. An investment banker. A teacher. A car wash owner. On the surface it seemed no one had much in common, but Lottie knew better. They all held a desire to share whatever Monica offered.

And they all knew Lottie already.

"We've read your article," Monica offered as an explanation as she guided Lottie away from a librarian, and Lottie's heel caught the corner of a thick carpet, sending her off-balance. Monica grabbed her arm and steadied her, and Lottie glanced down at the area rug as Monica guided her away. It was thick and white and made of bearskin. Out of place with the traditional Victorian house and the décor, but yet there it was, right in the middle of the room.

"We've never met anyone who has actual proof of a past incarnation," Monica went on. "I can't even begin to imagine what it feels like to see your previous life on display for everyone to see."

Lottie knew she was referring to the *NatGeo* article about the find in Egypt. "Believe me," she said, "I'm still getting used to it myself."

Monica stopped and gave her a long, meaningful look. "You've come across much skepticism and rejection since your regression," she said. "It must be harder, in some ways, with the article. I bet people think you're just trying to get attention."

Stuart Hanley came to mind and Lottie nodded. "How often do you meet?" She watched an older man share a joint with the schoolteacher she'd just met. The music shifted to an ambient acoustical guitar.

"As often as we can," Monica said. "We have regular meetings here on Saturday and Sunday mornings, and several during the week like we're having today. Many of us also meet on other days in other locations, so you can pretty much find a get-together any time you need."

Monica encouraged Lottie to take the one available chair adjacent to the wall, but Lottie declined. A girl who looked like she was barely a day past twenty came forward carrying a tray of small mugs.

"Tea?" she offered.

Lottie peered inside the small cups, which looked dark and innocent enough, and declined that, too. The gods only knew what was inside them.

"The tea will really help you relax," the girl said, lifting the tray higher and encouraging Lottie to change her mind.

"I bet it would."

As Lottie turned, she caught sight of the adjacent dining room. It was bold and colorful, filled with reds and blues and purples, and in the center of a round table covered with a lace cloth rested a vase of blue lotus flowers.

Lottie gasped.

Monica looked from Lottie to the vase. "Oh my God, I know, right? Aren't they the most beautiful things you've ever seen?"

Lottie nodded, but that was all she could do. The only

other places she'd ever seen blue lotus flowers were at Galen's condo and in the bouquet he'd sent her back in July—and in the red wine he'd given her on a balmy night over three millennia ago. When Galen was Kemnebi, and she was not Lottie but Shemei. He had offered a cup of wine and moved in beside her on the balcony overlooking the Nile. The wine looked as rich and red as the darkest pomegranate, with three blue lotus petals floating on top.

Monica took Lottie's hand again, tugging her out of the memory. "You look tense. Are we making you feel uncomfortable? Are you okay?"

It took a while for Lottie to find her voice. "I'm okay. I just feel a little strange being here," she said, still unable to take her eyes off the flowers.

"You're not accustomed to people who understand. That's normal." Monica's dark gaze sifted through Lottie's. The term *old soul* immediately came to mind, and Lottie wondered what those eyes had seen. Eyes that, Lottie noticed, were also glassy and bloodshot. "Try to open your mind," Monica added. "And just experience the experience for what it is, with no judgment. Then, see where the experience takes you. You just might be surprised where you land."

A middle-aged man lit up another blunt. The girl handed over two cups of tea to a young married couple. The music transitioned to tubular bells and piano. A wave of relaxation moved through Lottie and she blinked, the room momentarily splitting into two, then three. She inhaled, deeply, and felt her tension begin to shift.

Monica gestured for the group to gather together. "We're all at different stages of regression, Lottie. The worst thing you can possibly do to yourself is to fight it, so just be. Join us, listen to your heart and mind, and just be."

Three men moved the furniture toward the walls and everyone gathered in the open space, sitting cross-legged and holding hands around the bearskin rug.

"We're here to share experiences and to support each other. In some cases," Monica said as the group started a low chant, "people complete a regression. In others they find a new one. And sometimes people will actually share a regression of the same time and place."

Monica held out her hand, coaxing Lottie to join in.

Lottie hesitated. When she first learned about regression therapy in college, the courses taught hypnosis. For historical perspective, professors also taught mythology. But what she faced here was neither.

Smoke thickened, and the chanting fell into a low hum, and a sluggish, buoyant sensation tugged at Lottie's concerns, pulling them away. An image of Galen emerged, the sound of his melodious voice encouraging her to join the others and find herself.

"Do this," his voice whispered in her head. "Do this, or you will face even more regret."

Lottie watched the others close their eyes and drift off to some other place. Some swayed in time to the music, others kept chanting, and others continued smoking their blunts. Maybe they really were finding their way to a past life or figuring out how some other life fit in with this one. Maybe they just liked each other's company. Maybe they just liked smoking dope or drinking drugged tea.

And maybe this was all a hoax.

Lottie stayed for a while, watching, listening. But nothing happened. Whatever she'd been expecting, this wasn't it. She dug her keys from her handbag, walked out the front door, and got in the Jeep.

She headed back home, feeling lost, empty, and misunderstood.

Chapter 6

By the time I pulled into HQ's parking lot, I'd convinced myself that what I experienced during my hypnosis wasn't hypnosis and that I didn't witness Lottie's death. No one could see into the future and, logically, I knew the image couldn't be a snapshot of the past either. The only conclusion was that I'd remembered a scene from a movie and superimposed Lottie into it. There was probably a clinical term for what happened, but that didn't matter now.

I parked the SUV feeling a hell of a lot more upbeat than I did when I left the house, and went inside the four-story glass and steel building. Three levels of security later, I pushed through a set of reinforced doors and into the main office area in the sub-basement. PROs operated out of a small office managed by a few desk grunts and several ex-military and government officials who I'd met over the years. Except for Mommie Dearest. No one had ever seen her or knew how she got her nickname, or if she even had a real name, and there was a lot of speculation she didn't live in the States. A number of us were lifers who operated under PROs payroll and came into HQ when it was necessary, like me. All the other professional soldiers were consultants, on call for when their services were needed.

The office was fairly active for a Friday morning. I saw

Galen at the far end of a row of cubes talking it up with one of the admins. She was blonde, decked out in green, and definitely interested in Galen. She laughed, he laughed, she leaned in, he leaned in closer, and she whispered in his ear. I headed toward him. When the admin saw me, she pulled away, plunked down into her chair, and started typing.

"Where are we at?" I asked as I approached.

The admin jerked her head toward the corner conference room. "You're set for a conference call with Mommie Dearest in five." She still wouldn't look at me.

I shrugged her off and walked with Galen to the meeting. When we were out of earshot, I asked, "What's her problem?"

Galen was silent, and when I looked at him he was grinning. "You scare her."

We cornered the last row of cubes and I threw him a look. "I barely know her."

"You have a reputation in the office."

"For what?"

Galen stopped, apparently thinking about how he would deliver the explanation. "I believe the word she used was 'hardass.'"

I stopped and stared at him.

Galen stared back. "Don't tell me you're surprised."

Actually, I wasn't. And I didn't care. I started for the conference room again.

Galen quickened his pace to catch up. "You'll attract more flies with honey than with vinegar, Bellotti."

"I prefer bumble bees. And I'm not here to make friends, Galen."

"Even with me?"

I paused, mid-stride, wondering what the hell that meant. Galen and I worked together, but we had baggage, and all of it had to do with Lottie. I shrugged off that thought, too, and kept moving.

"And you?" I asked.

We headed toward the conference room glass doors.

"And me what?" Galen asked.

"The way that admin was hanging all over you, she obviously doesn't think you're a hardass. You hooking up with her?"

"Do you even know her name?"

I didn't answer.

Galen shook his head and pushed the door open, and we walked inside. "In response to your question, not yet," he said with another grin. "But hopefully tonight."

I grinned back but lost the mood again when I discovered an empty room. Galen moved in next to me and stood, hands on hips. The shiny glass and black lacquer table looked as polished and clean as the gray leather seats, and just as unused. No one had been here and, from the looks of it, no one else was going to be here either.

I turned to Galen. "I thought this was supposed to be a full team debrief."

MD's voice cut in from the speakerphone. "It's just the three of us. Sit down."

Galen did as ordered. I remained standing.

"Where is the photo, Bellotti?" MD asked.

I glanced at Galen and he shrugged. "You called us all the way here just for the photo?" I asked.

"I know the fifteen-minute drive to get to HQ killed you,"

MD said. "Now where is it?"

I fished the photo from my wallet and dropped it on the table. It slid across the polished surface like a hockey puck over ice.

"Did you see Bellotti take the photo from Sahin's wallet, Galen?"

Galen's head came up and he studied me from across the table. For the most part, he was an open book. He said what he meant and you got what you saw, but right now I saw caution in his eyes and that made me suspicious.

"Do you need to get your hearing checked, Galen?" MD asked.

"No." Galen straightened and refocused. "And yes, I saw Bellotti take the photo."

"Why didn't you stop him?"

His gaze moved from me to the photo, and I wondered if it was Lottie's likeness that captured his attention. I saw how he looked at Lottie whenever he was around her—Galen was as hungry for her as I was—and I had a mind to grab the photo and shove it back in my wallet so he couldn't stare at her anymore.

I clasped my hands behind my back instead.

"I sympathized with why Bellotti felt it necessary to take it." Galen pressed his mouth closed, and my suspicion edged up a few degrees. I suspected the photo dredged up memories or thoughts he wasn't about to share.

Galen looked at me, no apology in his eyes for wanting a woman he couldn't have.

"You work for *me*, Bellotti," MD said. "You do *not* take things you are not supposed to take. You get your orders. You follow them. You do *not* deviate. Am I clear?"

"Yes."

"You think I give a shit your lover is with another man?"

"No."

"You think I care that your precious male ego took a hit? You think that I'll give you a *poor baby* every time you question your lover's fidelity and overlook your stupidity?"

Galen's gaze returned to the photo and a wistful smile teased at the corners of his mouth before he reined the emotion back in.

I clenched my jaw. "No."

"Sahin went ape-shit when he discovered the photo was taken. I want to know why he had it and why it's important to him. We've killed his operation but we're not done with him yet. I want answers and, until I get them, all vacation, all time off, is canceled. This is intel I need *now*."

I cursed.

"You're in no position to argue about this, Bellotti."

I cursed again. This time louder. If Lottie was annoyed about my getting called into work this morning, this latest news was going to send me straight into the crapper.

"I heard that the photo had two people in it," MD said. "Lottie and another guy. Who's the other guy?"

I was working hard to keep my temper in check, feeling like I'd just been played. "His name's Jared," I said.

"As in Jared Sahin?"

Galen's eyes met mine, and the silence between us deepened.

"What the hell is your girlfriend doing with Zev Sahin's nephew other than screwing him?"

"She's not—"

"How close is she to him?"

"She's *not* close to him!"

"Famous last words from anyone who's ever been cheated on."

"Lottie's not cheating. She's not doing *anything*. She was at a party, and he happened to be there. He's a friend of her brother. She didn't—doesn't—know who he is."

"And yet you stole the photo. That tells me you don't trust Lottie. *How close is she to Jared?*"

"Are you even listening to me?"

"Watch the tone."

This was total bullshit. All of it. MD. Galen. The photo. And I intended to remind MD about it. "Just because you're at a party doesn't mean you're doing the guy you meet."

"Bullshit. Think back three years, Bellotti, to the gala you attended in London. And the woman you met there. You want to run that logic by me again?"

I slammed my palms on the table and yanked the speaker toward me. "That was different, and you don't know Lottie the way I do."

"Chauvinistic *and* pig-headed. You have the little woman wear little aprons when she cooks for you and beds you, too? *Open your goddamned eyes*, Bellotti! Think with the head above your waist!"

"I'm not—"

"Don't play stupid. It doesn't suit you."

"I think," Galen said, pulling the conference phone away from me, "we are overlooking something that could be even more important. And that's whether or not Lottie's brother is close to Jared Sahin."

"Is this your meeting now, Galen?" MD asked.

"It's more like an inquisition," Galen mumbled. He folded his arms over his chest and went back to examining the photo.

"Find out everything you can on Jared," MD said. "Dig up all of it, and when you think you're done, dig up more. And remember this. On paper he looks like a nice, respectable businessman. But he's linked to Zev and that means nothing is what it appears. I want details in two days."

Galen was still engrossed with the photo and I reached across the table, ready to take it back.

"Leave the photo where it is, Bellotti," MD said. "You don't need it anymore." Then she disconnected. End of meeting.

I threw open the conference room doors and strode out into the corridor. By the time I got to my SUV in the lot, I was furious and Galen was at my side.

"Don't start with me," I said, fishing my keys from my pocket.

Galen jammed his hands into his slacks and said, "MD most likely knows something we do not."

I sent him a look. "This is bullshit. She's keeping intel from us, from *me*, about that photo."

"It's not just a photo and we both know it. She's testing you to see just how personal you're making this, and you're failing."

"And it's not personal for you? You sat there and did nothing when I lifted the picture, Galen, and we both know why you kept your mouth shut."

"You need to calm down."

I stepped in, making sure Galen understood his place. I was his superior and I was the one who gave the orders. "Don't tell me what to do. Don't tell me how to do it. And last but most important, stay away from Lottie."

"This has nothing to do with me seeing Lottie. I stay away from her but I cannot help it if she—"

He stopped, and the suspicion that nagged at me in the conference room now turned into full-blown distrust.

I stepped in closer. "If she what?"

Galen shook his head. "I'm not getting in the middle of the issues you have with Lottie. I'm not your therapist, and MD was right. You don't have your head on straight."

"Remember that you work for me because I hired you, Galen. And my head is just fine."

"You approved my application because you felt guilty for what Lottie was going through at the time. That isn't something I can easily ignore."

"What you did for Lottie back in July was helpful but inexcusable. You wanted her, you couldn't have her, and you pretended to experience the same past life regression she did so that she would come to you—"

"I didn't pretend that I lived thousands of years ago among the Pharaohs, Bellotti. And you'll do well to learn from your own regression, your past, if you'd just open your damned eyes and let it happen."

I clenched a fist, thinking how good it would feel to crack it against his face. Instead, I unlocked the SUV, slid inside, and cranked over the engine. Then I turned up the heat, opened the window, and stuck out my head. "And by the way, the admin's name is Rebecca Lansdon. Middle name Arlene. Her birthday is April fifteenth and she loves Airedale Terriers. She also loved the flowers I sent her when she turned twenty-six this past year."

I threw the SUV into reverse and pulled away.

My heart was pounding and blood was rushing through my ears, courtesy of too many thoughts jamming up my brain. I jumped onto the main road and by the time I hit the fourth light, turned, and wove through the back roads home, a plan started forming.

I called my best friend, Nat. He served on my team at PROs and was a techno-whiz with skills I dreamed about. If he couldn't help me figure out the mystery behind the photo, no one could. When he answered the phone, I heard screaming in the background and a lot of rowdy laughter. His sons. I told him about MD's orders for me to find intel on the picture.

"Did you take a picture of the picture?" Nat asked.

"Yeah." I stopped at a stop sign and waited for a woman who looked liked she'd lived through the Ice Age to cross the road, and used the time to find it on my phone and send it to Nat. One of Nat's boys started complaining that Eddie wouldn't stop touching him. Carlos, most likely. Carlos complained about everything.

"Got it," Nat said. "You gonna call Michael about Jared, or you want me to?"

"No, I'll do it," I said, watching the old lady finish crossing the street. She might have been slow but she didn't look bothered, and I realized that was probably the point. I'd battled it out on the front lines, sat for hours in the dark scoping out the enemy, and sent men into ambush, and not once did I ever lose focus.

I'd lost focus now.

I drew in a long breath and held it, letting it all pass. The old woman turned around, waved, and smiled. I smiled and waved back. And slowly, I felt my skyrocketing blood pressure start to normalize.

"Be prepared," Nat said. "Michael's gonna get into deep, thought-provoking conversations about ollies and half pipes. Did he ever enter that skateboarding contest?"

"No idea." Michael was a nice guy but an airhead. His goal in life was to spend his days at skate parks instead of the law firm where he worked. How he got the job, I'd never know.

"Weird how that photo showed up in Istanbul," Nat said. "Any ideas at all why Sahin had it?"

"No clue." I turned onto Samsara Street and headed for my house. "But you know it isn't because of Lottie." I pulled up the driveway and waited for the garage door to open.

"And there's our starting point," Nat said as I pulled inside and killed the engine. "I'll cross-ref Jared against Michael Morgan. Maybe I'll also add Lottie in the mix just for kicks and giggles. See what comes up." Carlos started screeching and I had to hold the phone away from my head. Nat yelled for him to shut up. Carlos stopped for a few seconds then started screeching louder. The sound cut through and my ears started to ring.

"Wow," I said. "Can't wait to have a kid of my own."

"I thought you wanted kids."

"Do they screech like that all the time?"

"You have much to learn, grasshopper. Just you wait and see, D-Man. This ain't nothing. The profundity of children lies not in their shortcomings but in the life still stretched out before them."

"Nice quote. Who said it?"

"Me. Now let me get cracking on this pic before these kids drive me to drink more."

Chapter 7

I was thinking how to break the vacation news to Lottie, maybe with a home-cooked dinner and lots of candles and wine, when I found her in the kitchen standing at the counter, working her way through fistfuls of Lucky Charms right from the cereal box. Seemed like she couldn't get them in her mouth fast enough, and a bunch of them tumbled to the tile floor and rolled toward my feet. Lottie turned, saw me near the fridge, saw the mess on the floor, and burst out laughing.

"Hi," she said through a mouthful, and started laughing again. She chowed down on another bunch and licked her lips. I wondered what her lips tasted like. "You're back earlier than I expected."

I checked the clock on the stove. Actually, I was late.

"Want some?" She held out a hand and kept licking her lips, and I couldn't stop the wondering so I kissed her. She tasted sweet. With lots of marshmallow. Lottie offered a handful, but the cereal had clumped together in her palm. "Huh. Look at that. A Lucky Charms snowball."

"I haven't seen you eat Lucky Charms since we partied that summer before college."

"I know." She looked up at me, smelling woodsy and warm and…of something else.

I recognized the smell, put two and two together, and

grinned. "Have you been smoking weed?"

Her eyes went wider. Big, dark, and bloodshot. "Me? Nooo."

"Yes." I laughed. "You have." I peered inside the box and found half the cereal gone.

"No, I swear. Really, I swear. They were. I wasn't. I got hungry."

I shoved the box away. "You want to try that again?"

"I got sucked into a *really* big cloud, David."

"A cloud." Okay, this was going to take some work. "What kind of cloud was it?"

She rolled her red eyes. "Really big, David. You're not listening to me. It was *everywhere*."

Of course it was. "Do you remember where *everywhere* was?"

"Your meeting."

"No. I'm pretty sure I didn't smoke at my meeting."

"You can be so dense."

"And you're high." Speaking of which, "How did you get home? Did you *drive*?"

"Stop ignoring my questions."

"You're not asking any. I am."

Lottie huffed out her impatience. "How did your meeting go? I want to know. I wasn't there. That's why I'm asking. Questions."

"Of course you are."

"You're a complex man, David. You are not," she said, jabbing a finger into my chest, "an easy man to live with. Well, you're *easy*, but you're not easy."

"Is this going somewhere?"

Her gaze commandeered mine. "Do you want it to?" She moved in closer and pressed against me, all tempting curves and soft skin and silky hair. And I remembered this about Lottie: Whenever she got high, she got turned on. In a big way.

"I want this," she said, slipping her hands under my shirt and raking her nails over my chest. "Right now."

I saw no reason to argue.

She maneuvered me against the counter and kissed me, her hands moving from my chest to my hips and down, then she pulled away and stared up at me with all kinds of decadence in her dark eyes. She twirled her hair in her fingers and purred, "How do you want it, David?"

At that moment, any way I could get it was fine.

"Behind the trees in the vacant lot down the street?" she asked, tugging my shirt out of my jeans. "In the SUV at Applewood Mall?" She buried her face in my neck and nipped the skin. "Right here?" Her hands worked my jeans and she bit my neck again, harder this time.

A shock of pleasure jolted straight down, hard and fast and hot. I helped her shove off the jeans, and she got on her knees and down to business.

I was thinking *screw the public sex*, and then nothing at all, and then the image of a dark cave rushed in. Lottie was screaming. I was running toward her screams but couldn't get to her, and a brutal wind shoved me backward. I couldn't breathe. She screamed again.

I grabbed Lottie's hands and swayed, edgy from the vibe and not getting any air. My heart was pounding and I shivered over a cold sweat, and the screaming came at me again.

Lottie jumped up and grabbed my shoulders. I think she

might have been talking to me, but I couldn't hear the words. I gripped the counter and the blast of cold air barreled through once more. I shuddered, felt goose bumps break out, and chattered over the cold. A roaring noise plugged up my ears and the floor pitched underneath me.

"David?"

I was vaguely aware of her hands on me, trying to stabilize me on my feet.

"What's going on, David?" Lottie's face was in front of me, and she was staring at me, wide-eyed and pale. "You're like ice! David, say something. Are you okay?"

"I'm..."

I didn't know what I was.

"I'll get you some water. Can you stand?"

I must have nodded because she took off for the faucet, and I heard water turn on and off and then a cold, sweaty glass was pressed into my hands.

"Drink this."

I did.

"Do you want to sit?"

I shook my head. My internal radar was humming, but I didn't know what had triggered it. "Something feels off," I said. "Wrong."

I put the glass down, tugged my jeans back on, and stood there, feeling like I'd been plucked from one place and dropped into another. I knew I was in my own home, but something about it didn't feel right. Like there was something that didn't belong.

"You ever have a feeling like you know something's going to happen before it does?" I asked. "Something bad?"

Lottie nodded, but with caution. I wasn't an overly emotional guy, and talking about stuff like this was jumpstarting her internal radar, too.

"Just talk, David. Let it out. It doesn't have to be in perfect words for me to be able to help you."

The doorbell rang and Lottie and I stared at each other.

"Want me to get that?" she asked.

The bell rang again.

I shook my head. For some unknown reason, I felt drawn to the door and knew I had to be the one to answer it.

I walked to the foyer, the momentary fog starting to lift, but all I could see was the front door and a shadow moving behind the leaded glass, out on the landing. Lottie moved in at my side, watching me with a little wariness and lot of scrutiny.

The psychologist in her was back in business.

I grabbed the knob, swung open the door, and found a woman on the other side. She wore a sheer white blouse with a blue lacy bra underneath, tight black pants, and spiked blue heels. Her dark hair was cut short and looked striking against an equally striking face. A face, I realized, that had barely changed.

It was a woman I hadn't seen in years but that I remembered well.

Monica.

Chapter 8

Monica stared at me like she'd seen a ghost.

Her face lost all its color and her brown eyes went wide, registering the same shock and surprise I felt. As I moved aside to invite her in, she managed some composure and a smile emerged. It was a smile I remembered well and that, long ago, charmed me into doing things that should have been left undone.

"Wow." Monica stepped away from Lottie and met me halfway, still smiling and still looking like I was a figment of her imagination. She cleared her throat and then did it again. "Wow, wow, wow. I never expected this."

We hovered near each other in that strange space two ex-lovers would inhabit, neither one knowing how to ease the awkwardness.

I leaned in and kissed her cheek. "Never expected this either," I said, and my internal radar started humming again. This felt wrong. Meeting Monica in my house and having the three of us in the same room at the same time, but mostly seeing Lottie and Monica together.

An errant image of bearskins and a hut surfaced, followed by the sharp stab of anger. Only it wasn't mine. The anger seemed to radiate from Monica. But she didn't look angry. If anything, she looked pleased. *Too* pleased.

Lottie moved in and her gaze volleyed between the both of us. "You two know each other?"

"Yeah," I said. Dozens of long-buried memories surfaced and rambled through my brain. Some of them good. Some of them hot. Many bittersweet and confusing. "But it's been a while," I added.

Monica blew out a loud breath. "I, um, wow." She tracked me from head to foot and back up again. "I don't know what to say, David. Except that you've filled out."

Lottie looped her arm through mine and another image sparked to life. Two females near a cave, arguing.

"Well, it looks good on you, David," Monica said. "Really, really good."

I remembered the last time Monica said those words. We were in her backyard, and it was right before she yanked off my new jeans.

"So what brings you here?" I asked.

Monica said nothing, and I would have repeated the question, but her eyes went to Lottie and our entwined arms. "Lottie came to one of my meetings today and left her wallet behind. Must have fallen out of her handbag or something."

"Your meeting?" I was feeling slow on the uptake until it hit me. "Oh. The *meeting*."

Monica fished Lottie's wallet out of her handbag and handed it over. Lottie took it, but Monica didn't let go right away. They stood, locked in suspended animation and like they were sizing each other up, two women silently communicating a message I didn't understand. I reached in, tugged the wallet from them both, and dropped it on the side table just behind.

Monica moved in and squeezed my bicep, and her eyes lit

up with newfound fascination like she hadn't gotten a good enough look at me before. This time, when she explored my body, she did it more slowly.

"Thanks for returning my wallet," Lottie said. "I appreciate the favor."

Monica kept looking at me. "Aren't you going to invite me in?"

A low noise emerged from deep in Lottie's throat, and it took me a few seconds to realize she was growling. Then it took a few seconds more for me to stop staring at her.

"Oh my God." Monica pointed a finger at Lottie, and kept pointing as recognition fired in her eyes. "You're Lottie Morgan!"

Lottie's grip on my arm tightened. "Yes. We already established that in my office."

"No. No, no, no. Not the woman from *NatGeo*. You were the girl who lived down the street from David."

"You know me from somewhere before?"

"You bet. I can't believe I didn't make the connection. David told me a lot about you back in the day."

And I'd told Lottie nothing about Monica.

Lottie turned on me and blinked. "Back in the day?"

"I can explain later," I said under my breath and I refocused on Monica. "You've really caught us at a bad time here. We were just—"

"I haven't seen you for how many years, David, and you're kicking me out already? Don't you even want to catch up? Play the good host?"

She pasted on a smile for Lottie, like everything was okay, but I could see that it wasn't. I didn't know if Lottie and

Monica had gotten along at the meeting, but it was clear that the claws were out now. And I had to cut this short before things got ugly.

"We can catch up over dinner instead," I said, and Lottie dug her nails into my arm. "Or lunch. Lunch would be better. Or just coffee."

Monica studied Lottie and me, and Lottie's hand wrapped around my arm, and then Monica settled her own hand on top. "Don't worry. I promise I won't bark or bite or claw." She let go and went into the living room. "You have a beautiful home," she called out. "I love all the touches. But I never figured you for a domestic kind of guy, David. A home. A wife. A whole life carved out for yourself."

Lottie peered past me to look at Monica again, and the low growl returned.

"Why are you doing that?" I asked her.

"So how long have you been married?" Monica asked.

I held onto Lottie's hand and walked her into the living room. Lottie gave me a scowl and a look that said *Get her the hell out of here*, then she disengaged from me and went to the far side of the sofa where she could watch Monica more closely. I remained near the archway between the living room and foyer.

"We're not married," I said.

Monica had been fingering the dark wood furniture and her head came up. "Oh?"

Lottie's nostrils flared and her features darkened, a quick-tempered reminder that I'd said the wrong thing.

"Not married yet, anyway," I said, trying for a quick fix. "But someday."

Monica glanced at Lottie's left hand to confirm what she probably already suspected. No engagement ring.

"What about your husband?" I leaned against the wall, aiming for casual. "Greg was his name, right?"

"Divorced him over ten years ago." Monica went to the pictures on the sofa table. Lottie and me on the slopes in Crested Butte. Caught in an unexpected rainstorm at an outdoor café in Rome. Snorkeling in Bermuda.

Lottie edged in on the photos. Protective.

"I'm sorry," I said.

"Oh, don't be." Monica's hand went to a still of Lottie on the beach in a yellow sundress, her long hair windswept and knotted. It was my favorite picture. "I'm certainly not."

Lottie pressed her mouth into a tight line. So tight, the corners turned white. I held out my hands, telling her that short of being rude and throwing Monica out, there wasn't anything I could do.

Lottie scowled, and I knew I had to try better.

"Monica—"

"I guess you've been here a while," she said. "The house looks so nicely decorated. The grounds are beautiful, too. It's obvious you've been working at it for some time." She admired the crown moldings and high ceilings, then the turret to her right. "I missed this neighborhood, believe it or not. I got the house on Perkins after the divorce and rented it out. Moved to Northern Jersey so I could raise my daughter in peace and away from all the bad memories."

"You have a daughter?" Somehow, I couldn't picture her with one.

"I do. And she's a handful, too, but we do okay. Daddy

died a couple of months ago and left me a bunch of money so I moved back into the house here in Dix Hills. I figure maybe enough years have passed since the divorce for me to start fresh again. Not sure if it's going to be a permanent thing yet, though." She went silent, still fiddling with the edge of the sofa. "Those were fun times that you and I had." Monica paused. "Good memories."

And they had no place here.

"Monica," I said, walking toward Lottie and placing my hand at the small of her back, "this really isn't a good time. Seriously."

Monica turned and smiled again, but this time something sad lurked behind it. "Yeah, yeah. I get the message." Her chin lifted and she drew in a sharp breath, forcing that sadness from her face. Then her voice and her eyes turned soft. Almost resigned. "I'm happy that you're happy now, David. You deserve it."

I pulled Lottie in close and wrapped my arm around her shoulder. "Thank you."

"Well, um. Yeah. This is becoming awkward." Monica tried for a laugh that fell short of its mark. When it seemed like she didn't know what else to say, she started digging around inside her handbag again. She pulled out a piece of paper and handed it over to Lottie.

"For what it's worth, I'm hoping you continue with our meetings, Lottie. This is a list of the folks who host meetings like I do. I want you to have it so you know there are other places you can go to for support. But mostly I wanted to apologize for today. I guess I didn't exactly prepare you for what to expect. I'd like you to come back to the next meeting tomorrow, and hopefully the ones after that."

Lottie ignored the paper. "I appreciate it, but I think I'll pass."

Monica nodded and the sad, forced smile returned. "You sure I can't change your mind? You can bring David with you, if you want."

Lottie tensed under my touch. "Thank you. That's very nice of you to offer."

Monica hiked her handbag over her shoulder. "Well, then," she said, "I should be going, but I really do hope you change your mind, Lottie. I'd love to have you with us. I'd truly like to get to know you better."

Lottie and I escorted Monica into the foyer. Monica opened the door, paused, and turned. "David? It was a trip, really. If you're up to it, I would love to do coffee sometime and catch up on all the years. I think we owe ourselves that much, don't you?"

Monica's gaze lingered on mine.

Then she closed the door after her.

Chapter 9

The next morning, I woke with half of Lottie and all her hair sprawled over me. My body hurt in places I didn't know could hurt, and I shifted under her weight, trying to get more comfortable. Lottie stirred, opened her eyes, and looked at me.

"Good morning," she said, blinking away sleepiness. "It is morning, isn't it?"

"Yep." Because we'd spent the whole previous afternoon and night in the bedroom.

I brushed her hair from her face and kissed her. Her eyes met mine and we stayed that way, looking at each other, not saying anything, cozied up under warm blankets and feeling like nothing else mattered in the world.

And all I kept thinking was that I could do this every day.

Lottie nuzzled into my neck, gave a lick, and pulled back. "Is that what I think it is?" Her eyes widened, her sleepiness long gone. "Did I *bite* you?"

I felt the tender area on my trapezius. "More like you were trying to mark me."

Lottie touched the bite mark with her fingertips, careful not to hurt me more than she already had. "I'm sorry."

"Don't be."

She shook her head like she was having a hard time forgiving herself for what she'd done. "I don't know what got into me."

"Pot," I said. "Along with a hefty dose of jealousy."

Lottie pulled away, tugging bedding along with her until she saw the scratches on my chest and thighs. "Did I do that, too? Why didn't you stop me?"

I shrugged. "We've gotten rough before."

"But I don't remember doing any of it. David, some of these marks are deep."

"You were...insistent last night." I stroked her arm, enjoying the feel of her soft skin under my fingertips. "But what was with the growling?"

Lottie grimaced. "The girlfriend in me couldn't help it. The psychologist in me knows it was a primitive response to a threatening stimulus."

I sat up. "You think Monica's a threat? Why?"

"I saw how you looked at her."

"Because I haven't seen her for years. It was shock more than anything else."

Lottie's eyes went to the scratches again.

"Come on, Lottie. You're the psychologist. You of all people should see what's going on."

"Maybe. And you should have told me about her."

"I didn't because I didn't think it was important. It was an affair. It was kept a secret. And by the time you and I got together, I didn't see any point in bringing it up. I wanted you, not her. I've always wanted you. Monica was just a fill-in." I cringed when I realized how crass the remark sounded. "She was just about sex, Lottie, and she was only there for that moment in time. She knew it, too. She knew you were the competition and she knew there was no point in even trying for anything more with me." Lottie's hair, which was thick and long, fell forward. I brushed it away, partly because I wanted to see her beautiful face and partly because I loved the feel of her hair. It was like silk, only better.

"Hey." I inched in closer and took her face in my hands. "You're stronger than this. What happened to the opinionated, independent woman I love?"

Lottie's smile barely reached her eyes. "Monica still wants you. And I, for some reason, am feeling particularly vulnerable about it right now."

I felt my eyebrows go up. "After all these years? I don't think so." But I realized I was just saying that to make her feel better, which was stupid. Lottie was a big girl and more than capable of taking care of herself. "Okay, maybe she does want me, but it doesn't change how I feel about you."

"I know." But Lottie didn't sound certain. "I've been through a lot lately, David, with the regressions and all the emotions I've been trying to understand because of them. I feel like I'm on emotional overload. It's given me a bit of a thin skin and these people who are coming into our lives lately…"

She looked away and, for a second, guilt passed over her face. Some darker, deeper part of me, the place where I kept things I didn't want anyone else to know, flickered to life. She may have been thinking about Monica before, but I knew she was thinking about Galen now.

Before I could tempt the conversation further, I slid out of bed. The room felt cool on my skin and I stretched, working out leftover kinks. I took my cell phone off the nightstand and surfed it for messages, texts, and emails.

"Is that work?" Lottie asked.

I tensed at the question, realizing I still hadn't told Lottie that MD had revoked all vacation until I resolved the photo and Zev Sahin. I hesitated, too long, and Lottie answered it with a disappointed sigh.

"Okay," I said, "here's the deal. MD rescinded my vacation until I settle an open issue with the photograph I swiped from the op. Seems the connection between the photo and the op goes a little deeper than we originally thought."

Lottie straightened. "But I'm in that photo."

"I know, and it's nothing to worry about. I just have to close up some holes. That's all."

"What holes?"

I wished I could tell her. I leaned down and kissed her again, this time with the hope of erasing all her worry. "Trust me on this. It's not a concern."

Lottie studied me with caution, but I could see the lover's uncertainty overshadowing the psychologist's convictions. "So what does that mean? No trips of any kind at all?"

"For now, and then I'll make it up to you." I held out my hands. "You know I'm good for it."

"Good and full of yourself," she said.

There was anger in her voice and it sounded, what was the word Lottie liked to use? Displaced. Something else was still on her mind. Or rather, someone.

"Lottie, we've been down this road before. This is my job. It's what I do. I can't ignore orders. Would you ignore a client that needed you, even on a day off?"

"If it's just a photo," Lottie said, "then why do you have to do this? Why can't someone else?"

"Because I was the one who stole it and MD wants me to

do penance." I walked around the bed and sat down next to her. "We can still take a vacation once I get the intel MD needs. She wants it in two days. It's not like this is going to eat up my entire vacation."

"I waited while you were in Turkey, David. I was here. Alone."

"You weren't alone the whole time. You have friends and I know you saw them."

"That's not the point."

This wasn't like her. Whatever she was feeling she was keeping close to heart, and I wondered why she didn't feel comfortable talking about it now. She was a psychologist. And talking was what psychologists did. I put my hand to her chin, making her look at me, and lowered my voice, making it as gentle and understanding as I could.

"What's really going on, Lottie?"

"Not now," she said, straightening with conviction. "Do what you need to do."

I was thinking of pushing back, but Lottie didn't give me the chance to argue. She rolled away and pulled the covers over her body so I couldn't see any bare skin. Her annoyed position.

Okay. Better to let this one go. I headed to the bathroom and freshened up, and after I was done I called Lottie's brother, Michael, leaving an urgent message when voicemail kicked in. I didn't explain why.

I changed into running gear, went outside, and stretched, and my mind wandered to Monica. Again. I hadn't thought about her in years and now that she'd resurfaced I couldn't stop. Maybe it had to do with the fact that Monica reappeared in my life so unexpectedly. Maybe it was because I'd reconnected with her through Lottie. Maybe it was something else. As much as I'd told Lottie the truth—I wasn't interested in Monica at all anymore—something about her still nagged. By the time I pushed through the first mile and headed into the second, I was sweating hard and still not at peace. When I hit the fourth mile, Monica had pretty much jammed up my head. And when I rounded the last few blocks to my house and finished the sixth mile, I was drenched and feeling even more jittery. So much for an endorphin high. So much for clearing the mind.

I paced the driveway to bring down my heart rate, and the garage door opened. Lottie stepped out in bare feet, wearing a thick, yellow robe and holding a phone.

"Nat," she said, handing it over.

"Two minutes," I said. I ran into the laundry room, stripped down to my shorts, and wiped off the sweat with a towel from the hamper. In the fridge I found a chocolate protein shake and a large bottle of filtered water. I grabbed both and dove into the shake first.

Lottie followed and when I took the phone, Nat sounded freaked. "I need your help."

I swiped an arm over my forehead, still sweating. "Is this about the photo?" I asked.

"Yes and no. She gave me a *list*, D-Man."

I finished the shake, stumbling over the cryptic message before figuring out what he meant. "Who? Lori?"

"Yeah. She wants me to go *shopping*."

I dumped the empty container in the garbage and hit the water. "And?"

Lottie motioned to me with her hands, like she wanted to know what was going on.

"For her and the boys," Nat said. "She wants me to go to the supermarket and *buy stuff.*"

I sipped more water and noticed that Lottie had folded all the laundry, which was now sitting on the kitchen table, ready to be put away. I gestured to it and mouthed a *thank you.*

Lottie pressed her lips together, turned, and walked away, still pissed off about the cancelled vacation.

"I'm going to take a stab at this," I said to Nat, heading into the foyer and peering up the stairwell so I could watch Lottie's legs as she climbed, "and say you've never shopped at a supermarket before."

"No. And I don't want to."

So this was the deal. Nat stood about three inches shorter than me and carried twenty pounds more muscle. I had no doubt that if it came down to it, he could kick my ass and send me to a hospital. And yet he was scared of the supermarket.

Someone screamed on the other end of the line and Lori, Nat's wife and Lottie's best friend, yelled at one of the boys. "What did you just do? Carlos, did you pour finger paint down Leo's shirt?" There was some thumping, a door slamming shut, and rustling noises with the sound of a car engine turning over.

"You gotta help me, D-Man. I'll be at your house in ten."

"What? Wait—"

He hung up.

I raced upstairs and found Lottie tugging a pink bra with lacy flowers out of the dresser. "Have I seen that one before?"

"No," she said, pulling out matching panties. "And you're not going to."

I sighed.

"So," she said, shoving clothes around the drawer. "Are

you going to stand there all day or is there something else I need to know?"

I hesitated.

Lottie faced me head on. "Don't bother to explain. You're heading out with Nat, right?"

"Yeah, but he's working with me on getting intel on the photo. And, um, he needs help food shopping."

Lottie stared at me. "Food shopping."

"I know that doesn't sound right, but—"

"Don't bother, David." Lottie brushed past me and headed into the bathroom. "I'll entertain myself. I've done it before and I'll do it again."

She shut the bathroom door, leaving me standing alone in the bedroom with a boatload of guilt.

I grabbed clothes from my closet, raced through a shower in the hall bathroom, and changed in eight minutes. True to his word, Nat sat idling at the curb in his red Mustang. I walked out the front door to meet him while he drummed his fingers on the steering wheel. After buckling in, I gave him a long look. His jeans and navy shirt were splattered with red paint.

"You suck," I said.

"Thank you," he said, navigating a U-turn. "And you're going to help me even though you're in a pissy mood because Lori's got a bug up her butt that I don't help out around the house enough."

"You don't," I said. "And for some reason Lori still loves you."

We jerked to a stop and Nat turned his exasperation on me. "Whose side are you on anyway?"

"You really want me to answer that right now?"

"Bastard," he mumbled.

We kept going despite Nat's irritation and mine, and pulled into a parking lot ten minutes later, finding a spot just outside the supermarket entrance.

"What's so hard about this anyway?" I asked as we walked toward rows of shopping carts just outside the door. Nat stared at them like they were diseased. "Grab one," I told him.

He refused.

"Tell me something," I said, snagging a cart and moving aside so a woman with a toddler could take one, too. "What did you do when you brought down Sahin's compound?"

"Oh man." Nat puffed up his chest, looking all fired up and like he was ready to go at it again. "Major artillery. Rocket launchers. Flash bangs. M-240s. Huge explosions. Best freaking explosions I've seen in months. I swear my ears are still ringing."

I moved in on him so we stood toe to toe. "And I gave myself the job of pinching a wallet in a nightclub so that everyone else on the team could do what they're good at. I hated it, but I did it anyway, and that's exactly what you're going to do. So shut up, go inside, and shop." I grabbed him by the shirt and shoved him through the door.

"No need to get so testy," he said over his shoulder.

I rolled the cart to a stop near produce. "So what intel did you find for me?"

Nat handed me a piece of paper. I unfolded it and scanned its contents. Instead of details about Sahin or the photo, I held a shopping list.

"Are you kidding me?" I asked.

Nat took the cart and started for the melons. "You shop. I

share intel. It's the way of the world. The yin and the yang. The—"

"Pain in my ass."

"It's what you love about me most, D-Man."

I gave the list a good read and said, "Lori wants cucumbers."

Nat held out his hands like he didn't know where the cucumbers were, so I guided him over. Nat looked at them like he didn't know how to pick one either. While I selected, Nat grabbed a few grapes from a nearby display and popped them into his mouth. "What's next on the list?"

"Salad. Bagged."

We moved over two rows. Nat surveyed the dozens of prepackaged bags with a blank look. I guessed, grabbed one, and threw it in the cart. Out of the corner of my eye, I noticed a thirty-something blonde in a suit and heels watching us while she shopped for apples.

"So what did you find out about the photo?" I asked.

We turned the corner, moved down the next aisle, and stopped in front of the coffee. The blonde followed, passed us, and surveyed the tea. I grabbed French vanilla decaf, ground.

Nat moved in close, his expression serious and his voice just above a whisper. "MD's right. That's Jared Sahin, Zev Sahin's nephew. He owns Trendz, an upscale men's clothing store in New York City on Fifth near Central Park."

"Big bucks."

"Yep."

The blonde edged in a few steps closer, looking like she was listening, then backed away and rolled toward the cookies.

"But wait. There's more," Nat said, nodding his head like

he couldn't give me the details fast enough. "Remember Monica?" He grabbed the cart and guided us down the next aisle for more privacy.

The blonde followed.

"Zev Sahin is Monica's brother."

Blood rushed into my ears and I froze.

"Yeah." Nat glanced side to side. Probably checking for the blonde. "My reaction exactly. I guess you never knew Monica's maiden name?"

I shook my head. Never knew her married one either.

My chest felt tight and all of a sudden I couldn't breathe. "I need air," I said, pushing the cart forward.

Nat raced after me. "Hey, what gives? You okay? Shit, D-Man, you okay?" He yanked on my arm, forcing me to stop.

"No, I'm not okay. And why didn't all this come up when we researched Zev for the op?"

The blonde inched in a little, pretending she was interested in crackers. I nudged Nat so we could move away.

"There's something you need to know," I said, lowering my voice so no one else could hear. "Monica's back in my life."

Nat didn't blink. "No shit?"

"No shit."

Nat paled. "Aw crap, David. How can you do that to Lottie? She loves you, and I thought you loved her, too."

"No, no. It's not like that." I dropped my voice lower. "Lottie met Monica at a meeting yesterday. She's into all that regression stuff and found Lottie because of the *NatGeo* article and contacted her. I think she's trying to draw Lottie in."

"Into what?"

"I don't know. But she came to my house last night." And knowing she was related to Zev Sahin didn't sit well with me. She was a Sahin and, like MD said about Jared, when someone was linked to Zev Sahin, nothing was what it appeared.

Nat rubbed a hand over his buzz cut then the back of his neck, cursing under his breath. When his cursing ran out of steam, he looked at me. "Lottie knows about the two of you?"

"She does now. And she got super possessive."

He rubbed his head again, this time thinking. "What did Monica want?"

"Lottie left her wallet at Monica's house and she came by to return it."

"That's convenient."

"I know. She also said she wanted to see Lottie. Seems the regression meeting wasn't what Lottie was expecting, and Monica tried to convince her to come to more of them. She definitely didn't expect to run into me, and she definitely didn't make the connection about who Lottie was until she saw us together. I don't think she had a clue that she'd meet me again."

Shelves of water stood behind me and I grabbed a bottle, snapped it open, and drank. Tequila would have been better but they didn't sell that in the supermarket.

"So a woman you had an affair with is now trying to make friends with Lottie," Nat said. "Her brother is a huge drug lord and now this woman, the *drug lord's sister*, knows where you live, and came to you after you killed his operation and ended up with a photo that somehow links back to Lottie."

"Yeah. That pretty much sums it up." I dropped the empty bottle into the cart so I could pay for it later and hunched over, a heavy, sick feeling churning in my stomach.

"You think Monica's got the goods on what you did to her brother?"

"No idea."

"Think he knows you had an affair with her?"

"No idea."

"Think Monica's being up front with you?"

"No idea."

"You gotta figure this out, D-Man."

I peered up at him. "You think?"

"You gonna tell MD?"

"Hell no. Not yet, anyway."

"Who else knows about the photo?"

I straightened, not liking the answer. "Galen."

"Oh. Great."

"Yeah. My thoughts exactly."

"You gonna share this with Galen? Coz he knows you took the photo, right?"

"I'm not saying a word."

"Think Lottie might say something?"

I wasn't sure. It wasn't something I'd thought of until now. "Lottie doesn't see Galen anymore."

"Meaning?"

"Meaning nothing. She doesn't see him."

Nat looked like he didn't believe me. "You're in denial."

"This isn't denial," I stressed. "She doesn't see him."

Nat pressed a hand to my shoulder and stared at me, dead-on. "Do you trust Lottie?"

"Of course."

"No, I mean do you *trust* her. As in, is she faithful to you?" Before I could dismiss the question, Nat added, "She came close to falling into the sack with Galen a few months ago."

"And nothing happened," I reminded him.

"That's not answering the question."

Because it was a memory I wanted to forget. I'd caught Lottie with Galen once, looking like they might have taken things further if I hadn't interrupted. It was during Lottie's regression. Lottie and I were in a bad place in our relationship and Galen took advantage. It never happened again, and Lottie and I never discussed it further. Neither did Galen.

"You know I love her, right D-Man?"

I nodded.

"But you also know something ain't right and it hasn't been since Lottie started with those episodes. I know you want to believe nothing happened, but you gotta admit that she and Galen got a weird thing going with that past-life crapola. She ran to him for help, not you, when it started hitting the fan and I think they're using it as an excuse to meet."

"Galen knows better than to throw away his career like that." I remembered the day I told Galen what would happen if he stepped out of line with Lottie. He battled me over it, insisting that I shouldn't worry. "He wouldn't risk it."

"And what if Lottie persists with him? Goes after him anyway?"

"She wouldn't do that."

Nat went silent for a minute. "And you swore when you were eighteen that you were just going to help a woman named Monica clean up her yard after a storm."

I said nothing.

"You're an idiot, David. You really think you can trust

Galen? With anything?"

"I trust Lottie. That's all that matters."

"Yeah? And what happens now that Galen's back from the op?"

"Nothing's going to happen."

"Lottie's trying to build up her practice, man. Don't you see it?" Nat shoved us off to the side so an older couple could pass by. "She's not gonna use Monica to help her do it, for obvious reasons, so who's left that believes in her, D-Man? Hmm? It's not you. It's Galen. It's always been Galen." Nat grabbed a jar of peanut butter off the shelf and threw it into the cart. "You're a sorry son of a bitch. Smart as hell and still the most stupidest guy that ever lived."

Nat took the cart and pushed it down the next aisle. Soups, pastas, and sauces. "And now," he said, checking out the shelves of canned soup, "you're stuck. You tell Lottie about this intel, she's gonna want details about Sahin, and you can't share that info with her. And if you tell Galen, he's gonna step back in and get close to Lottie again, saying he just wants to protect her like he did in July." He reached for a can of chicken soup, read the ingredients, shook his head, and put it back on the shelf. "You're screwed."

A burning sensation sprouted in the base of my neck and started moving up. A headache. And a bad one. I shrugged my shoulders, trying to ease the growing tension. It didn't help. I closed my eyes and rubbed my temples.

"So what are you going to do about Monica?" Nat asked.

"There's nothing to do."

"You're just hurtin' for trouble, aren't you?"

Someone tapped me on the shoulder. The blonde had

moved in and was smiling in an embarrassed way. Like she wasn't sure she was welcome but wanted to talk to us anyway.

"Excuse me," she said. "I'm sorry I was following you, but I have to say that I think you two make a really nice couple."

Nat and I exchanged a look.

"I couldn't help but notice that it looks like you've been arguing since you walked into the store." She dug through a fancy handbag and pulled out a business card. The name read Susannah Grant, Couples Therapist, and listed out a bunch of credentials, a phone number, and an office location. "You've both got the classic, representative body language of challenges in your relationship, and if ever you need to talk, call me. Okay?"

Her smile widened and warmed, then she patted my shoulder again and took off with her groceries.

Nat turned bright red and stalked off.

I stood behind, nursing a headache and thinking I would have laughed if the situation were different.

I took the cart and went searching for Advil.

Chapter 10

Lottie pulled her Jeep to the curb, rolled to a stop, and thought about why she'd showed up at Galen's condo again. It had been three months since she last saw him, and despite everything she and David had been through, here she sat, tempting fate once more. Of course, she could always turn around and just head back home but then she wouldn't have answers. And she needed those desperately.

Lottie cut the engine and stayed in the Jeep, studying the square-cut hedges and the golden colored foliage that framed Galen's condo. A breeze blew through, rustling tree leaves, their brilliant color reminding Lottie of an oversized ebony bed with images of trees and gods carved into it. She remembered her life in Egypt not as if she'd lived it thousands of years ago but as if she lived it yesterday. She remembered herself as Shemei, David as Bakari, and Galen as Kemnebi. She and Bakari had loved each other, deeply, and were excited for their pending marriage. But he was Pharaoh's General and often went away to battle, sometimes for months at a time. Following one of their biggest campaigns, thousands of Egyptians heralded Pharaoh's return with his army. Shemei stood at the edge of the Avenue of Sphinxes, anxious to find Bakari safe and whole, but Kemnebi had found her instead. Bakari, he said, didn't make it. Shemei was crushed, devastated to learn that she would have to live without the only man she'd ever loved. But it was what happened after she learned of Bakari's death that haunted her most—when Shemei took solace from Kemnebi and invited him into her bed, losing her grief to the fire he ignited within her.

And now here Lottie sat, preparing to face him again.

She grabbed her bag, locked the Jeep, and strode up the brick walkway to the front entrance, determined to leave certain memories behind and find support and answers ahead. After ringing the bell she waited, and waited some more. She considered leaving when the door opened and Galen, looking freshly showered and dressed in khakis and a silk brown shirt, greeted her. But not with enthusiasm. For a second, Lottie wondered if he was getting ready for a date. His eyes were dark and unreadable and his lips were pressed together, and she felt like she was the last person he wanted to see.

The rich, spiced scent that Lottie now recognized as unique to them both slammed into her like a blast from an oven, hot and potent. Another image swept in, the two of them exhausted and entangled in fine linen sheets, a rare Egyptian breeze brushing over their sweaty bodies.

Swiping away beads of perspiration from her upper lip now, Lottie cleared her throat and asked, "Can we talk?"

Galen hesitated. "We've talked before and it has caused many problems. I don't think this is a good idea."

"I need your help, Galen. Please."

"Each of your visits seems to start out as a plea for help, but they always end with trouble for the both of us."

His voice, so smooth and cultured, moved through her like heady red wine. "Galen, I have no one else to talk to."

"Words I've heard before." He shook his head. "I work for Bellotti now and do not want to face this temptation. Please go."

He made to close the door but Lottie shoved back. "I think David is starting his own regression."

Galen paused. "I'm very glad to hear that."

"I also think he needs your help."

His face darkened, like she was infringing on his time and he didn't want to be bothered. When he spoke, his voice mirrored the edginess in his expression. "I'm not a girlfriend with whom you should share your deepest thoughts, Lottie."

His biting words stung. His snub even more so. Galen had always been receptive toward her, never hiding how much he wanted her despite her relationship with David. She guessed she shouldn't have been surprised by his reaction now. David had made his displeasure over Galen's involvement with her very clear, and it seemed as if Galen intended to make good on his promise to stay away.

Still, Lottie refused to give up. "David needs help with his regression, and I'm too new at this to be able to guide him."

"You are more versed with past lives than you give yourself credit for."

Galen tried closing the door again and, like before, Lottie shoved back. "I think something is wrong. He's facing emotional conflict he hasn't faced before, and is refusing to acknowledge the thoughts and feelings that are consciously intolerable to him."

Galen folded his arms over his chest, looking like he was thinking about what that meant. "You feel lonely."

Lottie didn't want to admit it but she did.

"And yet you remain with Bellotti despite this loneliness. It's a very interesting choice that you've made in men, don't you think?"

"That wasn't fair."

"What's not fair is turning up on my doorstep and playing games with me."

"These are not games, Galen." Lottie frowned, showing her impatience. "You know my heart belongs to David, but that doesn't change the fact that you are a big piece of my life, of all of my lives, and that I'm a large part of yours, too."

Galen said nothing.

So Lottie pressed on. "I know you've felt alone, too. For all I know, maybe you still do. But I'm having trouble finding people who understand me and what this feels like, and because of that I don't think I can help David." She shifted on her feet as the first shivers of doubt started moving in. "David doesn't believe me no matter how hard I try with him. My boss doesn't believe me and has threatened to fire me. Even my best friend doesn't believe me so I've stopped talking to her about all of this. So how can I help David when I can't even find help myself?"

"The way is easy if you simply look."

"I've been looking for months."

"And I was looking for more than a year," he snapped.

A gust of wind chilled the space between them and Lottie shuddered.

Galen sighed and rubbed his forehead. "I have a feeling I'll be made to pay for this, but I can't stand seeing you out there in the cold." He motioned for her to come inside and gestured toward the main living area.

Lottie went in, letting herself take in the serenity of Galen's personal space. She had been here several times before and under similar circumstances. Uninvited, underprepared, and uncertain. She noticed that nothing had changed in the three months since she last visited. Decorated in jewel tones and heavy, masculine woods, the rooms carried Galen's personal touches that she understood well. Framed Egyptian artwork. Replicas of faience pottery. Mirrors beveled with coral and lapis and ebony. A vase filled with fresh blue lotus flowers.

Another evocative and very old memory surfaced. Kemnebi had held up two cups of red wine and offered one. Inside, three lotus petals floated, the outer edges of their bright blue color stained a deeper shade of red. He held his own cup and his eyes met hers, and in his gaze she saw an unspoken promise of what was to come. And, for the first time in her Egyptian life, she invited another man into her bed.

The memory disappeared and Lottie drew in a breath, heart racing, body flushed and humming to the tune of Galen's, and took a few distancing steps away.

Galen settled into a deep, navy sofa and looked up at her, still waiting on her story. His gaze searched through hers, peeling away what little defenses she had left.

"Tell me what's going on with Bellotti."

Lottie watched Galen's mouth, the way its soft curves formed the words, and turned, focusing on the vase of lotus flowers instead. Anything to help clear her mind and keep her focused. "How do you handle this?" she asked. "How do you manage the solitude as you try to find people who are just like you?"

The air around her shifted, warm and growing warmer, as his voice wrapped itself around her as he spoke. "It isn't easy," he said. "Especially when you're the only person with whom I'm truly connected."

Though he sat ten feet away, Lottie felt Galen's pull. The part of him that called out to her, binding them in a way most people would never understand.

Against her better judgment, she turned and faced him. "You also have a connection to David," she reminded him. "As well as others."

"And yet you and I always end up coming back to each other." Galen stood and moved in closer, and Lottie felt the heat intensify. She took a step in retreat, a tantalizing sweat spreading over the small of her back.

"I'm curious, however, as to why you're discussing this with me and not Bellotti."

"Because he doesn't understand."

"No." The challenge in Galen's sand-colored eyes made Lottie pause. "He doesn't understand *you*."

Lottie studied the thick carpet, wrestling with the truth. And it hurt to admit it. "No," she whispered. "David doesn't."

Galen moved toward the foyer. "Your issues are with Bellotti and not me. I can't help you, Lottie. You have not found peace and I'm not the one who can find it for you." He opened the front door, encouraging her to leave.

She didn't want to even though she knew she was here for selfish reasons only. "Please, Galen."

Galen ignored her appeal. Behind him, the open door marked a way toward the dark night and the unknown. Outside Lottie saw only the troubling and unfamiliar. Inside with

Galen, she felt reassurance and comfort. And something else.

"We can help each other, Galen." Lottie approached him with tentative steps. "I think it's a mistake not to."

"What we share goes far beyond the physical, Lottie, and that, I believe, is what frightens you more than anything."

"We can talk to David together—"

"That won't help."

"Please."

She grabbed his arm and the memory that surged forward this time squeezed the air from her lungs. She was sitting by a roaring fire that smelled of pine, hearing the snaps and pops as the wood burned. People circled around the fire, chanting. Dancing. Celebrating. A black sky dotted with thousands of sparkling stars hung overhead. A man came over and brushed the hair from her cheek and past her shoulder. His hands looked roughened from the hunt. A fresh injury showed on his chest, three claw marks swiped across and down. His eyes caught hers and she understood what he wanted. What they both wanted. He took her hand and coaxed her from the group, using a fiery torch to light their way through thick brush and trees. She trembled under his touch, more from fear of the unknown rather than fear of him. Out there, in the black distance, in this new place they had found, were strange and unfamiliar things. Things that lurked in the darkness that were dangerous and life-threatening if they were not careful. But with him she knew comfort and protection. And as he maneuvered her onto the soft, sweet-smelling grass and took her, she thought about another man and wondered what it would be like to lay with him.

Galen pulled his hand away and came back into focus.

"Did you see that?" Lottie asked, her heart hammering so hard she swore Galen could see it banging against her chest. "It was a different memory. A new one, of the two of us."

Galen pressed his lips together, a faraway, clouded look in his eyes.

"Tell me you saw it," she demanded.

He didn't. Instead, he opened the door wider, refusing to meet her gaze. "I think you should leave, Lottie."

"You were there. I sensed it. I *saw* it, and I know you saw it, too."

Galen would only stare out into the front yard. "This conversation is over."

"Galen—"

"There is nothing for us to talk about. Please go."

Lottie stood in place, waiting for Galen to change his mind. But he didn't.

With a resigned nod, Lottie walked out the door.

Chapter 11

Nat pulled the Mustang to a stop in front of my house and I reached for the door. He tapped my arm.

"Hold on a sec." He tugged another piece of paper out of his jeans pocket and handed it over. This time, it wasn't a shopping list. On the paper, Nat had scribbled Monica and Jared's names along with their phone numbers and addresses. "Found them in the database at work," he said. "Never knew they were there 'til now." Because we didn't need to know until now. "Not a lot to find on them. They've kept a low profile, which is why they didn't surface in our initial reviews. We were only looking for the big guns. Not sure if that's good or bad."

I gave the paper a cursory glance and said, "Thanks." Then I got out of the car.

The passenger window opened and Nat's voice followed. "D-Man?"

I hung back and peered inside.

"Be smart about this." He didn't mean the intel.

I stared at him and nodded.

Nat took off and I trudged up the walkway, unlocked the front door, went inside, and disarmed the alarm. The house felt warm and tranquil. And empty.

Lottie wasn't home.

Nat's warning kicked around in my brain.

I headed to the kitchen, fired up my laptop, and cracked open one of four Dos Equis beers we had in the fridge. It was a little after two, but I didn't care. It was Happy Hour somewhere in the world.

At the kitchen table, I kicked off my sneakers, stretched out my legs, and went straight to the PROs website. Once I logged on, I tapped through a few rounds of security, sorted through the databases until I found the one I needed, and got to work. By then, half the beer was gone.

I discovered that Monica J. Sahin was born forty-five years ago in Istanbul, Turkey, on January twelfth. She had two brothers, Zev and Damian, and one deceased brother named Stephan. She married Greg Boseris on February fifteenth when she was thirty-one. She divorced four years later and had one daughter, Ada. More information in ten seconds from a government database than I got during the months I spent with her. Not sure what that said about me, but I was eighteen at the time and didn't have my head on straight.

I found Jared S. Sahin next. He was born in New York City on April twenty-eighth, was twenty-five years old and was the son of Monica's deceased brother, Stephan. Files on Monica and Jared told about college education, investments, businesses, and real estate owned. Neither had any outstanding warrants or appeared on any FBI most wanted lists. Out of the entire family, Monica and Jared were the only two who moved to the States to live permanently, which probably explained why they dropped off the radar. Monica and Zev's brother, Damian, was known to travel the world and, according to files, was an avid collector of ancient artifacts. According to bank statements, all three were loaded. Family drug money most probably, courtesy of Zev Sahin.

Now I had to fill in the blanks.

I dug out a second Dos Equis and, using the contact information Nat gave me, called Monica first. While her phone rang, a knot formed in my stomach. During our affair we weren't always discreet, but we weren't reckless either. Now, I felt exposed. Handled incorrectly, this situation could blow up big time, but I never got the chance to find out. Voicemail kicked in, putting my objective on hold.

"Hi, Monica. It's David." I paused because the situation felt weird, reminding me too much of our first morning after when I called her, wanting more. "Call me back when you get this message." I left my cell number and hung up.

I was about to dial Jared next when the phone rang. It was Lottie's brother.

"Dude," Michael said. "Got your message and I got one minute before I have to run. What's up?"

I heard scraping and grinding in the background, followed by grunts and cheers. A skate park. "Jared Sahin," I said. "You know him?"

"Haven't seen him since last winter. We're not really tight." Someone called Michael's name and Michael shouted that there was no way in hell he'd let the other guy use his board. Then he came back on the line. "Wannabes. Always asking to borrow my goods, you know?"

"You hear from Jared at all?"

"Nah. Went to college together and did the occasional party. Kinda went our separate ways. He's a client of the law firm I work for, in the Private Client Group. You know, the guys who work with the guys who have more money than they know what to do with."

I reviewed the computer screen to make sure I got the details right. "I heard he owns Trendz on Fifth. Know anything about it?"

"Pricey men's clothing store." Michael laughed. "Owned it for a few years, I think. Want me to let him know you're coming in or something? It's been a while since I saw him and I think he'll still remember me, so maybe I can score you a discount."

This was the risk I took by talking to Michael first and giving him a heads up. But it was either that or risk not finding Jared at all.

"Not necessary," I told him.

"Okay. We cool, then?"

I told Michael we were, and he said to tell Lottie "hi," and we both hung up. I noticed the second beer was empty now, too, and wondered how they kept disappearing. I went through another half hour of research and was halfway through the third Dos Equis when Lottie walked through the kitchen door. She looked at me, looked at the beer, and headed for the wine rack and grabbed a bottle of red. Her posture was rigid, her shoulders looked knotted, and I knew right away something was wrong. I shut down the laptop while she went to the bar in the den and came back with a wine glass.

"Where were you?" I asked.

Lottie ignored me, instead putting all her focus on opening the Pinot Noir, filling a glass, and drinking.

"Lottie?" I shoved the laptop aside, got up, and reached for her.

She pulled away. Her nostrils flared and her mouth clenched, looking like she didn't know if she wanted to cry or rage. She finished off the wine and poured a refill, and I waited until she got herself together. When she did, there was a tremor in her voice.

"I really don't want to talk about it, David. You wouldn't understand."

She'd been saying that a lot since July and I hated it. "Try me."

She studied me over the rim of her glass like she wanted to believe me and couldn't. It was a disappointing look and it made the knot in my stomach tighten. She shook her head, turned, and walked away. "I need to be alone right now."

I didn't need to be a genius to understand what was going on. I'd seen Lottie in this kind of mood on only a few occasions, and it always came from the same source.

I squared off, working hard not to lose control but demanding an answer anyway. "Where did you go this afternoon?" I repeated.

She walked another ten paces before turning and squaring off, too. "I went to see Galen."

Silence and seconds ticked by. In that time, Nat's words hurtled around my head. *She ran to him for help, not you. Do you trust her? Is she faithful?*

"That look on your face right now?" Lottie came back, grabbed the bottle, and poured while she walked away. "It shows me that you're still not open to discussing Galen even though you keep asking about him."

I came up defensive. "I didn't say anything."

She came up annoyed. "You don't have to, David." She

was breathing heavy and her skin was flushed, and I could see the effect Galen had on her.

Jealousy stabbed through my heart. I bit back on the ugly emotion as well as my growing impatience. "Tell me what happened while you were with him."

Her eyes flashed with irritation and she laughed—with equal impatience. "David, I honestly don't think you could handle knowing it."

I opened my mouth and then closed it. Nothing good was going to come out if I responded to that comment without thinking. I spied the Dos Equis, debating if I should have another and get hammered along with her. After I found enough patience for the both of us, I tried again. "Just talk to me, Lottie."

Lottie swayed while she thought about it. The alcohol was kicking in fast. "Okay. What the hell." She came back to me, but her mouth was set and her eyes were hard and her knuckles were white from clenching the wine glass. "I think you're going through your own regression and that you're in denial about it. I went to Galen and asked him to help you through it, only when I was there I had another regression of my own. Or rather, *we* had another regression. Together."

I leaned against the counter and rubbed my temples, feeling the headache gnawing its way back in. "Not this again," I mumbled.

"Yes, this. Again." Lottie shook her head. "You have issues with Galen, and serious ones, and your refusing to acknowledge them along with your refusal to accept that regression is a reality will make the situation between us worse. I'm not sure how you can't see that because it's as plain as day to me."

"Did you ever think that I just don't see life the way you do?"

"Yes," she said. "And until recently it didn't matter. We used to feel like soul mates, David. Like we were lock and key regardless of how we viewed life. But lately?" She shook her head and her hair fell forward. I wanted to brush it off her face and feel her soft skin, but Lottie's body language screamed *back off*. "It's like we're heading on two different planes."

"And what does that mean?"

"I don't know." She tossed down more wine and stood in front of me, swaying again and battling demons she wasn't willing to share.

I couldn't resist anymore and took her face in my hands. "What did Galen do to you, Lottie?"

"It's always about Galen to you, isn't it?" Lottie's eyes became glassy, and not from the wine. "Did it occur to you that this is just about you and me?"

"It can't be about just you and me when you keep inviting Galen back in." The words came out with more antagonism than I intended and I gritted my teeth, trying for calm again but it was failing me, fast. Too much pent up emotion, too many months of trying to hold it in, too many days spent ignoring Galen's hold on Lottie—all of it was coming to a head. Whether we acknowledged it or not, he'd become the third person in our relationship.

Lottie pulled away. "It took me three months, David, and I'm still not complete." Her face lost all color and her body started to shake. "Three months of trying to work through all the anxiety and confusion. Of not knowing if there was really something wrong with me. Of trying to convince the people closest to me that I wasn't losing my mind and trying to come to terms with the loneliness and abandonment."

I straightened. "You think I abandoned you?"

Lottie backpedaled toward the slider. "I understand not understanding the concept. Believe me, I do. You thought I was going through a phase. But I needed guidance and help, and without Galen, I never would have survived."

Meaning, I wasn't there for her.

I glanced away, feeling for the first time like I'd failed the woman I loved. "Galen," I whispered, and the name felt heavy on my tongue and heavier in my heart. "Of course it was Galen. It's who you run to."

"Only because you leave me no other choice."

"And had I not walked in on the two of you back in July? Were you doing what you were doing because you had no other choice?"

Lottie's eyes narrowed. "That wasn't fair and that was different."

"You almost slept with Galen."

"But I didn't."

"Because I *walked in*!"

Lottie looked ready to snap back but stopped herself from mouthing off. A smile appeared but it was one of bitter realization. "You think I would have slept with Galen if you hadn't interrupted us."

I didn't take the bait.

"Admit it, David."

I wouldn't.

"Say it." She held the wine glass and pointed a finger at

me. The wine bottle at her side sloshed in agitation. "You think I would have slept with Galen if you hadn't walked in. It's what you're thinking. It's what you believe, so you might as well get this over with and come to terms with what's really bothering you—"

"Yes. I absolutely, positively believe you would have slept with him if I hadn't barged in. I felt like I had my insides ripped out when I walked in on you." I hurtled the beer bottle into the garbage. It shattered against the others, the sharp sound piercing the distance between us. "I still see you together in my mind, and it makes me insane to know he wants you as much as I do. Happy now?"

The glass panes on the kitchen windows vibrated from my anger. My jaw was clenched and I was breathing hard, and I knew right then that I'd done the right thing but in the worst possible way. And I couldn't take any of it back.

Lottie stared at me a long while, the psychologist in her picking me apart with deadly, demanding silence. "And what about Monica?" she challenged. "How do I know you won't pursue something with her?"

"I already told you there's nothing going on."

"You've got her name and number on the piece of paper right there next to your cell phone," Lottie said. "Don't even try and pretend that you didn't contact her."

"You're misreading what's going on with her."

"Then maybe you should tell me."

"Yes, I called her. About *business* related to Jared, who happens to be her nephew. I'm not interested in Monica that way and there's no reason not to trust me."

"And *every* reason not to trust *me*?"

I blew out a long, ragged breath and stared up at the ceiling.

"Want to know what I think, David?"

All of a sudden, I felt very tired. "What?"

"I don't think this is about you, or me, or past lives, or regressions, or Monica, or anything else. I think this is about Galen and only Galen. I think he got under your skin and you can't handle it, and it's manifesting itself in other ways."

"I was thinking the exact same thing about you."

Lottie's silence mushroomed like a nuclear detonation. I'd hit the target and taken out both of us.

"No matter how hard I try," Lottie said, "I can't get it through to you that it's what Galen and I shared in the past that serves as the glue between us. Not the sexual attraction."

I looked at Lottie, wanting to believe her.

"But at least I acknowledge who he is to me," she added. "The only reason you accepted Galen to your team was because you wanted to keep your enemies closer. It wasn't to help me during my regression or to show maturity or understanding in our relationship. It was a selfish decision, plain and simple, because you wanted to keep an eye on him. And someday, when you get over yourself and figure out what's really bothering you about him, you'll come to terms. And only then will you and I be able to move on."

Lottie opened the slider and went outside.

Alone.

Chapter 12

I stood in the kitchen, staring at the slider and the empty space Lottie had left behind. I could have gone after her but doing so would only have made things worse. She'd said that things were changing between us and I had a feeling, a bad feeling, she was right. But she was also amped up on wine, and liquor never fueled mature, calm conversations between anyone. If I focused on my goal and gave Lottie her space, we could come back together and make our relationship right again.

Without Galen's help.

While Lottie stayed outside, I called Trendz, hoping to make headway with Jared Sahin on the phone. A woman answered with a throaty voice that sounded like she should have been working phone sex instead of a men's clothing store. Then again, maybe that was the idea. I asked for Jared and immediately got pushback.

"Mr. Sahin only meets with his clients in person."

"But I'm unable to make the trip," I said.

"Can I have your name? I can speak with Mr. Sahin and have him come to your home for private consultation."

Not what I wanted. "No. That's fine. I'll figure out something else."

I hung up and moved on to Plan B. Thirty minutes later and after taking a shower, I was ready to tackle Jared head-on.

Again, the house felt quiet—too quiet—and I traipsed around the rooms searching for Lottie. As a last resort, I checked the backyard and found her sitting in a lounge chair, now wearing a heavy sweatshirt and with her hair hanging over the back, a hand dangling over the armrest and holding the wine glass. The bottle of Pinot sat on the brick patio beside her, almost empty, and the late afternoon sun reflected burnt orange off the dark green bottle.

I approached from behind, careful not to startle her in case she'd passed out. Lottie could drink with the best of them when she wanted to, but I'd never seen her finish a whole bottle on her own before. Her head lolled to the side when I appeared and her eyes skittered as they tracked me. Not passed out but definitely toasted, and definitely seeing more than one of me.

"I'm going to Trendz to see Jared and get this PROs business out of the way," I told her.

Her eyes scanned me from top to bottom and back up again, and the brief flash of heat in her eyes had me thinking of pushing off Jared for another hour. She held up her glass in mock salute, her face glowing from the liquor and the sun.

"I don't know when I'll be home, but it shouldn't be late." It was closing in on three-thirty now. An hour into the city, an hour with Jared, an hour back. Longer if I hit traffic.

I crouched down beside her, brushed the hair from her face, and stroked her bottom lip with my thumb. "We can go out to dinner if you want." Her head lolled away and she focused on the blue and purpling sky, either preferring the view or fed up with me. I was betting the latter. "Or we can stay home and I can cook. Your choice. As long as we spend time together. I know this isn't working out exactly the way we planned, but I want to make it up to you."

"Whatever."

Right. Whatever.

I headed for my SUV in the garage and jumped on the expressway, trying to figure out what the hell had happened with Galen that had her in such a mood. She'd said that she'd experienced another regression with him but I wasn't buying it. Something else was eating at her.

Disappointment. That's what had Lottie all fired up. Disappointment in me.

The ride into Manhattan was trouble free but the more I thought about Lottie, and us, the more I couldn't get her out of my head. Part of me kept thinking I shouldn't have left her alone and part of me wondered how much worse things might get between us. We'd argued before, and had bad times, but this felt different. Lottie had never shut down like this. I spent most of the ride analyzing what had gone down and trying to find a solution, but short of claiming that I believed in something I didn't, I wasn't sure there was anything I could do to fix this.

I pulled onto Fifth just before five and found a parking garage a block away from Trendz. It was heated and cost thirty-two fifty. Welcome to the Big City. I passed store windows displaying three thousand dollar suits and eight hundred dollar shoes and felt underdressed for the occasion. Black merino slacks, a Ted Baker shirt, and Italian loafers didn't make enough of a statement in this part of town.

Trendz was decorated with polished marble, subtle lighting, and a full bar with bartender. Several salespeople were working with customers, laying out suits or slacks with shirts and ties and making suggestions. Some were with wives. Others were with girlfriends. All of them held either a highball or a glass of wine while they shopped. None of the salespeople were female.

A man in a tailored gray pinstriped suit approached. "May I help you, sir?"

"I'm looking for Jared Sahin."

"I'm sorry, sir. He's unavailable right now. Did you have an appointment with him?" The guy had light brown hair that hung just below his collar and wore a watch that looked like it cost as much as the suit. He was clean-shaven, square-jawed, and lean.

"Is he with another customer?" I asked.

"Client."

Okay. "Is he with another client?"

"He is unavailable right now."

"How long will he be busy?"

"Perhaps I can help you instead. My name is Paolo. What, specifically, are you looking for? Most of our work is custom, which I think would benefit you. Your build isn't suited for off-the-shelf."

"Actually, I just need to talk to Jared." I leaned in and lowered my voice, making sure he got the point. "It's a personal matter. If he's with a client, I'll wait. If he's not, then find him. Now."

Paolo shrank back a few steps, intimidated by the six inches and thirty pounds I had on him. "That won't be possible."

"Tell him Michael Morgan is here," I said, hoping that dropping Lottie's brother's name would get me in the door.

"Michael Morgan."

"Personal friend. He's not expecting me but he'll want to see me." I dropped my voice even lower, like I was letting him in on a conspiracy. He leaned in, wanting to hear it. "Tell him it's about one of the documents being drafted for him at the law firm, related to his business transaction."

Paolo peered at me. "Which document should I say?"

I shook my head. "Confidential."

He looked like he was caught between believing me and not wanting to screw his boss over and pay for it later. I pulled away and spread my hands. "Your call, but I wouldn't want to be here when he finds out you made a business decision on his behalf, and it was the wrong decision."

Paolo fussed with his tie. "I'll see what I can do."

I passed the time toying with fabric samples, dismissing two more requests for assistance and an offer to drink while I waited. Jared emerged from a back room, looking nothing like he did in the photo. He was nearly my height and had brown hair pulled into a ponytail and a goatee. A tatt curled up the right side of his neck. He wore expensive jeans, a silk shirt, and a huge grin that said he was excited to meet up with an old friend.

He stopped when he saw me and not Michael and the grin disappeared. His lips pulled back in disgust, like I was something that rolled out of a landfill and had been stinking up the place for days. He considered me for a while, his features turning unreadable, and strolled toward me as if he had nothing better to do. Two bodyguards flanked him, one tall and bald, the other with a nose that looked like it had been broken once. The bald one shifted his suit jacket, flashing a nine-millimeter.

I stood my ground.

"David Bellotti," Jared said. "I wondered when I'd finally meet you and here you are, in the flesh."

I kept my mouth shut, trying to play catch-up and figure out how he knew who I was.

"That was pretty ballsy of you walking in like you did," he said, circling me as he spoke, and I watched the guards watching me. "And I just bet you're dying to know how I know you."

"Zev," I said, my gaze tracking back to Jared.

"Scored it in one," he said. "Should I be impressed?"

He moved in so we stood toe to toe. I had a good five inches on him and could take him down with one quick shot, but he didn't seem threatened. Having muscled guards at your side will give you that confidence.

"You're more intimidating in person," he said, digging out his cell phone and doing some quick fingering. I scanned the store. Everyone was still shopping, oblivious to the threat going on near the front door. Jared shoved the phone in my face and a digital photo stared back at me. "Your picture doesn't do you justice."

I bit back a reaction, wondering how he got his hands on my PROs ID photo.

"I'm more resourceful than you realize," Jared said, tucking the phone into his suit jacket. "Have to be, now that you've destroyed my family. My uncle is in prison because of you and, well, that puts me in control now." He cocked his head and pasted on a satisfied smile. "How convenient is that?"

None of the intel I'd seen on the Sahin family hinted that Jared was in position to take over if Zev went down. No connections. No history. It was as if he didn't exist until now.

Jared's eyes narrowed and he tut-tutted me. "Missed that day of school, did you? Didn't get all the intelligence you needed, did you?" He leaned forward and lowered his voice. "I'm going to make Zev look like chicken shit."

I pasted on a satisfied smile that matched his. "Only because you're full of it yourself, Jared. We both know you're lying."

"Why? Because my face isn't plastered all over the place like my uncle's was?"

"Because if you were a serious player, you wouldn't be holed up in a clothing store. You'd be hiding right now, trying to avoid the same fate that took your uncle."

Jared's fist came up and I grabbed it before it made contact with my face. The bald guy made to pull out his gun but Jared hushed him back into place. Jared shrugged out of my grip, his face burning with rage.

"You have no idea what you've done," he said under his breath. "But know that you will find out."

There was no point in playing this any further. I sent Jared and his men another smile and walked out the glass doors to the street. I managed my way back to the parking garage and my SUV, paid, and pulled out. I clenched the steering wheel, my nerves in a sudden free fall. Someone honked from behind and I pressed the gas and wove my way around the city until I ended up near the entrance to the Midtown Tunnel. I didn't remember how I got there.

I called Nat and got right into it. He whistled when I finished the story. "How's Jared know about you and Zev Sahin?"

"Guess news travels fast in that family," I said as I queued up for the Tunnel, "and now it's a problem." I gripped the steering wheel and cursed. "He knew who I was, Nat. Knew I led that mission. He had my PROs ID photo. My goddamned *PROs ID.*"

"The guy did his homework. And I doubt he did it alone."

Hacked in. Knew someone on the inside. Could have been anything. And none of it was good.

"Get to Lottie," I told him. "Cover her until I get home. Make sure she's safe."

"You think Jared will do something?"

"Not sure. But my gut says something else is going on, and I'm not going to sit back and wait for it to happen. He never surfaced when we dug through the intel, Nat, and that worries me."

"I got your six, D-Man. Drive safe and I'll keep the little lady safer."

By the time the Tunnel spit me out the other end and I was merging onto the expressway, I had a plan. I called Lottie next, the ideas racing through my mind as fast as the cars speeding beside me. She sounded groggy when she answered, like I'd interrupted a deep sleep.

"Nat's on his way over," I said.

"Now?"

"Now."

"Why?"

"I'll tell you when I get home."

She drew in a sharp breath. "What's going on, David?"

"I promise I'll tell you. Just not now. I have another call to make."

"You're scaring me."

Good. Scared meant she'd be on alert. "I'm sorry. Just sit tight until I get home. Everything will be fine."

A red BMW cut me off and I nailed the horn, then it swerved into the left lane before charging past two minivans up ahead. I motored along, doing seventy, thinking tonight's drivers might kill me before the Sahin family did. Just as I started figuring out my next call, the phone rang. A number I didn't recognize displayed on the dashboard and I thought things through for two more rings before taking the call.

Monica was on the other end. "I got your message. I was surprised you called me, David." She sounded cautious but excited, too, and I now regretted contacting her. "I really didn't expect you to reach out to me again."

Again. Like I did years ago.

"Now's not a good time, Monica." I swerved to avoid a small Honda with a kid texting behind the wheel. "I'm in the middle of something."

"Oh." She paused. "Is Lottie there?"

"No." I wondered if Monica knew what Jared knew. And I wondered why Lottie was suddenly so important to her. "It's just not a good time."

"Well, I may not have good timing but *you* do." Her voice sounded playful. Upbeat. "I've been thinking about you all day and I was hoping we could get together. I'd love to take you up on that dinner."

A cop car flashed his lights, blipped his siren, and ripped past, chasing a sport bike that was going twenty miles over the limit. I knocked it back ten, grateful he wasn't coming after me.

"I'm with Lottie," I reminded her.

"I know that." Monica laughed, but it didn't hide her disappointment. Then her voice turned cheery again. She was working me, hard. "I'd like to catch up. That's all. Since Daddy died, I've realized a few things. Good things. And I'd like to make amends. Close old wounds. Start over again."

"That's very nice, Monica, but there isn't anything to amend."

"It'll be innocent, David. I swear. You were young and I was confused, and I handled us badly. I shouldn't have taken off the way I did. Without saying anything to you."

No, but it didn't matter now. And, if I thought about it, it didn't matter back then either. There was nothing to apologize for. Nothing to second guess. A bad choice that came with big consequences, though more for her than me.

And now I had two options. Pass on a get-together and wonder what Monica wanted to say or take her up on her offer and try to obtain the intel I couldn't get from Jared. If she knew what I did to her brother, Zev, I might be able to make the meeting work in my favor. If she didn't, then I had to get to her before Jared did.

"Okay," I said, thinking through all the options. "I can't do dinner, but we could do something else tomorrow."

"I'd love that." She sounded way too pleased and that bothered me. Her excitement made me feel deceitful and unfaithful, even though I had no intentions of playing out either. "I have a regression meeting at eleven, but we can meet after if you want. Spend some time, relive some memories. Ada will be with the babysitter, so we'll have the whole afternoon for ourselves."

Reliving memories was out of the question. So was time

alone. "How about I come to the meeting instead? See what it's all about? Then we can talk after."

She paused. "Is Lottie coming?"

"You already invited her so, yeah, she'd be there."

Another pause. And more disappointment. "I guess it's okay. I'll see you tomorrow."

I disconnected feeling like a scumbag. I hated playing people like that because it never ended well. Someone always wound up hurt.

By now it was almost six-thirty and the sky had darkened. Streetlights kicked on, lining the expressway like an airport runway. Three more exits, one more call to make, and then I'd be home. It might be my most difficult conversation yet.

MD picked up on the first ring and I wondered if she had ever walked away from her phone.

"I have a problem," I said, getting right into it. I told her about my run-in with Jared and MD listened, silent. For a while I didn't hear anything from her end and I began wondering if I had lost the connection. I was reconsidering hanging up and redialing when MD broke in.

"He's talking payback."

"Yeah. And I'm starting to worry about what he might do."

"I know what you want and I can't give it to you," MD said. "If the Sahin family hits, it could be tonight, in a week, or in a month. It could also be never. And I can't, and won't, spare the resources to watch someone who isn't on my payroll."

Because, in MD's mind, Lottie was collateral damage.

"It's interesting to me that Jared flashed firepower but didn't make a move," she said.

"We were in a public place," I reminded her. "He's not

going to do anything with witnesses around. But it makes you wonder what he's planning. He sounded convinced that he could take over for Zev."

"Let him try," she said, "but I agree with you. He doesn't have the resources and he's probably blowing hot air. If he were critical to Zev, we'd have discovered it before we hit Istanbul. Still, we need to keep Jared on our radar."

"That doesn't make the situation any less lethal."

"No, it doesn't," she said, and the meaning behind that simple word was clear. I was facing an unknown factor that, with even a fraction of Zev Sahin's leverage, could still send me to an early grave. Situations like this always came to a head because situations like this didn't die. Only the people involved did.

"Regardless," MD said, "I'm pulling you out of the post-mission operation, Bellotti. Effective immediately, you're officially off the grid on this one."

"You know Jared's going to keep me involved and that means I can't just take off. I'm on his radar now."

"I know."

I motored off the expressway and made my way through the back roads.

"You have a license to carry concealed," MD said as I navigated home.

"I don't carry."

"Then it's time you did."

Chapter 13

Lottie met me just inside the kitchen door, wearing her yellow robe and holding her large mug with the smiley face. The air around her smelled sweet, like hot chocolate. Her hair was pulled into a ponytail and she had dark circles under puffy eyes. Could have been aftereffects of the liquor but I was guessing it was more from anxiety. Nat stood behind her, watching. The lights were on in the kitchen and den but outside was dark. Dark enough for someone to hide and spy. I draped my arm around Lottie and kissed her, shoving the growing paranoia deep down and away. Paranoia made you stop thinking and when you stopped thinking you made mistakes.

"Thanks for coming over," I told Nat.

"No big. It's been an uneventful evening but this one's got a jackhammer of a headache." He jerked a thumb at Lottie and grinned. "So what's the deal now? Did you talk to MD?"

"Yeah, and I'm off the post-mission op." I tossed my keys on the desk and searched the fridge, thinking of having a beer but changing my mind. Thai sounded better. "But, the damage is done."

When I closed the fridge, Lottie was back at my side. "Tell me what's going on, David."

For a minute I was caught between the confidentiality I swore to PROs and the promise I made to the love of my life. I gave her enough details without compromising the situation and told her about the operation and Zev Sahin and that Monica was a member of the Sahin family. I finished with my run-in with Jared.

I was glad MD wasn't there to hear it. It wasn't everything, but it was enough to get me fired.

Lottie soaked up every detail and there were moments when I wondered who was listening, the girlfriend or the psychologist. At times her eyes clouded with unease. During others they sharpened as she analyzed every fact. She sipped her hot chocolate when I finally ran out of gas, thoughtful while she blew away the steam, and walked toward the center aisle where she stood. Quiet.

Nat and I exchanged a glance, neither one of us knowing what to make of her silence.

After several minutes, she put down her mug, planted her hands on the counter, and regarded me with determination. "So what do we do now?"

"Now, we keep our eyes and ears open," I said. "We plan. We remain vigilant."

"Plan." Lottie said the word like it soured her stomach. "Which basically means living a life so cautiously that we don't live? We've done that before and neither of us liked it."

"Not necessarily."

"Oh?" She straightened, challenging me to prove her wrong.

"Let your plans be dark and impenetrable as night," Nat said.

"And when you move," I answered, "fall like a thunderbolt."

"Sun Tzu's *The Art of War*," Nat explained to Lottie.

"Poetic," Lottie said, "but it doesn't answer my question."

She sounded impatient and annoyed, and I couldn't blame her. My life was built around war. I fought for what was right and took down those who stood in the way. She lived by ideals, wanting to make people whole. Preparing for battle, physical or emotional, went against everything she believed in. It wasn't her fault that she wasn't an ex-Marine or a professional soldier, or that she wasn't trained to kill or survive without food and water. Only that she loved a man who was.

"Then maybe this will answer the question." Nat slammed a hand on my shoulder. "I dug around while you were manning it up with Jared and found some stuff you probably want to see." He strode to the kitchen table, flipped open the laptop, and tapped it out of sleep mode. I followed, leaving Lottie to her thoughts. There would be more conversation for us later.

Nat settled into a chair and I pulled one up next to him. "I checked out Jared's and Monica's and Damian's accounts. Wanted to see what was what. Damian uses his money to go on expeditions and find relics and artifacts and stuff like that. Seems on the up and up. But I found something primo you'll find interesting." He shifted the laptop so I could see. "Check this out." He pointed to one of Jared's bank accounts, which showed a steady progression of hefty deposits over the past year. It had a balance of just over sixty grand. "This one's tied to his store, so I'm guessing this moolah is business related. But then I also found this." He minimized the screen and expanded another. "This is an investment account that's linked to another account. It's Zev's. Or was, anyway. It was transferred in full to Jared about a year ago, around the time they had their falling out, and ever since then there's been no activity between the two men. The deposits coming in don't originate from anything related to Zev."

"Laundered?"

"That'd be my guess."

I let out a slow whistle. Over two million invested. Just shy of one hundred grand in secondary checking.

"And that's just one investment." Nat launched another screen. "There's more out there, but this one just screams *Look At Me.*"

Lottie took a chair on the other side of the table and pointed to the laptop. "Where are you getting this information from?"

"Databases we have access to," I said.

"Is it legal?"

Nat and I stared at her.

"Call it a job benefit," Nat said and he turned back to me. "Jared's got a steady stream coming into the first investment account and he's been building it up for over a year."

"No indication why?" I asked.

"No. But there's a steady stream going out, too."

"To where?"

Nat pointed out the debits. "Have a look-see."

I did, and I wasn't sure what to make of it. "Monica?"

"Yep."

"Why?"

"Dunno."

I sank back in the seat and folded my arms over my chest. "I poked a hornet's nest when I brought down Zev Sahin."

"But do you really think Jared's gonna try and take over

the family empire? He's on the grid now, D-Man, courtesy of him facing you down. He can't fart anymore without someone noticing."

I nodded. "Maybe that's why Jared got so bent out of shape."

Nat nodded. "Otherwise, why get all pissy with you, right?"

"Vocal doesn't necessarily mean dangerous," Lottie said, peering at us over the edge of her mug.

Nat and I looked at her again.

"I see this type of behavior in therapy very often. People who are most vocal are those who are usually trying to compensate for shortcomings. The guy who brags about his sex life but has erectile dysfunction. The woman who buys tons of designer clothes but lives in a tiny apartment and can't pay the rent."

Nat and I kept looking.

Lottie put down the mug. "In my experience, it's not the one who's in your face that you need to worry about. It's the one who's quiet and slips under the radar."

"Then why is Jared so full of bravado?" I asked. "What's he compensating for?"

She shook her head, unsure. "Without counseling him, I couldn't say. Maybe he was close to Zev Sahin before Zev cut all ties and he's hurting. Maybe he never thought something like this could happen to his family. Or maybe he's delusional, which could explain why he thinks he can take over where Zev Sahin left off."

It sounded reasonable enough.

"I can do more checking, but I gotta let go of the reins and get on with life." Nat shoved away from the table and squeezed my shoulder. "I have officially led the horse to water. It's now your turn to drink. Let me know what else you find on these guys."

"Say hi to Lori and the boys," Lottie said.

Nat saluted her with two fingers. "Will do. We're supposed to watch *Finding Nemo* tonight and I can't wait. It's my fave movie and Dory's the best freaking character ever. I love how she talks whale."

After he let himself out, Lottie sat quiet and thoughtful and I kept sorting through Jared and Monica's accounts. We were buying time, Lottie and me, avoiding The Big Conversation because neither one of us wanted to tackle what was going on between us. Something had invaded our relationship in the past few hours, something that we weren't prepared to handle.

By the time Lottie finished her hot chocolate and my eyes had gone blurry, Lottie announced she was going upstairs to watch television. I used that as an excuse to shut down and join her.

"I haven't eaten since breakfast," I told her. "Want to order in? Maybe Thai?"

"Maybe later."

I followed Lottie upstairs, admiring the way her calves worked each tread. When we got to the bedroom, Lottie scoured around for the remote and I went to my closet, stripped to a pair of shorts and a T-shirt, and stared at the gun safe. When I first joined the Marines, I ran through the backwoods of the training camp with my team, rifle in hand and a thirty-pound rucksack on my back. I was drenched with sweat and grunting, pushing myself forward, determined not to fail. When we reached the ten-mile mark, Sergeant Ledbetter barked for another ten. A wiry kid from North Dakota tripped over a branch and fell and the rifle dislodged from his hands. Ledbetter screamed at him. "That goddamned weapon is your lover! Treat her sweet or end up dead!"

I disengaged the locking mechanism on the safe, chose the Kimber, and loaded two magazines. Like all the other weapons I owned, I'd treated it sweet, but it had been a while since I held this one in my hands. I tried remembering the last time I used it, and wondered if I was going to have to use it again.

I had just relocked the safe and was checking the safety when I sensed movement behind me. Lottie was leaning against the doorframe, her arms folded over her chest. She stared at the Kimber, turned, and left.

I followed, settled the gun on my nightstand, and connected my cell phone to the charger. Lottie untied her robe, let it drop to the floor, and turned toward me. She was wearing one of my button-downs, the first four buttons undone, the shirt hugging all the right places and teasing at what was underneath.

"That shirt looks better on you than me," I said.

She didn't smile. Only looked at the gun. "Just how much don't I know about you, David?"

I didn't understand the question.

Her eyes came back on me, demanding an answer.

"If this is about the gun—"

"It's about everything," she said. "I'm seeing things and hearing things that I don't understand. I know that your job is all about the secrecy, but even after you told me what's going on with Jared and Zev Sahin and the photo, I'm thinking you still haven't told me all. You have years-old scars on your body that you've never fully explained and that I'm not sure I want to know about. And while you and Nat were working at the kitchen table, all I could think was, *I don't know who this man is anymore.*"

All of a sudden, it felt like I had that thirty-pound rucksack on my back again.

"Why are you bringing this up now?" I asked. Because she'd had dozens of opportunities before.

"It doesn't matter why. It's just that—" She tugged down the bedding. "Something feels different between us and I can't identify what it is."

"I think I can," I said.

Her eyes lifted. "I know what you're going to say and you're wrong. Galen isn't an issue for me."

"It isn't just Galen. And he *is* an issue for you."

Her mouth twitched.

"I don't hide anything from you, Lottie. Not even about Monica."

"Really?" Lottie sank onto the edge of the bed, her back to me.

"After all these years, how can you think such a thing?"

"You know, I used to wonder what you did when you went away on missions. Tried to imagine what you were capable of." I walked over and sat down next to her. "I've wondered what your eyes have seen and what decisions you've made and what lives were lost." She paused. "And what lives were taken." She stared ahead, like she was imagining the things I'd done. "Maybe I've just been in denial about your job and, now, your job has invaded our lives."

"I didn't mean for that to happen."

"I try to tell myself that. And part of me wants to believe it."

"You can. I'm not lying to you, Lottie."

"Just like you weren't lying to me about what happened while I hypnotized you the other day?"

I didn't have an answer for that. I knew I'd been avoiding it, trying to convince myself that I'd experienced something else instead, and with everything going on it was a pretty easy thing to do. But now I'd been backed into a corner.

"You remembered something and, like other emotional challenges in your life, you're ignoring it. And this is the side of you I don't understand, David. You face everything else head on. Full force. Take no prisoners. But this?" She shook her head. "I don't get it. Why not just accept that this is the beginnings of a regression? Why not let the people who've been through this, like me, help you?"

"Because I can't."

"Why not? What are you afraid of?"

"I'm not afraid."

"I think you are."

Lottie took my hand and an icy jolt shot up my arm and raced down my spine.

Lottie gasped. "My God, David. You're cold again."

I trembled, sensing the earth shift under my feet and seeing an image of something…something hanging on the fringes and just out of reach.

"David?"

White rain. A burning fire. A hut, with bearskins. A woman with a fiery spirit and long, wild hair. The images triggered in rapid succession, one after another, like fleeting snapshots in time.

I sniffed, a familiar smell easing into the room. Something woodsy with a hint of green. It was Lottie, but *more*. I inhaled deeper, trying to place why it seemed so familiar, and the vague emotion shifted into an image. The point of a spear. A dark cave. And screams.

"David. Stop. You're squeezing too hard."

I looked at Lottie but wasn't seeing her.

"David. Did you hear me? David, please. You're hurting me."

In my mind, I was running toward the screams, trying to find her. Her voice was shrill and desperate, the sound coming from the left, then the right, then from behind. The wind carried her terror from every direction and I spun around, again and again, trying to lock onto her voice. She screamed one last time, sharp and piercing, and then the sound was cut off. The wind howled past and in my heart I knew that if I didn't find her, she was going to die.

"David!"

The image dissolved and I was looking at Lottie's hands in mine. Her fingers had turned blue, my knuckles white. I released her, got up, and stalked to the phone.

Lottie followed. "What just happened to you? What did you see?"

"I'm calling for Thai," I said, dialing the restaurant for delivery. "Pad Kra-Prao and Mee Krob sound good?"

"David—"

The restaurant answered and I gave them our order. After I hung up, I kissed Lottie and turned for the television. "How about downloading a movie? There's some new stuff that's just released that looks really good."

"*David!*"

Lottie had yelled at me. My temper flared but the misplaced reaction didn't last long. I sank down on the bed, elbows on knees, and stared at the carpet. The television was playing in the background, some commentator going on about the country's latest mortgage problems, but all I heard were the screams that were still alive in my head.

"You can't keep shutting down, David." Lottie's bare legs came into my field of vision but I refused to look up at her. If I did, I was scared she'd see just how afraid I was. "Please," she said, sounding desperate now. "Please tell me what you saw."

My eyes went to the gun on the nightstand, and it felt like forever before I could answer her. "I saw me not being able to save you."

"From what?"

I dug up the courage to finally face her and swallowed down the terror. "From me."

Chapter 14

The next morning, I woke up feeling the heaviness again.

Lottie had persisted in psychoanalyzing what I'd experienced the day before, but I'd shut down on her. We ended up eating in silence and falling asleep without talking. It wasn't fair and it wasn't respectful, but I had no other choice. If I showed Lottie any weakness, any sign of fear, then she'd become even more afraid. And I couldn't have that. I was there to protect her. It was who I was, how I looked at life, and how I viewed our relationship. Old-fashioned but I couldn't help it. Some deeper part of me, the part Lottie called the subconscious, had this overriding need to make sure she was always safe. If she wasn't, that reflected on me.

I stared at the ceiling, listening to Lottie's soft breathing, trying like hell to get comfortable with where we were at. I kept seeing the image of the fire and hearing Lottie's screams, and no matter how hard I tried I couldn't get either out of my head. It felt like a message of some kind. A warning that I had to be vigilant and now, more than ever, ready to protect her.

I rolled over, looked at the gun, and sighed. Home was supposed to be a safe haven. A sanctuary. Not a place for war.

Lottie stirred as I slid out of bed. My shirt that she'd worn last night was crumpled in a ball on the floor. The sheet and blanket barely covered her but that was okay. It was another nice view, an outline of long legs and curvy hips and a narrow waist. Of a flat stomach and firm, small breasts. Then the small heart-shaped birthmark on her shoulder disappeared and the long hair became short and I wasn't looking at Lottie anymore but Monica.

I blinked, trying to shove the image away. She rolled over and I was aware of brown eyes observing me. Not Lottie's near-black eyes but lighter eyes ringed with green. I scanned the woman's face and her pouty mouth and blinked again, logic telling me that this was a figment of my imagination while emotion seemed determined to send a different message instead.

It was a message I wasn't ready to tackle.

"I'm heading to Monica's meeting today," I said, grabbing fresh clothes from the dresser. "I want you to come with me."

Lottie pushed up from the bed and the sheet fell down to her waist. But it wasn't Lottie's breasts I saw. I focused on the boxer briefs and socks in my hand.

"Why?" she asked.

"Because I want you to see that I'm not interested in her." Even though she was the woman I was seeing right now and couldn't get out of my head. "Because I want to talk to her about Zev and Jared Sahin and because I think she might know things that can help me."

"Because of MD's orders?"

I nodded and shut the drawer, ready to hop in the shower. "Yes."

"Does Monica know why you're visiting?"

"No."

"So she thinks you're looking to reignite the flame."

"This isn't a booty call, Lottie." My back was still to her and the irritation in my voice sounded way too clear. But it wasn't Lottie that bothered me. I'd become a coward, unable to face the very thing that I couldn't understand.

"Does Monica know that?" Lottie asked.

With a deep breath, I sucked it up and turned around, forcing myself to concentrate and appear normal, like nothing was wrong. Lottie regarded the clothing in my hands and then me. She was quiet but her eyes said everything I needed to know. She was analyzing, stripping away my defenses to dig up what I was working hard to hide.

"That's a risk I'm willing to take," I said. Because Monica was all I had to go on right now.

Lottie got out of bed and headed for the bathroom, pausing just as she passed me. "Yeah, well, I guess we'll see where that gets you once you show up, David."

Now I had a problem. Lottie was in the bathroom and that meant no time alone for me to settle down and get my head back on straight. I could have used the hall bathroom but then Lottie would have grown even more suspicious so I followed, brushed my teeth, started the shower, and stepped into the jets. Another memory of Monica surfaced. I was in her bathroom, and she was brushing her hair at the mirror just like Lottie was doing now. Without thinking, I shifted my focus back to her. Her legs appeared longer, her waist more pinched, her breasts fuller and heavier. Her jaw became more angled and her neck lengthened, and the curve at the small of her back deepened.

Lottie started talking about what I should expect at the meeting, but I heard only Monica. I turned away, knocked the water temperature down to cold and stood there, using the pain as a distraction.

The shower door opened and shut, Lottie stepped under the water with me, and yelped. "David, geez! That's freezing!" She pushed the knob up to hot and grabbed the shampoo.

I worked at cleaning up quickly and efficiently, avoiding eye contact. When I finished, I toweled off and shaved. Lottie's attention stayed with me the entire time. Neither of us said anything. Once we were both dressed, I grabbed the gun, checked the loaded chamber, and rechecked the safety.

Lottie watched that, too.

We went downstairs and had coffee and yogurt in the kitchen. I read the day's news on my tablet. Lottie kept silent, still keeping vigilant watch over me. We washed the dishes and put them away, then locked up the house, set the alarm, and went to the garage. I popped open the trunk on my SUV, disengaged the combination on the gun safe in it, and slipped the Kimber inside. Not convenient but safe. I didn't want to walk into Monica's house with the thing stowed in the small of my back or in a shoulder holster.

Lottie got into the passenger seat and stared out the window.

I turned over the engine and fifteen minutes later was cruising past a Victorian house I hadn't seen in over a decade but that I remembered well. It was still purple and blue and accented with gingerbread that reflected Monica's colorful personality. There was no nearby parking and so I eased down the block and found a space in front of a ranch bordered with red-berried holly bushes. I cut the engine and Lottie grabbed my arm.

"How long will your gun follow us around?"

"I don't know," I said.

Lottie nodded but not because she liked the answer, and got out of the SUV. I followed her to the front door with my hand at the small of her back and rang the bell, aware of how much things had changed since I last came here. When Monica and I had the affair, I'd always snuck in through the back. This was the first time I'd ever used the front door.

Monica greeted us right away. She wore a tight orange blouse that showed a lot of cleavage and a black bra, tight jeans, and heels that brought her to my height. She looked good. Maybe even better than when she was thirty-three and teaching an eighteen-year-old about lust. She gave me a smile filled with innuendo but pulled it back a few degrees when she saw Lottie at my side. She ushered us inside, told us she was glad we came, and looped her arm through mine as she started introductions. I disengaged and took Lottie's hand instead.

The place was wall-to-wall people. Many of them smoked. Some even smoked cigarettes. Fog as thick as the kind you drove through before a summer storm filled the room. It smelled sweet and pungent, and I had a sudden memory of Lottie and me on the beach the month after we started dating, smoking and making love until the sun came up. My throat seized and closed, and if I didn't have another objective I would have made my excuses and gone home.

A guy came up offering a hit. He had long white hair, a long white beard, and straight white teeth. Santa, only high. "Opens the mind, man," he said when I passed on the offer. "You sure?"

"Positive. But thanks."

He offered to Lottie. She declined, too.

Monica went on with introductions, keeping her eyes glued to me as we circuited the room. A blond guy lit scented candles and incense, then piped in music that sounded like it came straight from a yoga class. Another blond, his twin, came out of the kitchen holding a tray full of small mugs, the kind you get in Japanese tea houses or sushi restaurants. While he worked the room the phone rang and Monica excused herself to get the call. The twin headed our way and offered us both a mug.

"Imported tea leaves," he said. "The best you can buy." I took a peek inside the steaming mugs and declined. If that was tea, I was blond, too.

He disappeared into the crowd, and Lottie and I were debating where to sit when Monica reconnected with us. She looked upset and even in the dim light her eyes looked dark with disappointment, her pupils sucking up almost the entire width of her irises.

"My babysitter is sick," she said, running a hand through her short hair. "Just what I need today. A house full of people and no one to keep Ada in check." She scanned the room as if a solution would pop up from the crowd.

Then she took off to find one.

Lottie nudged me with an elbow.

I looked at her and shrugged. "What?"

She flicked a glance at Monica and said, "Maybe you can help her."

I felt my eyes go wide. "You want me to watch Ada?"

"No, dummy, I want you to smoke weed." Lottie leaned in. "You're going to hate this meeting, David. You're not going to have the patience for it. But if you watch Ada, maybe you can find out information about Monica and then, after the meeting breaks, you can talk to Monica about what you need to find out, without an audience."

I pulled back, suspicious because this was one of those moments where we were speaking two languages and I only knew one of them. "I thought you didn't want me anywhere near Monica." Then I realized what she was doing. She wanted to keep her enemies close and at least temporarily away from me.

I took a step away, stopped, and reconsidered. "Am I going to get in trouble for this later?"

Lottie rolled her eyes and shoved me in Monica's direction. "Infiltration is what you do best, David. Why would this be any different?"

I felt Lottie's eyes follow me as I approached Monica. She was talking to the smoking Santa guy and I tapped her shoulder.

"David," she said, surprised that I was there, and I had a suspicion she was reading more into my following her than she should have been.

"I can watch Ada if you want," I said, risking a quick glance back at Lottie for reassurance but her expression remained indecipherable.

Monica's brows lifted. "Really?" Her surprise turned to calculation. "*Really?*"

"Sure." Only I didn't feel sure. I'd spent the better part of the morning figuring out how to handle Lottie, and Monica, and Lottie with Monica. Not a kid.

Monica grabbed my arm and jerked me toward the narrow, carpeted hallway and the stairs to find my charge. Just after

Monica called up to the second floor for her daughter, the front door opened.

Galen stepped inside.

Chapter 15

Lottie watched David head for Monica and felt jealousy spark inside her. When Monica looked at him and gave him a smile that hinted of things known only between the two of them, the spark flared and spread like wildfire. Only then did Lottie acknowledge that coming here with David had been a ploy, because she was doing the same thing she'd accused David of doing with Galen.

She was keeping her enemy close.

When she first met Monica, Lottie thought her offbeat and quirky. Now Lottie saw Monica as a threat, and as much as she wanted to believe it was because Monica was Zev Sahin's sister she knew it was more than that. Lottie recognized a hidden emotion at work between the three of them. Something deep-rooted. Something unspoken. And something very, very old.

She was considering going after David and calling the whole morning off when she felt an emotional shift in the room. A wave of longing so strong she staggered. Several hands grabbed hold and settled her into a chair. Someone's voice cut in and asked if she was okay.

Galen entered the room and Lottie felt his pull, the part of him that called out to the darker, primeval part of her that could threaten her sanity and her relationship with David if left unchecked. A familiar ache emerged, a desire so intense the temperature in the room surged. Their eyes locked and everything slowed down and faded away. For those few moments, when his gaze held hers, it was only the two of them, wrapped in fine linen sheets and each other.

A man offered Lottie a glass of water, disturbing the moment and the memory, and she watched Galen work the room while she drank. He looked comfortable and at ease here, and that made Lottie curious. When Monica returned and began gathering everyone together, two women struck up a conversation with Galen, talking about a trip they made to Scotland. Three hundred years ago.

Galen's glance skirted Lottie's way as they spoke, then he excused himself from the conversation and walked over. He wore black jeans and a tan wool sweater, an outfit that complemented his skin and physique, and Lottie drew in a composed breath as he approached, rising to her feet and steeling herself to the turbulent emotions she felt whenever he came near.

He leaned in and whispered, "I did not know you and Bellotti would be here." His breath felt warm against her neck and his voice moved through her like warm, spiced wine.

Lottie pulled back and fixed him with a steady look that was more to equalize than to spurn. "I could say the same of you."

A grin played at his lips.

Monica called for everyone's attention. "Welcome everyone!" She tugged a couple of chairs closer to the wall to make more room in the center. "So glad you could make it. Today, we've got some new faces and old faces," and everyone laughed at the joke, "and I'm very happy to announce that

Galen has joined us once again. We're more than pleased to have him back." Her announcement was met with a chorus of welcomes. "It's been, what, four weeks since we last sat with you?"

Galen folded his hands together and nodded at Monica, and Lottie became very aware of the relaxed control with which he held himself. The coiled snake, quietly waiting for the strike.

"Some of you may not have met Galen before." Monica gestured toward Galen and hesitated when she noticed Lottie beside him. A knowing smile curved at the corners of her mouth, hinting of some kind of realization. Or idea. "All I can say is, he's got a remarkable gift with regression that has been more than instrumental in helping many of us bridge the gaps in our lifetimes. He is definitely one person here you should get to know."

Lottie tilted her head and apprised Galen with new interest. "You're a regular here?"

He remained still, the snake still carefully coiled within. "I didn't realize I had to inform you of my social activities."

Lottie leaned in and lowered her voice. "I wasn't asking you to do that. Though you could have told me about these meetings when I went to your condo yesterday for help."

He shrugged and shoved his hands in his pockets, watching the group as it moved chairs and gathered in the room, and as if casual conversation with Lottie was an everyday occurrence.

"How do you know Monica?" she asked, shifting so that one of the blond twins could position several chairs in a circle nearby. "Have you known her a while?"

Galen motioned to an empty one just as Monica joined them. "Come, you two." She grabbed them both by the hands and led them in. "Sit."

Lottie did, aware of Galen's hard thigh pressing against her as he settled into the seat. Monica appraised them both with a smile. "You both look so nice together, like you belong." She paused. "How very interesting."

After she walked away, Galen leaned toward Lottie and whispered, "I've known Monica for longer than you can imagine."

His breath felt hot and tempting, and Lottie became aware that Monica was still watching them. She withdrew from Galen, steadied her breathing, and watched the activity around her as a diversion. Some sat in the chairs and some on the sofa, while others found space on the floor to form a circle around the room. Monica took the seat on the other side of Galen. Everyone seemed to know what to do and where to go. And everyone looked comfortable with who they were, where they came from, and how their lives tied together.

Everyone, but Lottie.

Lottie forced herself to focus on everything and everyone else around her, feeling as if she'd suddenly become a tool in some kind of psychological game. Only she was out of her depth and unable to understand what it was, or why Monica felt it important to play it.

She felt Galen press in again, his lilting voice and warm breath once again teasing her cheek and ear. "You will not find what you need by watching, Lottie," he said. "Here you'll only find acceptance, if you're willing to be accepted."

Lottie faced him head on but kept her voice low. "A

strange thing to say, considering that only yesterday you practically threw me out of your condo."

Galen nodded. "I know and I'm sorry for that. However, Bellotti cannot complain if we encounter each other at an organized meeting that neither of us planned."

Lottie had the feeling Galen was manipulating the situation, manipulating her, but she didn't understand why. "And you also promised him that you wouldn't pursue me."

"I am not pursuing," he said. "This is merely fate at work. And Bellotti cannot fight fate, much as he likes to try."

"Okay, everyone," Monica said. "Let's begin and focus. Deep breaths. Inhale in. Exhale out." She spoke in a soft timbre that Lottie found soothing but she was still too preoccupied with Galen to listen.

"David won't support the both of us in this, Galen," Lottie said.

Galen shrugged. Drew in a breath. Let it out. "Then move."

"Close your eyes and focus on the music," Monica continued. Piano and flute eased through the room.

Lottie watched Galen close his eyes, draw into himself, and relax. He looked at peace. Fulfilled.

"Or," Monica went on, "you can focus on the sound of my voice."

Lottie glanced around the room. She was the only one whose eyes were still open.

"Close your eyes and just *try*," Galen whispered.

But—"

"We are both here for specific reasons, Lottie, and now isn't the time to question them. Close your eyes and go with it.

Or leave."

Lottie closed her eyes. Her mind wandered at first but as Monica continued, Lottie found her attention drifting away from Galen and toward the calming cadence in Monica's tone, the rhythms that reached into her heart and took hold.

"You may hold hands if you wish," Monica said. Lottie breathed in, breathed out. "Let yourself go. Let yourself learn." Breathe in. Breathe out. "Open yourself to what is before you and behind you." Breathe in. Breathe out. "Open yourself to the experience today. To the possibility of merging with another. Let the images come. Let the memories move in. Relive them, and live them."

Lottie smelled the burning candles. The myrrh and cinnamon and cassia. She remembered those scents from a long time ago, when she used to wear a sheer linen sheath and light candles in her chamber before paying obeisance to Amun.

People started chanting, a low, rhythmic hum that reminded her of temple chants. The resonance vibrated through her skin and into her muscles, until it pulsed in time with her heart and settled deep inside her soul. Lottie drew in a breath then another. Monica's voice disappeared into the distance. The ancient Egyptian memory faded away until Lottie faced only a black, empty slate. The unknown.

Galen's hand wrapped around hers and an image exploded in her mind.

Everyone had gathered around the fire, bright against a black sky, celebrating the hunt. Skins hung from trees to dry and females cut meat with flints. Makra held up a large, bloody tooth from his kill, another trophy for all to see. They cheered and thumped him on the back. Thanks to him, they had food now. Enough to last them through the first white rain. Makra had chipped a hole through the tooth and slid it onto the leather band he wore around his neck, one of many that showed his power and skill in the hunt. Some of the hunters also wore bands but none had as many trophies as Makra. Makra was *Einarr*. The warrior.

Lassia watched him through the dancing flames and tendrils of smoke, mesmerized by how his body moved, as agile and powerful as a cave lion.

He did not notice her.

He never did.

The elders spoke of carving this achievement into The Cave of Triumphs when light returned, marking Makra's victory among his many others. It was because of Makra that their tribe survived and grew. It was because of him that rival tribes stayed away.

She watched Makra tie the leather band around his neck. The muscles in his chest and stomach bunched and released as he moved, the hefty teeth fitting against his powerful body. On any another male, they would have looked awkward and graceless. Even too big. Makra laughed when another male moved in close to share a story meant only for the two of them, then his laughter died when something else drew his attention away.

Lassia watched Cilla approach, her body moving in a way that Lassia envied. She held Makra's attention, every male's attention, and knew it. She was beautiful in a way Lassia was not beautiful. Could please Makra in a way Lassia never learned.

And Lassia wanted to learn.

A little girl followed behind Cilla, shy and quiet in the moonlit shadows. When she reached Makra, he picked her up and swung her around, making her squeal with laughter. She played with the new trophy on his neckband, clasped her hands on his cheeks, and laughed again. He put her down and patted her behind, encouraging her to join the elders who sat on the other side of the fire. Then Makra took Cilla by the hand and led her into the darkness. Alone.

Lassia wondered what Cilla would do to him that night. What magic she would perform that would keep him under her spell. She did not notice that Ayak had sat down beside her until he nudged her out of her thoughts, an offering of berries and dried meat in his hand. She took them and ate greedily, and when she took in her last bite, he nudged her again. She looked at him, the curve of his mouth, the mischief in his eyes, and immediately understood.

He stood and held out his hand. She took it, eager to be with him because she had missed him while he was gone with Makra on the hunt. And, with Ayak, she could continue to learn the ways of the female. She followed him through tall, golden grass into darkness, to the edge of a cave where they would find solitude. She loosened the pelt from his waist and let it drop to the ground, found him ready, and smiled. He had missed her, too. He pulled her down and beneath him, and Lassia's hands followed the contours of his strong back and arms while he pushed up the furred hide she wore around her waist. She arched when Ayak thrust into her and molded against him, moving with him and urging him to go deeper. They needed no fire, no food, no water. Only this heat that they shared.

Ayak gasped, grabbed her thigh, and quickened the rhythm. Lassia felt her passion swell and his need grow more urgent. His mouth took hers and they climaxed together.

In the distance, Lassia swore she heard Makra climax, too.

Lottie's eyes flew open. Sweating and out of breath, she jerked her hand from Galen's and swallowed over a dry, tight throat. Galen remained calm in his place. Others were still chanting though most seemed at peace with their own thoughts. No one had realized what had just happened. Acoustic guitar now piped through the speakers.

Quietly, Lottie got to her feet and slipped out the front door. A cool October breeze shocked her overheated skin and she shivered. She wrapped her arms around herself and leaned against a white Toyota parked out front, trying to catch her breath and calm her racing heart.

She realized her history with Galen was far more intense, and much more long-standing, than it seemed.

And she was going to have to deal with this, too.

She pushed off the car and headed to the backyard, looking for David.

Chapter 16

"Who are you?" Ada asked, grabbing my hand.

"I'm David," I said, keeping Galen in my sight until Ada and I walked down the steps from the kitchen and out the back door. I didn't think it was coincidence that brought him to Monica's door, but I had no way of proving it. And even if I could, I didn't think Galen would be honest about it.

Ada took off for a dogwood near the deck and the redwood patio set. She jumped on the tree and started climbing, and as she inched her way up I tried fitting more pieces together. I wanted to know how Galen knew Monica and for how long. I wanted to know how they met, how often they saw each other, and who else they knew that could be important to me.

Ada flipped over a branch and went down headfirst. My heart shot up into my throat and I shouted *"Ada!"* while launching off the bench to catch her.

She started laughing. "Oh my God!" She hung upside down like a bat, red-faced and enjoying herself at my expense. "You so totally freaked!"

I clutched my chest, sat back down, and muttered, "Damn near gave me a heart attack." Five minutes with the girl and I'd already lost focus because my mind had wandered. It was becoming a dangerous habit.

Ada studied me a long while, like I was an animal at the

zoo she'd never seen before. She wore black All Star sneakers, black jeans, and a black hoodie, and if it wasn't for the long, black hair that hung out of it, someone might have thought her a boy.

"So what did Mom promise you to get you to watch me?" Ada asked.

"Pardon?"

A helicopter passed overhead, its thumping rotors drowning out our conversation. I looked up to watch it, shielding my eyes from the sun. It was a Medevac en route to a nearby hospital. Ada's voice pulled me back in.

"Mom's always making promises to get people to watch me." Ada shoved shriveling, red leaves out of the way for a better view. "What did she promise you?"

"Nothing. I'm just trying to help out."

"Oh." She swung for a bit and said, "You look strong."

"Have to stay in shape for my job."

"What do you do?"

"I help keep people safe."

"Like a bodyguard?"

"Something like that."

Her hair swayed in time with her movement. "I want to be strong."

"You look strong."

"Mom says looks are deceiving."

"Your mom's right."

Ada went silent again, thinking about that. "Mom says you used to be a Marine."

I straightened. "Your mom told you about me?"

"Last night." Ada hiked a leg over a branch and

maneuvered to her left. "She said she ran into you and that you were an old friend."

"I am." Sort of.

A breeze rushed past, carrying the scent of burning wood. It smelled smoky, like pine, and I wondered if it was an indoor fire or an outdoor one, and if the person who built the fire knew that burning pine indoors was a fire hazard.

"I love that smell, don't you?" Ada took a long, hard sniff. "I wish we had a fireplace. Our old house had one and I loved sitting by it and listening to the crackle and pop. I liked toasting marshmallows in it, too. They're really cozy."

I agreed.

"So when did you meet my mom? How do you know her?"

She peered at me, her eyes intense and prying.

"Long story." One I didn't want to explain. "Do you get left alone like this a lot?"

"Yeah, but it's okay. Most times I have a babysitter."

"What about your dad?"

"He left when I was really little." Ada started humming a song that sounded familiar, by the Goo Goo Dolls maybe, and stopped like she suddenly had another thought. "Sometimes my cousin watches me. Sometimes my uncle, too, when he's around. He has a lot of money."

"Are you close to your uncle?" I asked.

"I have two. I used to have three, but he died and I don't remember him."

She may have been a kid but I had a feeling she knew a lot. I shifted forward, thinking I could make a lot out of our time together. I scrubbed a hand over my chin, thinking about how to handle this, and noticed I'd missed a spot shaving.

"What are they like?" I asked, keeping it easy. Keeping it conversational.

Ada flipped over, slid down the tree, and sat on its lowest branch. "They're protective," she said. She hung an arm over the branch and dangled her feet. It was then I saw the strong resemblance to her mother. She was a pre-teen but it was there, simmering beneath the surface, and five or six years from now she was going to be trouble. Guys were going to crawl all over her, giving Monica a dose of what she'd dished out herself. Ada had Monica's pouty lips and high cheekbones, the shiny hair and the dark skin, and the brightest green eyes I'd ever seen.

Only Monica didn't have bright green eyes like that. In fact, she didn't have green eyes at all.

I did.

I sat up and froze, doing quick math in my head.

And I didn't like the answer.

Chapter 17

Lottie swung open the gate and headed toward us. "I need to talk to you." She tapped my shoulder, but I couldn't drag my attention away from Ada and her green eyes. "David, are you listening?"

I got up and started for the back screen door. "Stay here with Ada."

Lottie pursued, hot at my heels, drilling me with questions. "Did you hear what I just said? I need to talk to you. Are you going to stop? David, I need you to stop."

"Not now, Lottie."

"David—"

"Not *now*." I swung around and Lottie came to an abrupt halt. Maybe it was the sharpness in my voice, maybe it was the sharpness on my face, but I'd irritated her and I didn't feel guilty about it. There were other more important things on my mind. "*Please*. I need time with Monica. Whatever you have to say has to wait." I started for the back door again, not breaking stride while I asked, "Is the meeting over?"

"I don't think so."

Didn't matter. I didn't care.

I threw open the door and it slapped shut behind me. I took the stairs into the kitchen two at a time, rounded the dining room, and headed into the living room. The meeting was still going, though I would have hardly called it a meeting. Smoke as thick as a blanket covered the room, which was silent except for some yoga-flute thing playing in the background.

I strode toward Monica. She sat next to Galen, holding his hand, the two of them part of a larger circle of people. I leaned down and tapped her shoulder.

"Monica."

She didn't budge.

I tapped again, harder, and whispered again, louder. "Monica."

Her eyes fluttered open and after a few seconds she peered up at me. Her pupils were large and black, and I wasn't sure she saw me much less heard me.

"I need to talk to you."

She blinked, and kept blinking.

I tried again. "We need to talk right now. It's important."

Her confusion lifted and she straightened. "Did something happen to Ada?" Her gaze turned wide and she glanced around the room, a quick check to make sure she didn't disturb anyone, and jumped to her feet. "What happened?"

"Ada's fine." I grabbed her hand and she followed eagerly as I tugged her toward the front door, away from the room and prying ears.

"Is she okay?" Monica went for the stairs, but I seized her before she could take off.

"Who's Ada's father?" I demanded.

She staggered, like she wasn't sure she'd heard right. "What?"

"Don't play games. There's no point in hiding it." I stepped in close so we stood breaths apart. "Who is Ada's father?" I wanted to know, needed to know, and yet didn't want to know. It was as if my whole life was balanced on this one point in time, and the answer would bring irreversible change.

I wasn't sure I wanted that change.

I held my breath, waiting for her response.

Monica wrenched out of my hold but only stared at me. In those prolonged seconds where her eyes held mine, twelve years compressed into heartbeats and the wild eighteen-year-old I used to be came face to face with the adult I was now.

Monica opened the front door and went onto the porch, motioning for me to follow.

I folded my arms over my chest and swallowed.

"I wanted to tell you back then," Monica said. A light wind passed, fluttering drying leaves and ornamental grass.

She sounded apologetic but I wasn't feeling all that forgiving. I raked a hand through my hair, feeling like the earth had just flipped on its axis and I wasn't able to hold on. "I'm Ada's *father*. And she doesn't know?"

"No. Ada doesn't know. She always assumed that Greg was her dad."

"Does anyone else know?"

The front door slammed shut and Monica and I both looked over to find Lottie and Ada standing on the porch with us. Ada was holding her balled-up sweatshirt tight to her chest, looking like she was afraid to move. Lottie stood by her side, but her eyes were focused only on me.

"Ada," Monica said, "go back inside."

"Is it true?" Ada looked from Monica to me to Monica again. "Are you really my father?"

"I said go inside, Ada."

"No."

"*Ada.*"

I went to the porch rail, grabbed on and leaned hard against it, working to hold myself together. Stay focused. I felt Lottie's hand on my back, and I think I might have said something, but I wasn't all that sure. In the middle of Ada and Monica's arguing, life as I'd known it had just changed forever.

"I'm not going to say it again, Ada. Go inside."

"No. I want to know—"

"Now's not the time, *Ada.*"

"So when *is* the time, *Mom*? Do I even get to know who the hell David is?"

"Watch your mouth!"

"Why? You curse all the time!"

I squeezed my eyes shut, trying to get a grip. Trying to come to terms.

"We will talk about this later," Monica said.

"When? After the meeting? After dinner? When I'm thirteen? Or sixteen?"

"We'll talk about this now," I said, turning to the both of them.

Lottie kept her hand on my back, but her show of support didn't match the expression on her face. She was angry. And hurt.

The door opened and Galen walked out. He hesitated once he saw the group of us together and sensed the tension buzzing between us. He stared at me the longest, like he was reading my mind and making all the connections without having to be told. Then he turned to Monica.

"The group is ready for discussion now," he said. "I can take the lead, if you want."

"No, it's not necessary." Monica started to go inside but Ada stopped her.

"He said we should talk and I want to talk!"

"Not now, Ada."

"But David said yes."

"And I said no."

Ada stomped her foot. "I hate you! I hate you hate you hate you!" She threw open the door and stormed up the inside stairs to the second floor.

Monica sighed and went back to her meeting.

Galen looked at Lottie before setting his attention on me. "I would offer to have you join us for our discussion," he said, "but it appears you have something else to tend to at the moment."

He left us alone on the porch.

And I had no idea what to do next.

Chapter 18

Lottie and I got into the SUV in silence.

Leaving Monica and Ada felt like a mistake, but I also knew that staying would have made things worse. They were both still arguing over me, and I wasn't happy about it. Nor was I in any frame of mind to step in. I was the outsider looking in, the piece that didn't fit, but I felt tethered to them in a way I couldn't explain.

Maybe it was the responsibility that came with being a father.

The word sounded foreign in my head, like the French my mother tried teaching me when I was young.

Lottie was staring out the window. "I can only imagine what you must be feeling, David. And thinking. Want to talk about this?"

I threw the SUV into gear and pulled away from the curb. "No."

The problem was that I didn't know what to say to her. *Sorry I got another woman knocked up, Lottie. I know I told you in the past that I only want children with you but, hell, I guess that's changed now.* Like that would go over well.

I came to the end of the block, made a right, and headed for the streets that would take us to my mom and dad's house and Sunday dinner. My eyes were focused on the road, my brain was focused on the daughter I never knew I had. I approached another stop sign and checked for traffic, the same thoughts rattling through my head, over and over. Monica was Zev's sister and Ada was Zev's niece and that meant, in some far-fetched sick way, that I was related to Zev, too.

My stomach soured.

Someone honked from behind and my brain shifted back into gear. I pressed on the gas to get the SUV moving again.

Lottie sighed.

I sighed, too.

I eased through quiet neighborhoods and tranquil curves and rays of sun that cut through orange and red and brown leaves. We passed a lone runner who looked like he was keeping a steady tempo pace. I wanted to run, too. Somewhere else, far away. Twelve years ago my life was simple. Party. Stay out late. Get laid. Get up the next day, recover, do it all over again. Now, twelve years later, I was paying the price for that stupidity and arrogance. Welcome to the real world of David M. Bellotti.

"Acceptance isn't going to come easily on this," Lottie said. "There's more going on here than you think, David."

"I know this hurts you, too, Lottie—"

"That isn't what I mean," she said, and I could hear the strain in her voice. Lottie was as dumbfounded as I was. "But remember this. It's not Ada's fault that she was conceived and born. So whatever you do, don't take out your anger on her. Or me."

"I'm not angry."

"Then maybe you should be. But at Monica. That's a hell of a secret she kept from you all these years." She was tapping her fingers on her knee, her mouth was tight, and her jaw was working overtime.

I pulled up in front of house and cut the engine. The house was a small clapboard split level where Mom and Dad raised four kids. I still wondered how we all fit.

"You ready to go in?" I asked.

"No, but what I feel probably doesn't make a difference."

I would have argued on that point but figured it didn't matter. Lottie needed to vent. I unbuckled my seatbelt but Lottie didn't unbuckle hers.

"I don't know how to react to this, David. I want to be supportive but there's a part of me that's refusing to do it. I know it's not fair, especially to you, but I can't help it."

She blinked her eyes, several times, and I realized she was crying.

Shit.

"We can go home," I said. "We don't have to do this."

"No." Lottie swiped the tears away and stared up at the roof of the car, like it would help stop them from falling. "We promised Rita and I want to do this." She wiped below her eyes once more and drew in a shuddering breath.

"Mom would understand if we pass up one dinner." I cranked over the engine but Lottie grabbed the shifter before I could throw the thing into gear, and I had the suspicion that Ada and Monica might not be the only things on her mind.

Galen was probably still in there, too.

"What happened at the meeting?" I asked.

Lottie's shoulders slumped and she looked at the front of my parents' house instead of at me. "I had another memory," she said, sounding as fatigued and as spent as I did. "When I was with Galen."

"Christ."

Lottie sent me a sharp look and I rubbed my eyes with my fingers. Back in July, when Lottie experienced her so-called regression, she claimed a meeting with Galen had prompted it. At first she was intrigued by Galen's knowledge about past lives, but when she realized he could give her more of the answers she needed about her own, she pursued him.

Lottie spent the first few weeks of that regression trying to explain how that past Egyptian life connected with our current one. "These lives are learning experiences," she had told me one night when we sat by the pool. "And the lessons you don't learn, with the people you are to learn them from, return in the next life. It's another chance to make amends and grow and move on. A life cycle, of sorts, until you're ready for the next realm."

It was during those days when Lottie was trying to make me understand and accept these concepts that I caught her with Galen. It was a day I wanted to forget, but the more I tried the more vivid the memory became.

So here we were, sitting in my SUV, facing a similar situation all over again.

"This new memory," Lottie went on, "is a very old one. Older than Egypt. I saw us again. You and me and Galen. Only this time, I think I saw Monica and Ada in that memory, too."

I leaned against the headrest and shut my eyes, letting her talk but thinking that this wasn't normal. People didn't believe in these things, and those that did often sought therapy.

"We have another unresolved connection," Lottie said. "I also think that Galen knows more about these new memories than he's letting on. In fact, I'm willing to bet on it. I think he knows about the five of us and I think that's why he goes to Monica's meetings."

Now I looked at her.

She twisted in her seat and faced me. "He's a regular, David. I tried getting more information from him but Galen was keeping it close to his heart. And I think it was because of you. You made it more than clear to him, when this all started back in July, that he better tread lightly around you and me."

I slumped into the seat feeling mentally and emotionally drained. I needed to run, to burn off energy and all the toxic crap churning inside me. "Were you able to find out how they know each other or how they met?"

"No. Monica started the meeting just as we started talking, and Galen made it clear he wasn't going to offer much, and then we joined hands and…"

Her voice died and she sat back to look out the window, trying to hide her reaction. But it was already too late. I saw her skin flush and watched her breath catch, and when she licked her lips I knew she was remembering something that didn't involve me.

Galen was starting to become a real problem.

"I expect he'll be at other meetings, David." Lottie was still staring out the window when she spoke. "And I intend to go to them."

I didn't want her to but there was nothing I could do to stop her. "Fine," I said, shutting off the SUV. "I'll go to them with you."

I swung open the door, cutting off a conversation I didn't want to have, and didn't realize how fast I was moving until

Lottie raced up the slate steps after me, grabbed my hand, and tugged me to a stop. A sharp October wind blew past and she pushed the hair from her face. Then her hair wasn't long but short, and those eyes turned lighter in color, and the dimple in her chin disappeared, and her Cupid's bow mouth became pouty, and her perfume became more citrusy, and I was no longer looking at Lottie but Monica.

I disengaged from her hold and headed for the door. "I think I need a drink."

Chapter 19

My mom raced out of the kitchen once the wooden screen door clattered shut behind us. Her tie-dyed dress fluttered and the sleeves billowed as she ran, and her hair looked even wilder than it did on Thursday. It was also now red. I smelled a glazed chicken and sweet potatoes cooking in the kitchen. On a second inhale, I smelled rosemary bread and buttered string beans.

"You're here. You're here!" Mom grabbed us and hugged us and then got on her tiptoes, pinched my cheeks, and dropped a dozen kisses on each of them. "I missed you."

I said, "You saw us Thursday night."

Lottie elbowed me in the ribs.

"Don't mind him, Jelly Bean," she said to Lottie. "It's a guy thing." She made me follow her into the kitchen and told Lottie to go into the living room because Dad and my sisters and brother were playing a bowling video game.

I took four steps into the kitchen and Mom rounded on me. The Moody Blues were playing in the background. "What's wrong? What happened? Tell me."

I hesitated a half second and that was enough to gas her up for more.

"Something's going on. Your aura is all wrong." She pulled out a bar stool from the center aisle and made me sit, and took the one opposite me. "What's going on, Bubbala? Are you and Lottie fighting?"

"No."

"Getting on each other's nerves?"

"No."

"Having trouble in the bedroom?"

"*No.*"

"Trouble at work? With friends? With colleagues?"

"Mom, can you give me a break for a few minutes?" She gave me an unsympathetic look like she did when I was thirteen and discovered I stole liquor from the cabinet. So I threw in, "Please?"

Her eyes narrowed but she didn't give up. "Your aura is so, so dark, David. Why is it so dark? It's murky, like the color of confusion."

Confusion. There was a word for you. My mother kept sex manuals on the kitchen bookshelves where cookbooks should have been, and she was telling me about confusion.

She dropped her head in her hands and stared at me, then abruptly sat up. "Do you want a brownie? I have leftovers from last night. They might make you feel better." She shoved a plate at me. Only two were left.

I was about to ask who ate them all and decided not to. There were things about your parents you should never know.

"I found out this morning that I have an eleven-year-old daughter," I said.

Mom stared at me and didn't move for a long time. She said nothing for even longer. Somewhere along the way, something kicked in and she went to the pantry and dug around her private stash of liquor, clinking and knocking bottles until she found what she wanted. She tugged out a bottle of Copas Añejo, planted it on the counter in front of me, found two highballs from another cabinet, and set those in front of me, too. She broke the seal on the tequila, filled each glass halfway, said *l'chaim*, and we both downed our drinks. She shuddered after she swallowed, refilled both glasses, and plopped down next to me.

"Monica?" she asked.

I choked on the tequila and my eyes watered. "How did you know?"

"I saw you. Once."

"When? Where?"

"It doesn't matter."

"It does to me."

"Of course it does. Now. But back then?" She shook her head. "Not so much." She patted my arm. "You sure the girl is yours?"

"Her name is Ada and yeah, I'm sure." Because looking at Ada was like looking at a smaller, female version of me.

I poured more Copas. The stuff was strong but it was smooth, and if I kept at it long enough I could get tanked. And then Lottie could drive me home and tuck me in. It sounded like a good plan.

"How's Lottie taking the news?" Mom asked.

"Not well."

"Of course she isn't. She's looking at this girl and thinking it should have been hers." Mom's eyebrows rose and she gave me a pointed look. "What? You think I don't see these things? You've been with Lottie forever and not even one mistake along the way?" She shook her head. "If she can't have children, Monica having yours is going to be really hard on her."

I pulled back. "How do you know Lottie and I never—" I shook my head. "Just because Lottie's never gotten pregnant doesn't mean she can't have kids, Mom."

She finished her Copas and poured more. "Of course it doesn't." But the look on her face seemed sad, like she knew something Lottie or I didn't.

Mom topped off my glass. "This isn't going to be easy for the two of you. Lottie's a tough cookie, but this will challenge even the best of relationships. Trust me on that." The timer sounded on the oven and Mom went to shut it off. She came back, drank more, and cocked her head. "Is Monica demanding money for Ada?"

"No. It's nothing like that."

"Hmm." She picked at a brownie. "I can see something else is going on here, David. Something else is bothering you."

I hunched, feeling the weight of everything press down on me, and spun my glass, watching the caramel-colored liquor catch the overhead lights.

"Is her ex-husband making noise? I wouldn't be surprised if he was. You're the reason they divorced, you know."

My head came up. "What?"

"Mmhmm." Mom gulped down more tequila and nodded. "We had our suspicions at first that that's what happened, but we eventually found out for sure."

"Who's we?"

"Daddy and me."

"You *told* him?"

"Of course I did. You're our son and I was concerned. So

we watched and waited to see what might happen, ready to step in if we needed to. But we didn't tell anyone else."

"Monica and I kept things low key. We were careful."

Mom gave me a long look. "'Careful,' Bubbala, is what got you your daughter. And I don't think Greg knew it was you who was cheating with his wife, but he knew someone was."

"Why didn't you ever say anything?" I asked.

Mom laughed. "David, you were so far up that woman's skirt, no one would have gotten through to you. And by the time Daddy and I were considering stepping in, Monica was gone. And looking back, I can see why she left. Seems she was already pregnant by then."

And the divorce came a little over a year later.

Mom slid her hand under my chin and tipped up my head to look at her. It was strange looking into her green eyes, which were my green eyes, which were also Ada's green eyes. "Something else is bothering you, hmm?"

"It's not just Ada." I went back to spinning my glass, trying not to sound dejected. "Ever since Monica came back into my life, I keep seeing her. When I look at Lottie, I see Monica instead. When she talks, I hear Monica. When I smell Lottie, I smell Monica's perfume." I cursed and gulped down what was left in my glass. "I don't like it."

"Unresolved conflicts. Probably unresolved sexual tension, too. Maybe something more than that. It's normal."

"It's *not* normal," I said. "I love Lottie and it kills me that Monica can so easily get into my head like that. And even though I know it's not Ada's fault that she's here, when I look at her I don't feel anything. At all. She's mine and there's nothing inside here." I tapped my heart, refilled my glass, and tossed that down, too, clenching my jaw through the burn.

"You expect to feel something right away?" Mom laughed. "I didn't feel anything for you for the first six *months*, David. And I knew about you from the moment I conceived you."

I didn't understand.

"Everyone has a door in the dark, David. And behind it is where we hide the things we're afraid to face. I think, on some level, you're still attracted to Monica or maybe still have feelings for her."

"That's ridiculous."

"Is it?" Mom waited for me to say something but I didn't know what to say. "I'm a *sex* therapist, David. It's my job to know these things."

Lottie and Dad started cheering in the other room and a round of high fives followed. It sounded like they'd won a good game. And here I was, feeling guilty and like I'd been cheating on Lottie. Maybe on some level I was.

"Oh, David." Mom tipped my face up again. "Open your eyes and see. You would do well to learn from your past if you let it happen."

A chill ran down my arms and the hair on them stood at attention. Those were almost the same words Galen had said to me the day MD ordered me to return the photo.

Mom held out her arms and looked heavenward, arms wide, palms up. "Embrace your past, David. Embrace what's inside you. You cannot fight these things, and they're important things, because they're who you are."

"Am I missing something here?"

She dropped her hands, looking exasperated. "Yes. You are. And it's probably because of me." Her mouth pressed into a thin line of disappointment, and for a few seconds I had the feeling she was trying to tell me something without actually saying it. Some cryptic message that I couldn't break. Then she waved off the conversation, and me.

"Let's get back to Ada. How did she seem when you met her? Well fed? Clothed? Normal?"

"Why wouldn't she be normal?"

"Oh boy. You really don't know anything, do you?" Mom poured more tequila for both of us. Half the bottle was already gone. "One of the reasons I was worried about you being involved with Monica was because she had a drug connection. And a big one."

"I know that." Well, I knew it *now*, and the knowledge was haunting me.

"Monica was a distributor, David. She sold drugs right out of her house."

I pushed back from the counter, wiping my hands on my jeans as I stretched my back, but the move was to buy time so I could think about this more. "You think Ada's caught up in something because of it?"

"Ada may be exposed to bad people. For all we know, she's also a user."

"She's eleven."

"And if she's your daughter, she's not stupid. But who knows with these things? And considering that makes her my granddaughter, that means I have to worry about her now, too. Which makes me worry about you even more." She picked at more of the brownies, looking preoccupied. "I should have said something," she murmured while she chewed. "Keeping my mouth closed was a mistake."

"What does that mean?"

She shoved the last of the brownie in her mouth. "Forget it. I'm just babbling."

"What else do you know about Monica?" Because if Mom knew about Monica, she might know about the rest of the family, and that information could work to my advantage.

Mom clicked her nails against her highball, thinking. "Not much. I don't think any of her family lives in the States."

"You know, it's possible that Greg didn't divorce Monica because of me. Maybe he divorced her because of the drugs."

"Oh no. The divorce was definitely because of you."

I forced a smile. Like that was supposed to make me feel better.

"Oh! I thought of something." Mom's eyes took on a sparkle I saw only when she talked about her job. Or Dad. "I remember that Monica had a brother who was super-protective of her."

"Do you know which one?" I asked.

"She had more than one brother? I thought there was only Damian. Dark guy. Packed his pants like there was no tomorrow—"

"Mom. Do you have to?"

Mom waved a hand, dismissing me. "Well he did. And I wonder what he looks like now. You know, many men, they get even better looking as they get older. Just like your father did."

Mom went on about Dad and what she thought of him now, but I wasn't listening. I was thinking about Damian. Nat didn't find much on him in the database and I made a mental note to check him out more thoroughly when I got home. After a while, I realized Mom had long stopped talking and discovered I wasn't paying attention.

"I'm not used to seeing you preoccupied like this," she said. "Again, it's that dark aura you're carrying. It worries me."

"Don't worry. I'll figure this out."

"I raised a smart boy. I have no doubts you'll figure this out. It's your safety that concerns me."

"Nothing's going to happen, Mom."

Another round of cheers erupted in the living room.

Mom took both my hands in hers. They were soft hands and I remembered them stroking my head when I was young and sick with a fever. "I know what you're capable of, David, much as I don't like to admit it," she said, "but I think there are people in Monica's family who are capable of more. Do you understand what I'm saying?"

I nodded and wanted to tell her again not to worry, but there was no point. Telling her not to worry was like telling Lottie not to worry. It was the price of sharing a life with me.

Mom studied the jagged scars that ran up the inside of my left arm from the wrist to the elbow. A memento of shrapnel I took in Iraq, trying to cover for a sniper who was angling for position. She dropped a soft kiss on the scars and caressed the old, ragged wounds. Just like she used to caress my head.

In truth, they weren't the only scars I had even when you accounted for the ones on the inside. And I suspected that by the time I was done with Zev and Monica and Ada, I would have even more.

Chapter 20

Dinner was noisy like always at Mom and Dad's, but I didn't engage much. I wasn't in the mood and no one was in the mood to bother me about it. Chris yammered on about his new girlfriend. He was in love, again, with a girl he met a few days ago. Maria complained about how boring freshman year of college was and asked me if she'd do better in the military. I told her not unless she wanted to give up sleeping around, partying, and shopping. Evie whined that there were no good men in the world and wanted to know why she couldn't find a decent twenty- or thirty-something with a good job. She was seventeen. And through it all, Dad kept his head down and his face buried in his meal.

But every now and then, Mom raised her glass to me when no one was looking. I knew she'd tell Dad about our conversation at some point, but she made it clear before we left the kitchen that what we discussed would only be between the three of us. At least until I decided otherwise.

After the last dish and wine glass were cleared from the table and the clock neared ten, I called it a night. Dad walked Lottie and me out to the SUV and tugged at my sleeve just before I opened the door. The streetlights played off his thick, silver hair. I remembered when it used to be dark like mine, and when he used to carry more muscle on his body and more playfulness in his brown eyes. But he looked at peace and happy. Maybe happier than I'd ever seen him.

He pulled me into crushing embrace. "We're here for whatever you need, David," he said, and he looked at me with a fierce loyalty only a parent could have for their child. I wondered if I'd ever feel that kind of loyalty toward Ada. He kissed Lottie goodbye, told her he loved her, and waved us off. Lottie drove home. We didn't speak and that was okay. Neither of us was in the mood.

Once the garage door closed us in, I unlocked the safe in the trunk and pulled out the Kimber. Lottie disarmed the alarm inside the laundry room and I placed the gun on the table next to the sofa in the den. I went to the kitchen while Lottie took off for the second floor, got a large glass of water from the sink, and drank it all. The laptop was still on the kitchen table and plugged in. I brought it to the sofa, prepared to work long and hard, and Lottie returned minutes later in navy sweatpants, a gray tee, and bare feet. She settled into the sofa beside me, remoted the television on, and stuck her cold feet under my thighs for warmth. I checked messages, email, and texts on my cell and found nothing urgent. While the laptop powered up, I dialed MD. One ring and she was there.

"There's something you need to know," I told her, and MD didn't go through the pretense of asking why I called her on a Sunday night when I wasn't on a mission. "When I was eighteen, I had an affair with a woman named Monica Sahin. She was married at the time and the affair didn't last long, maybe three months, and then one day she took off."

"Zev Sahin's sister," MD said.

"Yes, only I didn't know they were related until recently.

Monica has an eleven–year-old daughter, Ada." Lottie ignored the television and focused on me. "I found out today that Ada is my daughter, too."

Lottie sat up but didn't move in any closer. I thought about what my mother had said, about Lottie being able or not being able to have children, and tossed the thought away. It had no place in the here and now.

"Do we have a situation?" MD asked. By "situation" she wanted to know if PROs had to step in and do damage control. Or something heavier handed.

"No," I said. "I don't think so."

"This news doesn't change anything, Bellotti. You're still off this assignment."

"I understand, but it's not realistic to expect that I can stay away from Monica or Ada. I have a responsibility now."

"Bullshit. You have guilt."

"I—"

"Listen to me, Bellotti. Stay away from this." Her voice was sharp. Sharper than normal. "The DEA, DoJ, and Feds have control now. This job doesn't belong to PROs anymore. That's the arrangement we had with them and it sticks."

I didn't like being told what to do, and it seemed I was missing information. I liked that even less. "What happened? Has there been a new development with Zev?"

"That's not critical to you now—"

"That's a load of bull and you know it. This was *my* mission. I pulled it together and I commanded the team and even stepped back to steal a stupid wallet so everyone else could get into position. I deserve to know at least that much."

Lottie flicked off the television. The den fell

uncomfortably still except for the sound of blood rushing through my ears. I made it a point to breathe in and relax. Pissed off would get me nowhere.

"Zev is keeping quiet," MD finally said. "No surprise there. And the DoJ and Feds tried leaning on his wife, but she won't say much. Even though Zev's assets are frozen, there's the possibility we didn't find them all. There are ties that go deeper than what we already know."

I sat forward. The government was involved because I'd orchestrated the takedown with them, but I didn't think Zev's wife would be that unyielding. Jilted wives usually wanted payback, especially those that no longer had access to their husband's money.

"The Feds think there's money laundering involved through Jared and that someone in the family's investing stateside. The only thing Zev's wife would admit was that Jared and Zev had once been very close and that something happened about a year ago. She hinted that Jared isn't playing with a full deck, and Zev's been carrying the only photo he had of him since they had their falling out."

"The photo I lifted from his wallet in Turkey."

"Right."

I logged into my laptop and the PROs website, using that time to gather my thoughts. "Now what?" I asked.

"Now nothing. I already told you. You're out of this."

"I'm *in*, and I can help. I know these people. I have a daughter—"

"You have baggage and baggage costs lives. Stay away, Bellotti. I mean it. I'll inform you when I have more intel."

MD hung up.

I stared at the laptop for a long time. The PROs logo stared back, teasing me, testing to see what I'd do next. Lottie shut the laptop and, with a hand to my chin, turned my face toward her. I saw Monica in her place. The hair, the eyes, the body. Images, darker images, of the two of us moved in. We were in Monica's bedroom, against the wall, going at it hard. Her husband was due home any minute. Our climax was violent and loud.

I closed my eyes and shut down the memory.

"What is it?" Lottie asked.

I couldn't tell her.

"You saw something again. I know you saw it, David, and you keep fighting it. Look at me."

I didn't want to but opened my eyes anyway. The image shifted. I was approaching a dark cave, a feeling of dread working its way up from my stomach into my throat. I swallowed down the terror because I had to be strong. Something had happened inside that cave. Something bad. That's when I heard the scream.

I sensed Lottie move, and then she was on her knees in front of me. "Go with it, David. See what it is you need to see."

I was confused by the images because they didn't make sense. "What I see doesn't fit together. It's all over the place. Like different pieces of the same story."

"What exactly are you seeing?"

"It's Monica. It has something to do with Monica, but I'm not sure what it means."

An explosion sounded from the front door and I scrambled for my gun. The explosion came again followed by the splintering sound of wood separating from wood, and voices bellowed out, "Police!" I shoved Lottie behind the sofa, plastered myself against the den wall, and peered into the foyer. Six cops barreled inside.

"Drop your weapon!" they shouted. "Drop your weapon!"

I eased out from behind the wall and stared down the business end of nine millimeters and rifles with laser sights. Four red dots congregated at the center of my chest. My hands went up in surrender but I didn't know what I was surrendering for.

"I'm dropping my gun," I said, nice and easy. "See?"

I hung the Kimber from a thumb and slowly placed it on the tile floor. The red dots tracked me as I moved. Two cops edged in closer.

"Kick it away!" a beefier, older cop ordered, and I did. It skittered across the tile floor toward another officer whose badge read Simmons. He snatched it up. Lottie's voice cut in from behind, asking what in the hell was going on. I wanted to tell her to stay down, but the beefier cop grabbed me and slammed me against the foyer wall.

"You are under the arrest for the murder of Perry Wilcox."

"I don't know who Perry Wilcox is!"

The cop wrenched my arms behind my back, slapped on plasticuffs, and read me my rights. "You have the right to remain silent. Anything you say or do can and will be held against you in a court of law. You have the right to speak to an attorney. If you cannot afford an attorney, one will be appointed for you. Do you understand these rights as they have been read to you?"

I didn't respond.

Lottie stood at the den's archway, red-faced and arguing.

"This is absurd! He didn't kill anyone."

The beefy cop yanked me from the wall and shoved me toward the front door. Lottie ran after us, screaming they were going to pay for their mistake. I yelled, "Call Nat!" and then I was being herded down the front steps and toward the curb. Three black and whites were parked curbside, their flashing blue and red lights cutting into the dark like lasers. Neighbors stood out on the street watching the spectacle. Later, they would be talking about the neighbor who often went away on long business trips and who probably went postal. Who left a good woman behind.

I was shoved into the back of the middle black and white and saw Lottie standing in the doorway, her frame silhouetted by the lights inside the house. Behind her, one cop headed up the stairs to check the second floor. In the window to the left, another searched the living room. To the right, a third went through the dining room.

The beefy cop who handcuffed me squeezed in behind the wheel. His partner rode shotgun and radioed in that they'd caught the suspect.

"You have the wrong guy," I repeated, but I might as well have been talking to empty air. I cursed under my breath, trying to figure out what in the hell was going on and why this was all happening to me.

We arrived at the neighborhood precinct in five minutes. The cops yanked me out of the car, shoved me to my feet, and then forward. The beefy cop kept a crushing hold on my bicep to make sure I didn't run. He pushed me through the doors and toward the desk sergeant. The precinct smelled like freshly made coffee and industrial strength cleaner. I was booked and charged and fingerprinted. They placed my watch and wallet and cell phone in a plastic baggie, and patted me down one more time for other weapons. The desk sergeant watched me with sharp, gray eyes. The kind of eyes that missed nothing and made mental note of everything. I demanded my one call. No one was inclined to let me have it.

I was ditched into a small cell, the second of four in a row. The space carried the sharp smell of bleach that covered the stench of urine. A drunk yammered on in the adjacent cell, claiming the mother ship tagged his wife during dinner and that he had to go help her or she wouldn't find her way back to Earth. A single light fixture that buzzed like a wasp hung overhead. I wondered if Lottie was safe and if she'd been able to connect with Nat. I also wondered how she was managing with the police.

The cell door clanked shut behind me, and the cop took off for the small office area up front. A punk-ass kid with three hundred dollar sneakers, four hundred dollar jeans, a bald head, and gang tats on his arms and neck watched me from the bottom bunk in the corner. The top bunk was empty and I made it my target. The kid got up and blocked my way. I stepped around. He followed and blocked again.

"Bed's mine." He shifted from foot to foot, antsy. Tough. Daring me to take him on and prove his dominance.

I stepped around him and went for the opposite corner and he jumped me from behind. I ducked, wrapped my left arm around his neck, and squeezed him into a sleeper hold. He gagged and kicked but couldn't overpower me. Just as the kid was about to go unconscious, the cell door rattled open and two cops wrenched us apart. I was dumped into the adjoining, empty cell.

"Can I have my call now?" I asked, but they walked away.

The kid went back to his bunk and stared at me the same way Ada did earlier that day. Another animal at the zoo. I leaned against the cinder block wall and sank down to the floor to sit. And wait. I closed my eyes and listened to my heartbeat. Concentrated on my breathing. My body stilled, my pulse slowed, and all time disappeared. I would, and could, wait as long as it took, if I had to.

"Hey."

I heard the voice but didn't respond.

"Hey. I'm talking to you." It was the gang guy, and he sounded annoyed. "Hey asshole. I said I was talking to you."

I opened my eyes and looked at him. He was standing at the bars that separated our cells, watching me with new interest.

"Where you learn moves like that?"

I didn't answer.

He shifted on his feet again. "I *said*, where you learn moves like that?"

I still didn't answer.

"You a big dude but you quick. You an assassin or something?"

I closed my eyes.

"Can you teach me that shit?"

"No."

"Whatchu in for?"

"Bad manners."

He laughed, a loud, snorting kind of sound. "Hey." His voice was lower now, a harsh whisper. "I can hook you up, dude."

"Already got a woman."

"No. I meant 'roids. Get 'em cheaper than you're paying now."

I opened my eyes and looked at him again. "I don't do 'roids."

"No shit?"

"No shit."

"Day-am." He glanced right then left, making sure no cops were listening. "Listen up, yo. You change your mind, call me. I got the in, you know?" He tugged a card from deep inside his pants and flicked it my way. It landed at my left sneaker.

Another cop strode in, this one with buzz-cut blond hair, and stopped at my cell door to study the two of us. I shifted my sneaker so it covered the card. "What's going on in here?"

"Can I make my call now?" I asked.

The cop grunted and walked back to the front office.

"I'm guessing that's a no."

When the cop was gone I picked up the card and shoved it inside my sneaker. Then I focused on what I had to do next.

Chapter 21

A long time later I got my one call.

I used a phone near the desk sergeant while the blond officer watched my every move. MD answered right away. I told her what happened and where I was, and that someone had either made a big mistake or I was being framed. She listened in silence and spoke only when I had nothing left to say.

"You told Lottie to call Nat, but Nat hasn't called me," she said. "No one called me."

That was a bad sign. According to the clock on the wall, nearly six hours had passed since the cops invaded my home.

"I'll need time to fix this, Bellotti." Her voice sounded flat and that meant she wasn't happy, but it wasn't because I'd been arrested. It was because she was going to have to pull strings. "Has bail been set yet?"

"Haven't seen a judge," I told her.

She let out a short, clipped breath. "I'll get a lawyer on your behalf but it's going to cost us. You're ex-military and a professional soldier. They're going to consider you a flight risk, which means you're going to come with a hefty price tag."

"Isn't this where you say I'm worth it?"

MD hung up.

I spent the next sixteen hours in my cell. The drunk sobered up and was sent to a rehab center. The gang guy was transferred out. He pointed to my sneaker and the card inside it, and gestured that I should call him. I was left alone with the buzzing overhead light, and I worried about Lottie. I also wondered why Nat never connected with MD. I was given bathroom breaks but no food, and on Monday night the desk sergeant from the night before strode in. He stood with his hands on his hips, watching me from outside the cell door.

"You must have friends in very high places," he said. "Not only did you get put on top of the docket, two hours after the judge issued a million dollar bail through your lawyer, someone posted it. An hour after that, your charges were dropped."

He unlocked the door and it squealed open. I stood up and stretched the kinks out of my legs and lower back. The officer gave me hard cop eyes as I walked past him, but he didn't say anything more. At the front desk, I slipped on my watch, and checked the contents of my wallet and the missed calls and texts on my cell phone. I had one from MD saying that she'd arranged a ride for me once I was released. There wasn't anything from Lottie.

Not good.

The sky was dark with thick cloud cover by the time I set foot outside the precinct. I hesitated when I saw Galen's Audi convertible idling off to the right, puffing out a thick tail of exhaust that condensed against cold October night air. I'd been expecting Nat instead.

I shivered over the chill, dug the drug dealer's card out of my sneaker, ripped it up into pieces, and tossed it into the garbage can outside the precinct's double doors. Galen disengaged the locks and I slid inside the car. The heat was going full blast.

Our eyes locked and held.

Galen spoke first. "MD sent me to pick you up. She told me what happened." His jaw was locked, his breathing was shallow and fast, and his skin looked paler than normal.

"Did you stop by my house?" I asked. "Is Lottie okay?"

Galen swallowed. Hard. "Lottie wasn't there, Bellotti. I have no information on her. Neither of us does."

"Us?"

"Nat and me. I got a hold of him after MD called me. He said that Lottie had called him a number of times and left messages last night. The calls stopped just before midnight. Lottie did not call me, though."

Of course she hadn't. Because of me. "Fuck."

Galen's focus shifted forward and with each word he spoke, my heart sank lower in my chest. "According to Nat, Lori's mom came over to watch their boys so he and Lori could have a night out and alone. He had shut the phone off."

I swallowed down a dry lump, feeling adrenalin and dread starting to pump through my veins. "What time did you get to my house?"

"Late this morning. I had no idea that Lottie's absence might be an issue until I spoke to Nat."

I cursed again and stared out the window. Okay. Get a grip. *Think.*

But I wasn't okay. Something had gone wrong, and badly.

"We have to find out what happened to her."

I speared Galen a look. "Lottie isn't yours to worry about."

He shot me one back. "You can use my help and you know it. I—"

"No."

Galen turned on me and gave me cold eyes. "You're being pigheaded and stupid about this, Bellotti. If something happens to her…" His voice cracked and he looked away. "If something happens to her, you know you'll never be able to live with yourself. You'll always question what you didn't do but should have."

Jealousy pounded hard inside my chest. I didn't want him here, and I didn't want him wanting Lottie the way he did. I went back to staring out the window.

"I know what you're thinking," he said. "And it's not warranted."

"No, Galen, you have no idea what I'm thinking. And you never will."

Galen threw the Audi into gear and pulled out of the lot. Traffic on the main road was heavier than it should have been and it took a while for Galen to ease into the flow. "You need to get over this."

"What I need is for you to shut up and let this go."

Galen muttered something that sounded like *asshole*. After a few minutes of silence, he said, "You should know that I phoned Lottie twice from her landline and once from my cell while I searched the house inside and out." Galen sounded all business. And annoyed. "Her Jeep was there, and her bag and keys and cell phone were there. I realized then that calling her was pointless. The only thing that looked wrong was the damaged front door. Nothing else had been disturbed."

I kept staring out the window. We passed a homeless man on the side of the street beneath a street lamp, bundled under a blanket. He was holding a sign saying that he would work for food. He looked as helpless as I felt. "Where is Nat now?"

"Once he realized what was happening, he decided to investigate some more while I checked out things at your house." Galen made a left turn, heading through the side roads to my neighborhood.

"Someone took her," I mumbled.

"I have that same feeling."

My cell phone chirped and Nat's name showed on the display. I put him on speaker. Galen swung a hard left, taking me closer to home.

"It's gotta be Jared behind this, D-Man," Nat said.

That's what I was thinking.

"And I'll tell you why," he added. "Since Galen called, I've been doing some checking. That Perry dude? The one who got killed? His full name is Perry Adam Wilcox. Name ring a bell?"

I shook my head. "Never heard of him before."

"Well, get this. Perry Wilcox is the big guns for some of the Sahin family's investments but not Zev's. Know those accounts and transactions I showed you the other day? Wilcox manages them."

We made a right onto Samsara Street.

"Part of the laundering scheme?" I asked.

"Dunno."

Galen pulled up into my driveway and killed the engine. The porch light was on and I saw that a new front door had been installed, the wood frame still unpainted and conspicuous against the dark mahogany door.

I jerked a thumb at it.

"MD sent a team to replace it," Galen said.

I went back to the phone and Nat. "You have anything else?"

"Still working on it."

"Come over and do it here."

"Be there in ten."

I got out of the Audi, ran up the front steps, let myself in, and stopped. I called out Lottie's name even though I knew she wouldn't answer. The house was silent and still. When Lottie was home, I felt her presence like I felt my own heartbeat. Now, it felt emotionless and cold.

My eyes started to burn and I blinked and kept blinking. My chest felt as if someone had fired a twelve-gauge shotgun point blank at my heart. I leaned against the wall, pressed my hands against my thighs, and bent over, trying to hold it together.

Galen shut the door. "I had some guys help out and check for prints, Bellotti, but we found nothing. We asked the neighbors if they saw anyone other than the police and didn't get anything on that, either. We checked Lottie's phone and landline for messages or unusual calls." I straightened and looked at him with hope. He shook his head.

I stood in the foyer, my hands clasped behind my head, not knowing what to do. "I was set up. Someone, somehow, tagged me for a murder so that when the police got me, Lottie was left at alone and vulnerable. Then they took her."

Galen's response came out a strangled whisper. "Yes." He shoved his hands inside his pockets and slowly paced the foyer, head down, his back to me.

I fished my cell out of my back pocket and dialed MD, putting her on speaker phone so Galen could listen in. "Lottie's gone," I told her. "She went missing sometime between midnight last night and when Galen got to my house late this morning."

I turned and noticed that Galen had disappeared into the living room. He was staring at a photo on the sofa table. The one of Lottie on the beach in a yellow sundress.

I was ready to drag his ass out of there but MD's voice cut me off. "You were set up."

"That's what I'm thinking."

"You misunderstand. You were framed, Bellotti. For Perry Wilcox's murder."

"But I don't know who Perry Wilcox is."

"You're tied to him somehow and we have to find out why. You also need to know that right after you called me last night, I connected with the police. I know the Chief of Police personally. I called in a favor and asked them to run ballistics immediately, and your Kimber came up from a gun competition you were in a few years ago. Ballistics also matched what PROs keeps on file for you, which also matched the murder weapon."

She stopped, waiting for me to digest what this meant.

"Someone swapped out your original gun barrel when you weren't looking, Bellotti, to make it look like you committed the murder."

The information was coming at me too fast. "I kept the Kimber in the safe in the trunk of my SUV. The only way someone would have gotten to it would have been to pop the trunk and crack the safe while I was gone. On a public street."

The front door opened and Nat walked in. I motioned for him to get Galen out of the living room.

"How long was the weapon in the safe?" MD asked.

"I haven't used or removed the Kimber from the gun safe at my house since before I left for Turkey." Then I had to think back and recreate the day before in my head. "But it was in the SUV's safe between eleven in the morning and ten at night on Sunday. I went to Monica's and then my parents' house."

"Someone's got you in their crosshairs, Bellotti. I'm not thrilled you left the Kimber in the SUV's safe, but accessing it wasn't easy. Whoever did this took a huge risk. They went through a lot of trouble to send you a message."

That they were going to use Lottie against me. And that they had the power and resources to do it.

I swore to the gods that if anything happened to her, I would hunt down whoever was responsible and kill them.

Nat walked back into the foyer with Galen at his side. Nat looked at me with expectation. Galen didn't look at me at all.

"Do you know the time of murder?" I asked. "Are there any other suspects?"

"Perry Wilcox was discovered dumped in a scrub pine forest near a private beach in Southampton off Hornet Road. A nearby homeowner found him around six last night. There are no other suspects as of right now. Whoever dumped Wilcox wanted him and the ejected rounds to be found quickly. You sure you don't know the guy? Or have a quick run-in with him somewhere?"

I glanced at Nat. "Positive. Nat told me that he manages money for the Sahin family."

"That's right. He's a senior executive at Lassia Investments, a brokerage and investment firm in New York City," MD added. "Wife, three kids, upside down on his mortgage. Debt so far up his ass it doesn't see daylight. The police, for now, suspect he was killed either because of an investment deal gone bad or because he was embezzling, but that's only conjecture right now." MD's phone beeped with another incoming call. "I have to go, Bellotti, but one final word. I know you're not going to sit and wait for things to happen and that you're going to do whatever it takes to find Lottie. So know this: If you overstep your bounds, if you do something illegal, if you do anything to draw attention to PROs, I will deny ever having this conversation with you and will bring you up on charges to the fullest extent of the law. You will be done. Are we clear?"

"We're clear," I said, because I intended to find Lottie. At whatever the cost.

We disconnected and I turned to Nat. "Tell me about Lassia Investments."

He strode into the kitchen, took a seat at the table, and powered up the laptop still there. I pulled up a chair next to him. Galen flanked his other side. After a few keystrokes, Nat logged into the PROs database, found what he was looking for, and expanded the page.

"Check this out." Nat scanned through a bunch of other screens until he found one that outlined real estate investments. It was a list by location and purchase price. "You know that house MD was talking about? The one Perry Wilcox is upside down on?" He pointed to where Wilcox's contact information was stored, right-clicked the address and copied it, launched a map program, and dumped it into the search field. An aerial photograph appeared seconds later. "The house is in Southampton, D-Man. It's right down the block from Hornet

Road, where his body was found."

My cell phone buzzed. I grabbed it, hoping it was Lottie, but I didn't recognize the number.

"You miss her?" the male voice on the other end asked.

I stiffened and focused on Nat. "Who is this?"

"You destroy my family, and now I get to destroy you. Now you get to see who I really am."

"Jared?"

"You did pretty good for yourself. Out of jail in less than a day. On one mil bail, no less."

"Where is she?"

"Don't push me. I went through a lot of trouble to get you out of the way so I could get to her." Jared let out a laugh. "Now, let's see if you can keep this up. Let's see just how smart you really are. You have forty-eight hours to find her before I take her from you permanently. Starting now."

Chapter 22

"That was Jared. He's got Lottie and I'm going to Southampton to find her."

I went for the stairs and the second floor to gear up.

Nat followed. "How do you know she's there?"

"Jared's throwing breadcrumbs. This is one of them and I have to follow it."

"I'm going with you."

Halfway up the stairs I stopped, turned, and stared at him. Nat stared back. Galen was standing at the base of the stairs, watching.

"I'm going," Nat repeated. "And I'm ready." He lifted his jacket, showing a revolver tucked into a shoulder holster. "You can't do this alone and I won't let you, D-Man. I love her, too."

I was bouncing back and forth between feeling pissed off and upset, and thinking about the risk Nat was taking and what he stood to lose. "Give me five," I finally said. "Then we go." I peered past Nat's shoulder at Galen. "I want you to stay here. Just in case."

Galen paused, looking annoyed that he wasn't going along for the ride.

"You said before that you can help. This is how you will do it."

Galen straightened, still not happy. "Fine."

I took the stairs three at a time, rounded the hall, and went into the bedroom and my closet. I spun through the combination and grabbed an S&W .357 to back up the Kimber, along with ammo and a shoulder holster. I jammed the S&W into the back of my jeans, shoved the Kimber into the holster, and grabbed four extra boxes of rounds. On the way out I snagged a jacket and ran back downstairs. I hit the kitchen and swiped my SUV keys and cell. Nat was packing up the laptop from the kitchen table.

"We're gonna need this," he said. "Where's your car charger and wifi card?"

I opened the desk drawer, found both and tossed them over, and saw Lottie's smiley face mug on the counter near the sink. Something hard and raw punched through my chest as I wondered what life could be like without her.

I didn't want to know.

Galen watched us from the archway between the den and the foyer. I stopped just short of the laundry room door to look at him.

"Thank you," I said.

Nat and I pulled my SUV out into the street. It was starting to rain and heavy drops splattered on the windshield. I amped up the heat to fight the harsh chill and humidity. Nat jacked in the car charger and powered up the laptop to research the area where Wilcox's body was found.

He launched a map program and started hunting the area while I set Wilcox's Southampton address into the navigation system. Almost an hour later, after driving in silence and over roads slick from drizzle, we eased through the back roads of Southampton to a private community that harbored the privileged and influential. Hedges as tall as houses stood like sentinels at curbs, ensuring privacy and blocking the curious eyes of those who wanted to see how the other half lived. I dropped the SUV down to fifteen, careful not to draw the attention of local cops and speed traps. Old style, wrought iron streetlamps burned like candles against a heavy canopy of fog. I set the wipers to intermittent and killed the interior lights.

Nat rapped his window with a knuckle. "Turn right up ahead. That's the street where they found Wilcox."

I eased down a narrow, private road, plunging deeper into darkness. My headlamps illuminated the occasional mailbox, and the smell of salty, ocean air grew thick, even with the windows closed.

Nat pointed to the right. "GPS says this is the spot."

We rolled to a stop. Police tape demarcated the crime scene. It was a patch of undeveloped land filled with scrub pines and scrub oaks and lots of low-lying brush.

I nudged the SUV under two oaks near a hidden driveway where it wouldn't attract attention. We both got out and the first thing I noticed was the quiet. The second was the organic smell of decaying leaves beneath heavy seaside air. I pulled the collar up on my jacket to block the cold air, then dug out two flashlights from the trunk and handed one to Nat.

He checked his cell. "Four bars," he said, keeping his voice to a whisper, and his breath formed small vapor clouds as he spoke. "Service is strong and clean."

Something crackled to our left, the sound of footsteps breaking branches and disrupting the ground. I tugged the Kimber from the holster and pinned myself behind a tree. Nat did the same. A deer emerged, scented the air, then crossed the street and disappeared down a maple-lined driveway. Nat and I flicked on the flashlights and canvassed the crime scene without breaching the tape. There wasn't much to see.

A burst of heavier rain passed then disappeared, and I swiped a sleeve over my face. "I want to see Wilcox's house."

We got back in the SUV and Nat read off the address and directions while I drove. "He's dead ahead," he said, checking the laptop for coordinates. "Right on the water." I drove slowly, watching for more wayward deer. "That one. Number Two."

I idled at a gated cobblestone driveway and searched the area for a place to dump the ride but couldn't find anything. "I can't park here without being noticed. We'll have to go back to the main road and hoof it back here."

I K-turned and made the five-minute drive to a more established neighborhood filled with smaller homes, pulling in between a late model BMW and a Mercedes convertible. I grabbed two pairs of latex gloves and two pairs of booties from the trunk and we trekked back to Wilcox's street, using the dark, the trees, and the underbrush for cover. By the time we reached Wilcox's house, it was raining steadily and heavy. We flicked on the flashlights and covered the lenses with a hand. Our fingers glowed red against the dark, like the burning embers of a dying fire. There were no lights on in the house.

"I'm not seeing any video surveillance and perimeter alarms." Nat surveyed the area once, then once again. "Don't see any dogs either. They got a warning sign by the entrance that there's an alarm, but that could mean squat."

A drop of rain hit my neck and rolled down my back like an icy marble. I found a three-foot branch nearby that probably snapped off during a recent nor'easter and tossed it over the gates. Nat and I slipped in between the trees and waited. Fifteen minutes passed. No cops came. I signaled to Nat to jump the fence, and Nat headed left while I traversed right. Water streamed out of downspouts from the relentless rain, forming puddles around the house. I kept my footfall steady and even, careful not to leave prints. I figured the cedar house measured in at about seven thousand square feet, and worked my way around the right side of a wraparound porch, past a four-car garage, a double width chimney, a series of windows that framed a den half the size of my first floor, and toward the back side of the house. I met Nat on the rear cedar deck that overlooked a covered inground pool, a beach, and the Atlantic, and strode over to a set of French doors that opened into a massive kitchen.

"I'm betting they got an interior alarm," Nat said, "but I'm also betting no motion detectors."

Nat scanned the kitchen with the flashlight. It had an eight-burner gas stove, an indoor grill, two professional refrigerators, two double ovens, and miles of granite counter. He ran the light over the walls, down corners, and over moldings.

"No sensors," he said. "Probably an alarm wired to windows and doors, but nothing else."

I slid out of my jacket, wrapped it around my arm, and rammed my elbow into the French door. Glass exploded, giving us entry. No alarms sounded, but that may not have meant much. If a silent alarm had been tied to a central monitoring station, they'd have been alerted already.

I put the jacket back on, and Nat and I slid on the booties and gloves and went inside. "Work quickly," I told him.

"Bet this is Wilcox's summer home coz this place looks buttoned up for the season," Nat whispered. "I'll take upstairs."

I scanned the kitchen, the adjoining dining room, and den. Other than the kitchen, everything was white. White leather furniture. White large screen television. White walls. White brickwork bordering the fireplace. I crossed a white marble foyer triple the size of mine and moved into the living room, all white with the exception of three red pillows. The living room adjoined to a home theater. Next to the theater was an office with a white lacquer desk, two matching file cabinets, and four chairs. I took one step inside and set off a screeching alarm.

Shit.

Nat was at my side in seconds.

"Files," I told him. "Go through the files. Fast."

He took one cabinet while I took the other. In less than ten seconds I found a file labeled Sahin. In less than two minutes I had iPhone pictures of what was inside it. One minute after that, the files were replaced and Nat and I were slipping through the broken French door, sprinting down the length of the fence, and jumping the gate. Five minutes later, we were back at the SUV. When the police arrived at the scene, they would find only a broken door. No fingerprints or footprints. No other evidence that the house had been disturbed.

We took off our booties and gloves and shoved them under the seats. I gave Nat my iPhone and he uploaded the photos to the laptop while I drove us out of the neighborhood. It took him several minutes to find the details I wanted.

"Check this out," he said as I turned out of the back roads and headed toward the main part of town. "The heat was on Perry Wilcox for a possible Ponzi scheme. Investigation started a month ago." I flicked a look his way while he scanned to another photo. "He was definitely moving moolah for Jared Sahin, but he's investing with Damian Sahin, too."

"With? Not for?" I pulled into a Seven Eleven parking lot. It was well lit and active, and was a good place to blend in. I leaned over to study the photos.

"Yep. Funds expeditions to find artifacts."

"What kind?"

"Doesn't give specifics. Oh, check this out. Three weeks ago, Wilcox high-tailed it on a private jet to Turkey." He went on about the ticket Wilcox purchased and where he stayed. "Had drinks at that nightclub where you took down Zev."

I straightened and stared out the windshield, trying to make the connections. The rain had subsided to a drizzle. "Information that doesn't lead to Lottie," I said, and the empty feeling in my chest returned, along with the fear of what would happen if I didn't find her. I shoved the desperation deep down and out of the way. I would find Lottie if it killed me.

"And there's more," Nat said. "Wilcox and Damian took a trip to northern Canada on some kind of expedition just before that trip. What the hell is in northern Canada besides boatloads of snow?"

The lights from a passing car caught the droplets on the windshield, illuminating them so they looked like heavy, wet snow. A wayward thought came to mind. *White rain.* I didn't know why the words stuck in my head but they felt meaningful somehow. I rolled them around in my brain, trying to figure out where I'd heard them before and why they felt important now. A teenager emerged from the store and lit up a cigarette with a lighter, and the image of white rain gave way to a bonfire. I was sitting, cross-legged, in front of it. People dressed in thick fur and leather pelts danced and sang, their bodies silhouetted by the fire. A little girl climbed onto my lap and hugged me, and a female sat down by my side. She had dark brown eyes and black hair and looked like she could bear many strong children. The girl saw the female and scowled, and I scolded her for her defiance. She moved in closer, leaned her head on my arm, and said she was sorry. I kissed her head and ordered her to remain with the group. The female slid her hand inside mine and I led her away to my hut. I took her there, as I had often since that night she first gave herself to me. Outside the hut other voices grew loud, then louder. Another female's ill-tempered voice cut through. The flap was thrown open and the angry female stormed inside. She hissed the name of the female in bed with me.

Lassia.

The image gave way to Lottie, and I had a sudden sensation of her being nearby. I could smell her skin, taste her mouth. Feel her in my heart and soul. She was out here. Somewhere.

I straightened, my eyes refocusing on the windshield and the heavy, glittering raindrops.

"David? Yo, dude. You in there somewhere?"

One raindrop rolled down, cutting a swath down my line of sight. "Lassia," I whispered.

"Funny you should bring up Lassia Investments again," Nat said.

I turned in the direction of his voice, not really seeing him.

"Get this. The firm's managed by a guy named Gary Cooper." Nat swung the laptop to show me a sixty-something man with near white hair and striking blue eyes. It was a professional photo of him wearing a navy suit and a smug grin, the kind that came with arrogance and years of making heaps of money. "Damian Sahin owns a big-ass place here in Southampton. Bought it from Gary Cooper, who owned it before him. And guess where it is. Five minutes from Wilcox's house. Same neighborhood."

I cursed. "Can't check it out tonight. The cops will be all over the place because of the break-in at Wilcox's." And I hated that I was stalled because of it. I stared out into the rain again, the feel of Lottie still burning in my veins, the sense of her warm skin still pressed against mine. Something inside me stirred, wanting to protect her. Mark her. Make it known that she was mine.

Mine.

"What now?" Nat asked.

The inside of the SUV came back into focus and I checked the digital clock on the dashboard. It was just past three in the morning. Forty-three hours and thirty-six minutes left to find Lottie.

"Now I go to Plan B."

Chapter 23

Lottie jerked awake, sweaty, palpitating, and shaking.

She was in the same small room with the same white walls, thin mattress, cement floor, and bare light bulb that she'd been in since…she wasn't sure. She remembered David being arrested, trying to contact Nat, and then going out to her Jeep to find him. She remembered two men grabbing her once she opened the garage door. Then she woke up here with no blanket, sheets, or pillow. No handbag, shoes, or belt.

She'd been kept mostly sedated, left awake only long enough for sandwiches, water, and bio breaks. A man who stood taller than David, with brown hair and a nose that looked like it had been broken once, brought the food, watched her pee, and injected her again once she finished. There were no windows but the room felt damp, almost cold. It could have been a basement. It felt more like a cave.

Lottie wasn't sure how much time she had before the man with the broken nose returned and knew she had to act fast. She didn't know what was outside the door or who else was with her, but she couldn't risk not finding out. Inactivity meant indecision, and indecision meant she gave whoever brought her here all the control. Even in captivity, she owned her reactions and thoughts. David had once said that was the only power a hostage had, and only now did Lottie understand what that meant.

She rolled out of bed and tested the door lever even though she knew it would still be locked. It had one small hole in its center, where a pin or paper clip could be inserted to unlock it. Lottie scanned the floor, hoping to find something useful to disengage the lock and, again, found nothing. The place was barren and clean, and just as she was considering ways to dig out a spring from the bed, the door handle rattled as a key slid inside. Lottie raced to the bed and went limp, pretending to still be unconscious. She wanted to see what her captor would do when unable to wake her, and who else was around.

She heard the door close, the clatter of a tray being set on the floor, and shuffling footsteps as the man approached.

"Food is here," he said. He wrapped a hand around her bicep like a steel band and shook. When she didn't respond, he shook harder. Lottie flopped over but still didn't move. "Hey." He shook harder still. "Hey! Get up!"

She didn't.

The man let go, threw open the door, and called out, "Yo! She's not waking up!"

No one answered and the man called out again, this time from outside the room. Lottie opened her eyes and saw a view of a huge adjoining room with a pool table, a full bar with a marble counter, a large screen television, and two huge leather sectionals. Heat rolled in from the entertainment room, a welcome change to the cold she'd endured, and Lottie considered running until she heard pounding footsteps down a far stairwell and another voice she didn't recognize.

"What do you mean she isn't waking up?"

"Just what I said." Two men walked in and Lottie shut her

eyes. "She's not waking up. You try."

A hand cracked across Lottie's face. The right side of her cheek exploded with pain and when the other man struck again, Lottie rolled away to find safety on the far side of the bed.

"See?" the second man said. "She's awake."

Lottie glanced over her shoulder to look at her other captor, and froze. "Jared?"

He looked nothing like she remembered. His brown hair was longer and pulled back into a ponytail. He'd also grown a goatee and had a tattoo that curled up the right side of his neck.

Jared stared at her, saying nothing, then walked out and closed the door behind him.

The larger man shoved a sandwich and a bottle of water at her. Some kind of beef on whole wheat with lettuce and tomato. She wondered who prepared the meals.

She pushed the plate away, not hungry. "I want to talk with Jared."

He shoved the plate back.

"I want to talk to Jared," she repeated.

"Not going to happen."

Lottie studied the gun and cell phone that were clipped to his hip and the hypodermic tucked inside his shirt pocket. She considered grabbing the needle, sticking him with it, and running.

His eyes tracked hers to his pocket. "Don't bother trying," he said, and he pulled out the syringe and jammed it into her arm. She struggled under his hold but the harder she fought the faster her limbs grew heavy. Her eyelids fluttered closed, and the last thing Lottie saw before she sank into darkness was the man eating her sandwich.

A dream came almost instantly.

A fire blazed red and orange against the black sky, and the Clan huddled around it for warmth. Most of them wore heavy, brown bison skins as protection against the white rain and harsh cold, but some males danced naked, laughing and shouting and daring one another to see who could endure the icy frost the longest.

Lassia watched Makra play with his child, the girl, as he swung her around by her arms, kicking up white rain as they moved. The girl laughed each time it seemed Makra might let go, and the leather band of teeth at Makra's throat rattled with each thrust and swoop he made. Cilla watched them both with pride. Though Makra had not yet chosen Cilla as his Primary, the Clan expected it would happen soon. And once Makra chose his Primary, all other females in the Clan would fall into a lesser role with him until they chose another male for their own.

Lassia did not want this to happen to her.

There were other men, strong men like Ayak, but they were not Makra.

Through the roaring, crackling flames, Lassia watched Makra put down the girl and speak with Cilla. He turned for his hut and Cilla said something, and her voice sounded angry and sharp. Makra turned and responded, and though Lassia could not make out the words she could see that Makra had become annoyed. He stared at Cilla for a long while, perhaps to put her in her place, and then Cilla grabbed the girl's hand and the two disappeared into another hut.

Lassia saw her chance and took it.

She headed for Makra's hut, thrust aside the flap, and

found him removing the heavy fur from his shoulders and dropping it to the ground. A fire burned in the center and vented out a hole in the top, and the warmth inside the space was as soft and inviting as the sun's heat against bare skin. An area off to the side was piled thick with furs—spotted lion and rich brown bear—and served as Makra's bed. Makra had the largest hut of the entire Clan. Lassia wanted his hut to be her hut, too.

Makra narrowed his eyes and scowled. "You are not the female I requested."

Lassia stepped forward, determined to finally make him notice her. "I'm not leaving."

He studied her for a while, like he was trying to remember where he had seen her. Or if she even had a name.

"I am Lassia," she said.

His eyes skimmed past her and to the flap behind, as if he was expecting someone else to come in and might have to deal with that, too.

"Look all you want for your other female," she said, "I am still not leaving."

Lassia walked into the hut, slowly at first because she'd never seen Makra up close and because she wasn't sure how he'd react. If he was like any other male, he would not turn her away, but she couldn't be sure. She'd heard stories about Makra, brutal with the kill and quick with the temper, but she'd also heard stories about how he treated his females. And Lassia wanted to know why those females always wanted to return to his bed.

She circled Makra, trailing her fingers over powerful muscle and deep scars that must have taken many moons to heal. She was nervous, knowing she still had much to learn in the ways of pleasing a male, but she was determined. Makra was what she wanted, and had wanted, for a very long time. He was larger up close, larger than any other male in the Clan, but his size didn't intimidate Lassia. If anything, it intrigued her even more.

Makra's eyes followed Lassia as she circled him. Both times.

She stood in front of him, heart hammering on the inside but willing her body to remain calm on the outside, and ran a finger down the jagged scar on his arm. Then she bent over and swept her tongue over the old wound. She sensed him shudder and watched small bumps appear on his skin. Lassia took that as an invitation to lick again. She ran her hands over Makra's chest and trailed fingertips down to the criss-cross of scarred claw marks on his lower belly, just above the leather pelt at his waist. His breath caught and his nostrils flared. Lassia may not have been as experienced as other females but she wanted Makra like she wanted no other man. And she intended to use her hunger to make up for what she lacked in skill.

Her gaze met Makra's and stayed there. She traced the criss-crossed scars with her fingertips once more and proceeded downward and under his pelt. Makra did not move but watched her with green eyes that reflected the licking flames behind her. Lassia felt a rising heat she knew didn't come from the fire and, growing bolder, found she wanted with her hand. Makra responded quickly to her touch. With her other hand, Lassia yanked the pelt away and urged Makra toward the bed.

He picked her up and threw her onto the thick, layered

furs. It wasn't what Lassia had planned or wanted. Makra tried mounting her but she battled back, yanking her hands from his and kicking out from beneath his large body. They wrestled, rolling one way then another, him pinning her down, she using her legs to wrangle back on top, until Lassia shoved him down and clamped her thighs over his.

"Stay." Lassia was sweaty and breathless and determined to tame this *Einarr*. This warrior.

Makra grabbed her arms, prepared to wrestle her underneath him again.

"I said stay." She ground her hips against him so that he understood. "Stay there and do not move."

Small beads of sweat rolled off Makra's chest and to the spotted lion fur beneath him, and his chest heaved from exertion. Lassia clenched him with her thighs, holding him in place, and guided him inside her.

Makra went still. So did she.

They were a fit.

Lassia moved slowly at first, wanting to feel him. All of him. She kept the rhythm steady, her eyes fixed with his, determined to make him finally see her. To know her. He seemed unsure at first, maybe recognizing her inexperience, but it felt good, almost too good, and Lassia quickened the pace. She moved with him, provoked him, teased him, and the desire intensified, growing as hot and potent as the fire inside the hut. She urged him on, feeling the pressure build, and he shifted to drive in deeper still. He yanked off the fur that covered her body and ran his hands over her breasts and stomach and thighs. He slipped a hand between her legs and Lassia moaned for more and just as climax neared for them both, the tent flap was thrown open and a startled noise interrupted.

It was Cilla.

Makra growled at her, angry at the interruption. "Leave us," he said, and his fingers dug hard into Lassia's thighs as he fought for what little control Lassia knew he had left.

Cilla stepped forward, baring her teeth, a low growl rumbling from her chest.

"Leave us!" hc snapped, louder this time, "or you will never come to my bed again."

Cilla's eyes narrowed on Lassia. Then she thrust the flap aside and headed back into the dark.

Makra shifted his hips, urging Lassia to finish.

She refused. "There are two of us in this bed," she reminded him. "Not just you."

Makra grabbed her throat. "You are either a very foolish female or a very bold one."

Lassia swallowed, her heart thumping loud in her ears and hard in her chest. "No one has ever called me foolish," she said, aware that her voice and her body were shaking. But she stayed still, eyes on him, daring him to overpower her and take what he wanted.

He paused. "You are not like the other females."

Because she was bold enough to regard him as her equal. "No."

He seemed ready to grin but tamped down the reaction. "Who are you?" he asked, "and why have I not noticed you before?"

"I can show you who I am," she said.

Makra angled his head, studying her.

"You don't like a female on top?" she asked.

"I have never taken one in this way."

"So I am your first."

He laughed, a rich, powerful sound that came deep from inside his chest. Lassia decided she liked the way it made her body hum.

She shifted, bringing him in as deep as she could. His eyes turned as dark as night and his skin flushed again with sweat. His chest heaved, his jaw clenched, and his body went rigid beneath her. He was close.

And Lassia enjoyed holding this power over him.

He did not fight as she started moving again, instead fascinated with watching her as if she were nothing he had ever seen before. When he came close she pulled back, and Lassia sensed he enjoyed the tease. The tension. The knowledge that he had, until now, not experienced such a thing with another female. When she pulled back for the third time, he moaned her name.

She stopped, breathless. "Say my name again."

"Lassia."

"Again."

He ground into her and thrust upward. "Lassia."

She brought his hands to her breasts. "And again."

He thrust once more and growled. "*Lassia!*"

Lassia arched her back and took him, hard and without restraint, and when Makra sat up, bit her shoulder, and climaxed, Lassia knew she had succeeded.

Makra knew who she was.

It would only be a matter of time before he was finally hers.

Chapter 24

It was four in the morning by the time I got home and sent Nat back to his family. I'd trashed the gloves and booties in a dumpster near a restaurant along the way, and found Galen asleep in the den with the television on when I walked in. I wondered what Galen searched for in the house while I was gone. Didn't matter now. I had bigger problems.

He woke as I passed the den, heading for the foyer and the stairs. I gave Galen a rundown about what happened at Wilcox's house, that Wilcox funded expeditions with Damian to find artifacts, and that Damian had bought a house near Wilcox's that was once owned by Gary Cooper, the managing director of Lassia Investments. I added that I was heading into the city to meet with Cooper to get more intel, and that I needed him to stay put. Galen didn't argue.

I showered and shaved, and dressed in a power suit and a pair of Ferragamos. By the time it was five thirty I was on the road again, heading into Manhattan. I was focused and that was good. Focus kept my desperation in check and my mind sharp. It kept me from worrying about what would happen if I didn't find Lottie.

Traffic moved well, with professional commuters zipping into the city at a fixed seventy mile an hour pace. Just after six forty I was pulling into a parking garage off Water Street, the morning sun throwing a sharp reflection off downtown New York City's steel and glass high rises.

I found a Starbucks nearby with a half dozen people in line. A young woman who looked like she just graduated college took my order. Doppio espresso. With the exception of the few hours of sleep I had in jail, I hadn't rested since. I also hadn't eaten and knew I needed food. I ordered a pastry with enough sugar to power me through the next couple of hours.

"You look like you're having a bad day. And it's not even seven yet." The cashier was pretty and brunette and big-breasted.

"You could say that." I handed her a twenty.

The register opened and she counted out my change. "I get off at ten," she said, handing over the bills and her hand lingered on mine. "I bet I can take your mind off things for a while."

I pocketed the change and gave her a smile. "I bet you can. But I'm already taken."

Her gaze fell to my ring finger. "You're not married. Or you're pretending not to be." Her eyes, which were gray, met mine.

I looked at her. And kept looking.

"Right. Got it." She handed over my coffee and sighed. "Maybe in the next life."

I tipped my cup at her and found a table and chair near the window where I worked out a plan. At seven forty-five I was heading down Water Street toward Lassia Investments. The address housed a forty-three-story building with mahogany and brass walls and interior waterfalls that spanned the western side of the building. I strode toward the security desk, trying for attitude and impatience. It wasn't hard to pull off. I approached the desk and gave the lobby a quick scan for security cameras. Two near the security station. Six inset in the ceiling. One in each of the far corners.

"I've got a meeting with Perry Wilcox at eight," I told the security officers. "Where should I go?"

A slim, pale-skinned guard glanced at the slightly older one who was missing a finger, then refocused on me. Both were dressed in dark blue uniforms. He shifted on his feet, uncertain, and I knew exactly why. Wilcox was dead and everyone in the firm most likely knew it, only he was probably under direct orders to keep his mouth shut.

"I'm sorry, sir," he said. "His meetings have been canceled for the day."

"I wasn't notified about any cancellation. I'm here now. Find someone else."

"I'm sorry, sir. But—"

"Find someone else." I leaned in and lowered my voice. "*Now.*"

The guard exchanged another look with his partner. His hand hovered near the gun at his hip. And I was thinking about the Kimber tucked into my shoulder holster. Even with a license to carry concealed, it wouldn't go over well.

"Either find someone else who will invest my ten million," I said, "or I'll head to the investment firm down the street and have them invest it instead. And then, I'll call your managing director, Gary Cooper, and tell him he lost premium business because of you."

The heavy set guard moved in. "Identification, please."

"I've been here before. Call Perry's office upstairs. They're expecting me."

"Identification please."

I couldn't give them my identification because I couldn't risk someone linking me to Wilcox's murder. And I couldn't push this so far that they'd discover I was packing. I pasted on a tight, irritated smile that said I didn't like them wasting my time. Which they were.

"Call upstairs," I said, "and tell them Jared Sahin sent me here."

"You either have to provide us with valid identification, sir, or we will have to request you to leave the premises." The heavyset guard's hand now hovered near his gun, too.

I stared them both down but didn't get far because I couldn't take the risk. Better to end up the asshole that became the brunt of office gossip than to risk Lottie's life. "Gary Cooper will be hearing about this," I said as I tracked backward, toward the building's glass doors. "Along with the media and anyone else I can tell."

I spun around and hoofed it out of Lassia Investments, ready to jump on Plan C. Just as I grabbed the door handle to leave, a black Suburban that doubled as a limo pulled up to the curb and Gary Cooper stepped out. I recognized him from the photo Nat had showed me. He wore an expensive overcoat and shoes and was flanked on both sides by bodyguards. I saw my opportunity and took it, and bore down on Cooper as soon as I stepped outside.

"You should talk to your guards," I said, jamming a thumb toward the security station inside. "Disrespectful and arrogant. Do you know they turned down my money?" Cooper tried to bypass me but I kept at him. "I have ten million to invest and those assholes wouldn't let me inside to meet with Perry Wilcox. I heard great things about Lassia Investments, but my money isn't good enough for you? Why the discrimination?"

Cooper snapped his fingers and one of his personal guards moved in.

"I know Wilcox was brought up on that Ponzi scheme," I said, louder now so everyone on the sidewalk could hear, "but I really don't believe that Lassia Investments or you would allow such a thing to happen. A Ponzi scheme is bad for business, and you guys are clean, right? Wilcox swore the allegations weren't true."

It was enough to get Cooper to stop and turn. He studied me with sharp eyes that probably didn't miss much, took a step closer, and asked, "Do I know you?"

"Michael Morgan." I held out my hand but Cooper didn't take it. His guards boxed me in while employees with pricy suits and briefcases headed indoors. "You look like someone with half a brain," I told him. "Can you please contact Perry's office and tell them that his friend Michael Morgan is here to see him? He was really down last week, with all the Ponzi stuff going on, and I swear I was trying really hard to keep him off the tequila because the last thing he needed was to do something stupid while he was drunk, but—"

Cooper grabbed me by the arm and escorted me through the door, quickly, to get us out of earshot and the public eye. He said nothing while we headed for a private elevator paneled in burled wood and brass near the waterfalls, and when the doors closed us in I turned to the guards and gave them a big fat grin. Because Cooper was calling the shots, no one had bothered to check me for weapons so the Kimber was still tucked in my shoulder holster.

Cooper kept a cool gaze on me. "We've met before," he said. "I'm sure of it."

I tossed out a few names to knock him off the scent. "Richford's Gala in East Hampton this summer? The Children's Fund Live Auction? East End Summer Horse Show?"

His chin came up. He wasn't buying it. "No."

The elevator doors pinged open to the top floor, revealing a seating area big enough for twenty, with tan suede sofas, ebony tables, Waterford lamps, and thick carpet. Two assistant workstations with Macs and supersized monitors bordered a pair of ebony double doors that I figured led into Cooper's office. Cooper took off for it, snapped his fingers again, and the two assistants jumped into action. One in a pink suit with a fur collar took his coat and briefcase. The other, in a leather skirt and tight knit sweater and boots, handed him a cup of coffee.

"No interruptions for five minutes," he told them and he swung open his office doors and strode in. I followed. The doors whispered closed behind us.

"I appreciate your time—"

"Sit," he said, pointing out a leather club chair near a long burl wood desk. He settled into his own chair, a high-backed leather thing that looked like a throne, and planted his feet on his desk, balancing his coffee on his thigh. Ceiling-to-floor glass offered an unobstructed view of the Statue of Liberty, Brooklyn, and the mouth of the Hudson. The perks of living the high life.

I sat, and the cushion wheezed out a long breath of air underneath me. "Is Perry joining us here?"

"Don't do that again," Cooper said, and he tipped up his

chin so he could stare down his long nose at me.

"Do what?" I asked.

"That bullshit you did outside to draw attention. You want a meeting with me, you call and make an appointment like everyone else does."

"And yet here I sit. In a meeting. With you."

Cooper paused. Something that could have been a grin played at the corners of his mouth and then disappeared. "Why are you really here, Mr. Morgan?"

I had two choices. Tell the truth and risk Cooper contacting Jared Sahin and possibly hurting my chances of finding Lottie alive. Or, continue the lie and risk Cooper contacting Jared Sahin and possibly hurting my chances of finding Lottie alive. But I'd already grown tired of the game and decided it was time to confess.

"My name is David Bellotti and Jared Sahin, who invested through Perry Wilcox, is—"

"David Bellotti." Cooper slid his feet off the desk and stood. "*David Bellotti*. I should have known. I thought I recognized you." He checked his watch, a gold Patek Philippe, and opened one of the two massive doors. "Get out of my office *now*, Mr. Bellotti. Our discussion is over."

I didn't know what upset him so looked around the room, buying time, but I had the Kimber and knew I couldn't take any more chances. I got up and headed for the door, walking slowly but thinking fast.

I passed a framed diploma on a bookshelf that bore the name Gary Boseris Cooper. A crystal-framed photo beside it snagged my attention next, and Cooper's issue with me suddenly became clear.

It was a picture of Gary Boseris Cooper standing between a woman and a man, with an overhead banner celebrating New Year's Eve twelve years ago. The woman was a very pregnant Monica Sahin. The man was Greg Boseris, Monica's husband. Gary's son.

Chapter 25

Monica. Again.

I strode out of the building and to the parking garage where I picked up my SUV, thinking how she kept popping up when I least expected. In my gut I now knew she was the key. She was going to lead me to Lottie.

I blew through the Midtown Tunnel and jumped on the expressway and flew home, driving past my house and going straight to Monica's. I ditched the SUV at the curb, ascended the cobblestone walkway, and rang the bell. No one answered. I rounded the columned, gingerbread porch and scanned the driveway. No car, but that didn't mean much. I learned early on in the Marines that a place wasn't necessarily vacant just because it looked like no one was there. Off to my right, an interior curtain fluttered. I peeked inside the tall window and through the curtain but saw only antique furniture in the living room. A shadow appeared just off the doorway leading to the front hall, the movement broadening and contracting as if the person who was hiding was unsure whether or not to answer the door.

Ada.

I returned to the entrance and knocked. "Ada. It's me." I hesitated, not sure how to refer to myself. "It's David. Can you let me in?"

She didn't answer, and I knocked again.

"Ada, it's important. I need to talk to your mother. Please open the door or go get her for me." I glanced at my watch. It was just after ten, the hours left to find Lottie quickly ticking away. I closed my eyes and willed the girl to do the right thing. Seconds later, one of the double doors partially opened and Ada peered out. "I need to see your mother," I told her.

The door eased open and Ada stood guard in jeans, All Stars, and a leather trimmed sweater. She carried an iPod in one hand and had ear buds tucked in her ears. "She asked if you can come back later."

"This can't wait." I pushed past her and went into the living room, then followed the circuit through the dining room, kitchen, and back to the front hall. I was about to head upstairs but stopped. Something felt off. The house was too quiet and I quickly realized why. No one else was home.

I faced Ada. "Are you alone?"

She retreated a step. "No."

"I know you're lying." I edged in closer, careful not to frighten her, but when her shoulders straightened and her chin lifted in challenge, I knew this girl didn't scare easily. "Is anyone home? Besides you?"

Ada tugged out the ear buds and I heard Coldplay sing about closing walls and ticking clocks. "The babysitter had to go out."

I inspected the living room and dining room more closely and inhaled long and deep to scent the air. The furniture didn't look disturbed and I didn't smell remnants of breakfast from the kitchen. I retraced my steps to the kitchen but didn't find any dishes in the sink or the dishwasher or any telltale signs of leftover meals on the counters. I returned to the living room and hunkered down in front of my daughter.

"How often does your mother leave you home alone?" I asked.

Ada pressed her lips together. Pouty.

"Do you ever have babysitters at all?"

"Sometimes." She frowned and now she looked angry, like she'd been holding in the secret for too long. "But not today."

"Not today? Or not usually?"

Ada blinked and kept blinking, fighting back tears and refusing to let them get the better of her. "Does it matter?"

"To me it does." I spotted a smudge of blood on her sweater sleeve and on top of her left hand, and took her hand so I could get a better look at the injury. It had been cut but not deeply, and had started clotting. "That needs a Band-Aid," I said.

"It's fine."

"It'll get infected."

"I know how to take care of myself."

"I'll bet you do," I breathed, still holding her hand.

She didn't pull back or fight me and I had the strong feeling she craved attention and didn't often get it. "Mom keeps the Band-Aids upstairs in the bathroom." Ada's green eyes found mine and held. "If you want to get one."

An emotion I'd never felt before lurched in my heart and my first and only thought was to take care of this little girl.

"I'll be right back," I said. "Promise you won't take off on me."

Ada sank down on the sofa and folded her arms on her lap, the ear buds dangling on the carpet. "Where would I bother to go?"

An ache sprouted in my chest and swelled. I nodded, because I didn't trust myself to speak, and headed upstairs to Monica's bedroom and the en suite adjoining it. I took three steps inside and stopped, unprepared for the ambush of memories. The bed, the floor, the wall, the triple dresser. The décor may have changed to something more colorful and playful over the years, but the memories were as strong now as they were the day Monica and I made them. I shoved the images away and strode to the bathroom, intent on keeping the past where it belonged. The antique medicine cabinet held small soaps and deodorant and toothpaste. The cabinet beneath the sink held toilet paper and tissues and four makeup bins. I remembered the linen closet behind the door and checked it for Band-Aids, and moved towels and washcloths and sheets out of the way but found none. On the top shelf, behind pillowcases and a box of tampons, I found six bags of marijuana, five of what looked like cocaine and another three with an assortment of pills.

A more complete picture was forming in my mind and I didn't like what I saw. I went to the hallway bathroom and found Band-Aids in the medicine cabinet, and ran downstairs for Ada.

"You're coming with me," I said as I bandaged her hand. "Grab what you need for the afternoon, okay?"

"Where are we going?"

"I'm taking you to my mother's until I know someone will be here to take care of you." And even then, I wasn't sure that was the right thing to do. If Monica was a user, I didn't trust her around my daughter.

A minute later we were out the door and in the SUV. I called Monica's cell and left her a message, telling her that I had Ada and that we had to talk. I called Mom next and gave her a quick heads up, and found her waiting at her front door when we pulled up into the driveway. Mom and Ada stared at each other for a while, coming to some unspoken understanding of who they were to each other. Then my mother patted Ada's head and told her to go inside.

"I know you're going to talk about me and I want to stay here." Ada fixed me with a hard stare, daring me to override her.

I had no problem doing it. "Inside. Now."

"But—"

"This is me, not your mother. Inside."

Ada grumped but did as she was told.

"She looks just like you," Mom said once Ada disappeared. "Tell me what's going on, David."

I told her about the arrest and what I knew about Lottie's disappearance, and what I found at Monica's. I made sure to keep my voice level and even. I was worked up enough as it was. No need to get Mom worked up, too.

"I need you to watch Ada while I search for Lottie," I said. "I can't worry about the both of them, and she needs support and family right now because Monica isn't doing the job."

"You're always so focused."

Inside I was a mess, but I was ignoring it because I needed to focus on the goal.

"I'd love to talk, Mom, but I have to go." I made to turn but Ada's voice stopped me.

"You're leaving me?" Ada stood at the door with a book in

her hand. "I don't want you to go."

My heart wrenched at the sight of her wide eyes. She was strong-willed and determined but she was also vulnerable, having seen too much and been supported too little. I swallowed, to make sure she didn't see just how scared I was.

"I have to find Lottie. If I don't, something bad could happen to her. Do you understand?"

"Do you know where she is?"

"No, but I think your mother might know and I'm hoping she can help me."

"Mom is at my Uncle Damian's house in Southampton." Ada hiked the book she'd found under her arm. "She said she and my cousin Jared had grown-up stuff to talk about with him, but I know what that means."

"What does it mean?"

"Business stuff. Mom gets packages from Jared and then she makes the packages go somewhere else."

"Do you know what's in the packages?"

"She says that it's clothes from Uncle Jared's store, but I think my mother's lying."

I was thinking she was lying, too.

I crouched down and held Ada's shoulders. "You'll be safe here, Ada. And my Mom is a great cook and loves to play games. She can make you lunch and dig out all the old board games she used to play with me."

"I'd rather read this book." Ada tugged it out from under her arm and showed it to me. *Sex Manual for the Open Minded: Untold Pleasures for Him and Her.*

I stood and gave her a strangled smile. Then I gave my mother a long, stern look. "Keep it clean, please," I said under my breath. "And hide the brownies."

I headed down the cement walk to the SUV.

My mother called out after me. "Find her, David."

I stopped, my heart aching with desperation. Of course I would find Lottie.

I had to.

Chapter 26

Lottie woke and saw the silhouette of a man standing next to the bed. A man with short dark hair, bright green eyes, and a strong body.

"David?"

When she sat up and her vision adjusted to the overhead light, the image disappeared. There was no one else in the cold room. Only her.

She sat on the bed while longing uncoiled in her stomach and twisted up into her heart. She missed David, but more than that she wondered if he'd ever find her. And if he didn't—

Lottie shoved the thought away. She had to focus on the positive. Concentrate on hope. She'd read accounts in psychology journals about individuals connecting to someone else's dreams, and making telepathic impressions to plant messages another person's mind. Months ago, she'd have thought those concepts crazy. But learning about her past incarnations, and that life wasn't just what you saw in front of you, taught her to keep an open mind.

She opened her mind now.

And something nagged at her. A feeling. No, a presence. David's presence. It was as if he was inside her, one with her, breathing in time with her. Thinking with her, and wishing with her. Wanting her home.

She shut her eyes and drew him in closer. His scent enveloped her, a mix of warm amber and sultry sandalwood. His arms, so powerful and protective, held her steady. His heart, always devoted and faithful, kept rhythmic beat with hers. His body molded to hers, a perfect fit. As it had since they met thousands and thousands of years ago.

She remembered that first morning after, entangled in each other and nestled beneath thick blankets of spotted lion fur. His body felt warm, his embrace surprisingly tender. She had no idea how long they had slept, though it was clearly morning because she could see sunlight and blue sky through the vent at the top of the tent near the still burning fire.

Makra stirred, shifted on the pile of furs, and rolled over, taking the blankets with him. She shivered over the sudden cold but there was no way she could tug the blankets back. He was too big, and too strong. She started to get up with a mind to find her own coverings for warmth when his voice stopped her.

"Where are you going?"

The uncertainty she used to feel around him teased at her again, reminding her that maybe she'd made a mistake. Misunderstood his intentions. Maybe even made things worse. But he lifted the lion skin, inviting her to join him, and she did. He pulled her in close, inhaling her hair and nuzzling her neck, and when their eyes met she knew things would forever be different for them now. His chest rose and fell with hers. His scent had deepened, become even more enticing. And they did not need to speak to understand what the other needed or wanted.

In their short time together, they had bonded. She knew it

now, and from the passion she saw gazing back at her, it seemed he knew it, too.

They stayed in Makra's hut through the next rise and fall of both the sun and the moon, until exhaustion finally took over and Makra uttered the words that would forever change their lives.

Mine. For all eternity.

Chapter 27

I parked the SUV in the garage, strode into the kitchen, and an image of a woman with long black hair, perfect breasts, and a fiery spirit slammed into me. She was straddling me, bringing me in deep and then pulling back until I thought I would go mad, urging me to say her name.

Lassia.

She was tight and flushed and like nothing I'd had before, and when she slid her tongue over my chest and ordered me to say her name once more, I lost my mind. I grabbed her hips, sat up, and thrust in one final, furious time for a brutal and long climax.

My knees gave out from under me and I grabbed the granite kitchen counter.

Jesus.

I made my way to the faucet and threw cold water over my face, but it didn't do much to settle my boiling blood. My heart was pounding and my body was sending signals I didn't want or need.

I now knew that Lassia connected to Lottie, but I didn't understand why or how.

I went for one more dose of cold water, gritted through the arousal, and heard Galen rapping his knuckles against a wood kitchen cabinet.

"What happened at Lassia Investments? Did you meet with Gary Cooper?"

Galen was holding a sandwich, and a bottle of water sat open on the granite counter. Again I wondered what he did while I was gone—if he had wandered around the house, searching for personal items—but let the thought go. It was my idea to ask him to stay in the first place, and if he had stepped out of line? Well, I could always break his face later.

I filled him in about my meeting and finding Ada alone, keeping it brief because I didn't feel like talking. Then I went upstairs to ditch the suit for jeans, a T-shirt, and a heavy jacket. I wasn't feeling any calmer by the time I was done.

"I'm going to get Lottie," I told Galen as I wedged the .357 into the small of my back, and strapped a fixed blade dagger to one ankle and the Kimber into the shoulder holster. "You have your gear with you?"

Galen shook his head.

"Get it. We'll pick you up within the half hour."

I called Nat and told him what I was doing. He didn't waste time with questions. "I'd rather you didn't come here. It'd get Lori all upset. I'll be there in fifteen."

He made it in less.

We packed the SUV with more paper booties, latex gloves, and extra ammo. I updated him about my meeting with Gary Cooper and his link to Monica and her ex-husband, and what I'd done with Ada when I found her alone. I also told him that Ada said Damian was at his house in the Hamptons.

Nat grabbed my arm when I jammed in the last round of ammo. "You gotta relax some, D-Man. I know you want to get Lottie, but you look as electrified as a live wire."

I yanked down the cargo cover and slammed the hatch closed. I was still feeling Lassia all over me and my blood was still boiling and it was interfering with my ability to think. "I'm okay."

"Yeah. Sure." Nat leaned against the SUV, looking like he wasn't going to move any time soon.

"What?" I asked.

"Something else is eating at you. What is it?"

"Nothing."

I walked around the rear of the SUV and went for the driver door. Nat seized my arm. I rounded on him, fists clenched.

I didn't know what he saw in my face but he pulled back. "Whoa! Take it easy there, okay? You just got me a little worried coz you ain't looking right. No need to go all postal."

I dialed it back as best I could. "Sorry. Just feeling antsy."

Nat let it go but he didn't move out of the way. "So you think Lottie's at Damian's house?"

"I know she is."

"How?"

"I just do." I could smell her. Sense her. Taste her. She was inside my blood, tied to the primitive part of me that needed to take her and mark her as mine.

"Galen is coming with us," I added.

Nat cursed under his breath. "You tolerate Galen, D-Man, coz he's the best at what he does. So what's going down that you think we need a sniper?"

"Another gut feeling." And because I knew Galen had been right. I'd had my head up my ass because of jealousy, which could very well get Lottie killed.

When we arrived at Galen's condo, he was waiting at the front entrance and motioning to the open garage door. I pulled inside and Galen shut the garage once I keyed off the ignition. He packed the trunk with his M40 and extra ammo, and presented the M1911 with a suppressor tucked inside his jacket. I nodded. It was a good choice.

Once I shut the hatch, Galen hit me with the same question Nat did before. "How do you know for certain that Lottie is with Damian at his house?"

"Everything points that way."

"*Nothing* points that way, D-Man," Nat said. "I don't mind having your back when your orders make sense. But if we're wrong and we tip our hand, it could be deadly for Lottie."

I held up a hand to stop him, sniffed the air, smelling her, and my body started burning all over again with the insane need to get her underneath me.

Galen stepped in closer, ignoring Nat. "You saw something. What is it?"

I clenched my jaw, jacked up on hormones. I hadn't felt this crazed since I was sixteen.

"Bellotti?" I was aware that Galen was approaching me but with caution. "Can you hear me?"

I looked at him with the vague notion that it wasn't Galen in front of me. It was another male who looked and sounded like Galen.

"Go with it, Bellotti," Galen said. "This is a regression. Let the memory come to you and see where it leads."

"What memory?" Nat asked.

I wanted Lassia. I hadn't had her since sunrise and I needed to be inside her again, but the Clan was preparing for another hunt because food would soon start to run low. I sat on a stone outside my hut, sharpening my spear but thinking about what I did the last time I'd taken Lassia. I wanted to do it again.

The air was growing warmer now and tufts of thick, green grass were pushing through what little white rain remained on the ground. I wore a spotted lion fur from a recent hunt and enjoyed the day's warmth on my back while I worked. The sun was yellow and big and the sky clear and blue, and as I tested the newly sharpened edge a shadow moved in, blocking the light and heat.

I knew it was Cilla without turning around. She stood by my side and I felt impatience ripple off her like waves on a lake, slight on the surface but hiding something deadlier underneath.

"I heard the elders talking about you and Lassia, just after the sun rose today," she said.

I kept to my spear and didn't answer.

"They said you intend to make Lassia your Primary."

The point was sharp and deadly, and I tested it one last time by pressing a finger to its tip. A drop of blood surfaced on my skin and I licked it away.

"Is that true?" Cilla asked.

I rotated the spear, admiring my work.

"She is not worthy, Makra. How many full moons have passed since you have taken her to your bed and she still hasn't produced a child for you?"

I rose and moved in on her. "There will be no more talk of this."

"The Clan looks to you for strength, and to have children is to have strength. Lassia is—"

I stepped forward, forcing her backward. "I will choose Lassia as my Primary because it is my decision."

"There was a time when you were going to choose me."

"Not anymore."

My anger urged Cilla on. She stared up at me, chin raised, skin flushed. "You have not been spending time with our child either. She has not seen you since before the last rain."

"I will see her later."

"See her now."

"I am busy."

"Busy bedding Lassia. Busy hunting. Busy bedding Lassia again. Busy resting by the night fire. And then bedding Lassia once more—"

"Enough!"

The spark of a challenge appeared in Cilla's eyes. She pulled down the leather pelt from her shoulders, baring her breasts to me. She pressed against me and reached under the pelt gathered at my waist, working me in a way that would make me respond. It didn't take much effort.

But she wasn't the female I wanted to take.

"We were very good together, Makra," Cilla said. "Let me remind you how good." She tugged off her own pelt and tossed it to the ground, and lowered her voice as she pressed against me. Her hand made its way back underneath my pelt, this time determined to see the effort through to the end.

I pushed her away.

She stumbled but quickly found her footing. "I have heard you haven't taken any other females, either."

"So?"

"Or visited your other children."

I grabbed the spear and pressed it to the underside of her chin. "Stop. Now."

Cilla's eyes went hard. "You were my mate."

I leaned in, daring her to try again. "I was no one's mate, Cilla."

Cilla bared her teeth and a low growl came from deep inside her. "Think again about Lassia," she said, playing with the leather band of teeth around my neck. "She will not be around forever."

Cilla turned and walked away, every now and then looking at me over her shoulder like she was expecting I would change my mind, follow, and lose myself between her legs.

She would be waiting a long time.

"Cilla is angry."

I turned and saw Ayak approach and wondered if he had heard Cilla and me talking, and if he would try to use that in his favor. It was no secret that Ayak had feelings for Lassia, and I knew he would eventually confront me about her. I was *Einarr* and that meant Lassia was mine, but that didn't mean Ayak would not fight for her if he chose. And when he did, it would be a dirty fight. And a deadly one.

I glanced at my spear, making sure it was within reach if needed.

"I saw Lassia and Cilla arguing again when the sun rose today," Ayak said, picking up the spear to inspect the work I'd done. "About you."

I grabbed the spear and held onto it.

"They are arguing much more lately, Makra. Or haven't you noticed?"

"I have noticed," I said. "But I don't think it means much.

Females can become protective of their males like lionesses become protective of their cubs."

"But you are not a cub."

I drew in a deep breath and looked at the hill where Cilla had just been walking. It was thick with patches of yellow flowers.

"Cilla is jealous," Ayak said. "And that should worry you."

I kept staring at the hill. Ayak was jealous, too.

"Do not take Cilla's warning lightly," Ayak said, picking up the pelt Cilla had removed, turning it over to study it, and tossing it aside. "I have not seen Lassia since just after sunrise today. When was the last time you saw her yourself?"

"When she left to pick berries after I took her in the tall grass."

"Makra." Ayak's serious voice drew my attention away from the hill. "The females have returned from their picking, but Lassia did not return with them."

A stabbing alarm made me pause. My grip on the spear tightened. "You are certain?"

"Yes. I think something is wrong, and I think Cilla is responsible."

"How do you know?"

"Some females speak freely after you've been inside them. Last night, one of them said she overheard Cilla talking about getting rid of Lassia so that she could have you again."

I thought about Cilla's displeasure over my lack of attention and her disregard when I threatened her with my spear. As if she knew something I did not. A tingling sensation I felt only when I was on the hunt crawled down my back. The elders called it *voya*, sensing what was to come.

I grabbed my spear and urged Ayak to follow. We searched huts, asking other members of the Clan if they had seen Lassia. No one had. We hunted through the berry patches that grew on the other side of the hill as well as the lake and the nearby waterfall. With each passing step I grew more fearful. I remembered the Cave of Triumphs and how often Lassia liked to visit. It was one of her favorite places for us to be alone.

I raced forward, heading for the Cave and hoping she was there but realizing with every step I took that something was very wrong. She was no longer in my blood. I could no longer smell her skin. Could no longer feel her in my heart.

Ayak and I rounded a bend and sped over a short hill that overlooked the Cave and that's when I heard Lassia's screams. I ran hard with Ayak on my heels, but the field seemed to grow and stretch on forever, the distance between the Cave and me extending even farther.

When I heard Lassia scream again, I feared the worst.

That I would not get there in time.

The distant cave disappeared and the garage came back into view. Galen was standing in front of me again.

"Do not fight this, Bellotti," Galen urged. "Every image and memory ties into another. It's how we learn from our past. Now tell me. What did you see?"

I leaned against the SUV, still hearing the screams. They were distant remnants of another life but a warning for the one I lived now. A warning that things were no longer what they appeared.

I focused on Galen. "I'm out of time."

Chapter 28

Lottie came to and wondered what time it was. She had no sense of day or night and no idea when someone would return to the room again. She was being kept off balance with an unsteady schedule and sedation and only now, thinking about a similar situation David had been in when he first joined PROs, did Lottie realize why. It wasn't just to keep her from trying to escape and being found.

It was to keep her hidden from someone else that didn't know she was here.

She could use that to her advantage.

She went to work, checking the small mattress for tears or weak spots where she might be able to dig out a spring and use it to unlock the door or as a small weapon. But just as Lottie thought about tearing a hole, the door unlocked and Jared walked in.

Lottie sat on the edge of the bed.

Jared walked over and squeezed her cheeks, forcing her to look up at him. Her heart hammered hard in her chest but she refused to show him weakness. He studied her for a while and Lottie stared back, then he yanked her to her feet.

"Either Bellotti is very stupid or he doesn't care about you." His faced blossomed red and his other hand went to her neck.

Lottie gasped but she didn't fight back. Let him vent, if he needed. Angry people often made mistakes and she was counting on his.

Jared shoved his cell phone at her. "Call him."

His intentions became clear and confirmed what Lottie already suspected. She was being used as bait, with the sole purpose of luring in David. She'd use that to her advantage, too.

"Where am I?" she asked. "I'm guessing I'm inside a house but it's not yours. Otherwise, you wouldn't be working so hard to keep me sedated."

"Don't *push* me," Jared said.

Lottie dug up some bravado because fear would get her nowhere. "Or what? You'll kill me? You haven't yet, which means—"

Jared swung at Lottie but she'd been expecting it. She ducked under his arm and ran out the open door, through the media room, past the bar, and up the stairs to the first floor. She was wobbly from sedatives and stumbled twice, with Jared catching up fast, but found traction as she hit the wood floor upstairs. She rounded a hall, sped through a huge kitchen and into a great room that was two stories tall, and barreled into another man.

The man grabbed Lottie and stopped her, looking like he might hit her, too, but then his anger quickly transformed into curiosity. He steadied her with both hands and examined her face, fascinated and speechless. He wasn't a handsome man. He was beautiful, with dark curly hair, dark skin, and a lean body—all draped in European designer clothes.

"My God," he said. Lottie struggled under his hold but that

only made him more captivated. His hands were surprisingly warm, his touch almost reverent. "You look just like her. You look just like *Lassia*."

Lottie felt her eyes go wide.

Jared rumbled in. "Let her go, Damian. She's mine."

"How can she be yours if she's in *my* house?" Damian asked, scanning her face, her body, her hands and hair. But his attention didn't feel invasive. If anything, it felt appreciative. Adoring.

"Everything about you is her," he said, breathless. "Her eyes. The birthmark. The cleft chin. Her *face*."

"Then take her with you, please," another voice said and it was one that Lottie recognized. "For God's sake, I'm sick of hearing about Lottie every single place I go. She's getting in the way and I'd love to see her gone."

Lottie turned and saw Monica snorting coke from the quartz countertop that separated the kitchen from the great room, looking like she walked out of a fashion magazine. Her clothes were Fendi and her jewelry all diamonds, and her nails had been freshly manicured. She looked chic and trendy and high. An empty champagne flute stood on the counter next to a half full bottle of Krug Champagne.

Damian's voice filtered in. "She is not Lottie but Lassia, and she is coming with me back to Turkey. I cannot leave this woman here. It would be...wrong."

"She's staying here," Jared demanded.

Lottie's attention cut back to Damian and Jared. "David will retaliate if he can't find me, and he'll kill you," Lottie said, thinking, *I have to get out of here*. Her gaze flicked to the huge panel doors in the foyer behind Damian, and she remembered

Nat telling David that Damian held a passion for digging up artifacts.

Another idea formed.

"What do you know about Lassia?" Lottie asked, giving Damian her full attention. "Do you know Makra, too? Because I see them both in my dreams."

"Enough of this," Jared said, grabbing Lottie's other arm. "She stays with me."

Damian stood his ground. "You know of the legend?"

"Oh Christ, here we go again." Monica poured another glass of Krug and slapped the bottle onto the counter. "Legends. Stories. Myths. She's playing you, Damian, *so she can get out of here*. And personally, I'd like to *see her go*."

"Not legend. Truth." Lottie stared at Damian, willing him to listen, hoping he'd be the way to buy time until David found her. *If* David found her. "Makra was *Einarr*," she said, talking quickly now. "He wore a leather band around his neck and had scars on his chest and belly from animals he hunted. Lassia was his mate."

"Yes." Damian nodded. "The legend of Lassia, who carried a fierce passion for a man. One that was so overwhelming she couldn't resist pursuing it, until it destroyed her life as well as the lives of those closest to her. The legend says that Lassia keeps returning, life after life, trying to reunite with that man and that passion."

Lottie shook her head. "Not a legend but the truth."

"For God's sake, Damian, I have no time for this." Jared pulled out a gun and pressed it to Damian's chest. "I need her so I can finish business with David Bellotti."

Lottie's heart skipped then double-timed, the front doors

and escape now seeming miles away.

Damian stilled, all his interest transferring to Jared. "Give me a little more time. I want to hear what she has to say. Give me that, and then we can decide what happens to her."

Lottie glanced from Damian to Jared.

Jared shifted. "Why should I?"

"Because I need to show her something important," Damian said, letting go of Lottie, and Jared gripped her harder. "And if you don't and kill me instead, the money stream from me stops and you'll have no way to fund yourself and try to take over what Zev started."

"This isn't about trying. I will do this."

Damian shrugged. "Only if you keep me alive."

Lottie watched as Damian fished his cell phone out from his slacks and cycled through the photos. He held up one of himself and another man inside a cave that was lit by several spotlights. Lottie recognized the other man from police photos shown to her the night David was arrested. It was Perry Wilcox. Beside them was a very old but perfectly preserved image of a man and a woman. The woman had long black hair and a heart-shaped birthmark on her shoulder. The man had a leather band of teeth around his neck.

Lassia and Makra.

"This man, Perry Wilcox, is a friend of mine who found this cave last month after years of research. We have been pursuing the legend for decades." Damian's eyes lifted and met Lottie's. "And you are that legend. It is said that Lassia still walks this earth." Damian caressed Lottie's cheek and shook his head once, as if unable to come to terms with the truth. "*You* walk this earth."

Lottie had become so mesmerized with the photo that she almost missed something important. Damian had referred to Wilcox in the present tense.

"Did you know that Wilcox is dead?" she asked. "Jared had him murdered this past Sunday. He framed David for the murder and then kidnapped me."

Damian went still. In the kitchen, Lottie heard the refrigerator compressor hiss and kick on.

"Is this true?" Damian asked.

"Perry was skimming from our accounts," Jared said.

Damian slammed Jared into a wall. The gun clattered to the floor. "Perry was my friend, you bastard."

Lottie turned and ran.

Right into Monica.

Monica's eyes were dilated to near black. She grinned, moved in closer, and lowered her voice. "You would have been better off with Galen, Lottie, when you came to my meeting. If you'd have gone with him, you wouldn't be here now, counting down the minutes left to your life."

Lottie stared back. "What are you talking about?"

"Think back, Lassia," she whispered. "You died because of Makra, and you will die because of David now. He's mine, and always will be."

"It took you twelve years to make this decision? I can make one a lot faster."

Lottie shoved Monica, threw open the front door, and fled.

Chapter 29

I pushed the SUV east on the expressway, hovering near seventy on the speedometer. Nat sat shotgun. Galen had the back. My heart knew Lottie was at Damian's. My head argued I had lost grip with reality.

None of us spoke for most of the ride. We were focused and geared up, and when my cell rang and Mom's number popped up on the hands free dashboard display, my heart skipped a few beats. She knew where we were and what we were doing, and knew not to interrupt unless it was important.

She didn't wait for my hello. "They took Ada, David. Two men came to my house and took her."

I straightened. Passed a cop car perched on the center median. "Who? Did you get names? Faces?"

She swallowed loud enough for me to hear. "They knocked. They were polite." Her breath hitched. "One was really big. Had a nose that looked like it had been broken once."

I remembered seeing him at Trendz. Jared's muscle. "When?"

"A few minutes ago. Oh Jesus, David. They had a gun."

"Are you okay?"

"Yes."

I glanced at Nat. His eyes were sharp and alert, his jaw

was locked. He was thinking the same thing I was. Jared was changing the rules of the game.

"Did they say where they were taking her?" I asked.

"No. But Ada. Oh my God, Ada. She was screaming, David. She didn't want to go."

"Did you call the cops?"

Mom paused. "Not yet."

"Don't."

"But David—"

"Try to stay calm and sit tight, okay?"

I blew past another SUV. Ahead of us, dark clouds were moving in, shoving the afternoon sun behind them. Another storm was on its way. Nat tapped my arm and pointed to the speedometer. I was flirting with ninety. Not something I wanted to do with a trunk full of weapons and three armed men inside. I eased up on the gas, drew in a breath, and held it for a count of five.

"Did Ada recognize either of the men?" I asked.

"Yes, but she didn't say any names. I'm so very sorry, David." Mom was crying now.

"It's not your fault. I'll take care of this."

"How?"

I had no idea. Yet. "Stay put and let me know if anything changes."

"Call me when you find them both."

"I promise."

I disconnected, pulled off Montauk Highway, pressed through back roads, and got stuck behind Bentleys and BMWs that refused to go over speed limit. It took almost thirty minutes to get to Damian's street and thread past mansions I could never afford. The road narrowed to a single lane, and for a moment I wondered if I'd made a wrong turn. Several fat drops of rain splattered the windshield.

"This is it," Nat said.

The scrub pines that marked the entrance to the road had disappeared. Huge trees that had been shipped in and planted to line the street canopied over the gravel road. Red, green, and yellow leaves covered most of it. We passed one black mailbox. No name. No address. I killed the headlights and left the fogs on for illumination.

"Keep going," Nat said. "About another five hundred feet."

A chopper thwumped overhead, descending for a landing. I slowed the SUV down to five and lowered my window, listening for position. "The chopper's bearing is dead ahead," I said.

Galen leaned forward. "Damian's house?"

Nat nodded.

I eased down a curving, gravel driveway and crunched my way up to a scrolled, wrought iron gate that guarded the entrance to the mansion and that had been left open. I stopped the SUV.

"Kinda weird that the driveway gate's open," Nat said. "Folks with digs like this usually want their security."

Exactly what I'd been thinking. I pulled off to the side near an ornamental tree that was shaped like a corkscrew, killed the interior lights, and cut the engine.

Her scent wrapped around me as soon as I got out of the SUV. My body responded and I breathed in long and deep, filling my lungs with the warm, woodsy smell I knew only as hers. I was going to find her, I was going to mark her, and no one was ever going to take her from me again.

"She's here," I said.

"You okay?" Nat asked, stepping in beside me. "You got that strange look on your face again."

I nodded, staring at the three-story mansion with its hilly lawn, double-sized porch, and four-pillared front entrance. Heavy raindrops dropped on my head. Nat flanked my right. Galen took my left. I remembered standing in front of the Cave of Triumphs, fearing the worst and finding it. I wasn't going to let that happen again.

"What do you see now?" Galen asked.

"The cave." I breathed in, scenting the air one final time. "I can feel her. Smell her."

"Your past life is revealing itself. Follow it."

One of the front doors was thrown open and Lottie barreled out onto the porch and down the steps. Her hair was wild and her legs gave out twice before her feet found the landing.

Jared chased her.

I took off, motioning for Galen to go left and Nat to go right, pumping my legs hard and fast to get to Lottie first. I was closing distance but Jared was closer. He snagged onto her arm, pulling her to a stop. He spun her around to face us and jammed a revolver to her head.

I halted, chest heaving, eyes locked with Lottie's. I was looking for a weakness. Trying to find the way to Lottie through Jared. I would kill him if I had to, but he'd used Lottie as a shield.

Nat angled for a better position. Galen drew his gun and

locked in his target.

I broke contact with Lottie long enough to catch Galen's attention and flick a glance Jared's way. If anyone had a chance of taking Jared down, it would be our sniper.

Galen shook his head once. No clear shot.

I held out my hands and took one step forward. "I'm here now, Jared. Let Lottie go."

Galen moved a step farther to the left, steady on foot and sure with his aim. Jared swung his way, watching him, the gun still at Lottie's temple. Nat moved a step to the right. Jared swung back toward him.

"Move or she dies!" he said.

A fierce possessive streak clawed at my stomach. No one was going to touch my female.

"Let her go," I said again. "You can do more with me than with her."

Lottie was staring at me, wide-eyed and unblinking. Trying to hold it together. The bold female I'd always known her to be.

The front door opened and I cast a quick glance to see who was joining the party. Monica was walking down the stairs and over the lawn toward me. Another man walked onto the porch and stayed there. I recognized him from photos I'd seen. It was her brother Damian. Monica slipped her arm through mine and smiled, looking loaded and ready for a good time. I pulled away but she grabbed on tighter, stroking my arm with her fingers.

"I'm not leaving you this time," she said. "I won't let you get away again."

Jared retreated, taking Lottie with him. "As I see it,

Bellotti, you have two choices. You can have Lottie or you can't have Lottie."

He was playing games, only I still didn't know the rules. "How do my choices play out?" I asked.

Jared cocked his head. "You're a smart man. You've already figured out that this isn't as simple as it looks." He turned his head toward the gate leading to the backyard and called out, "Bring her here!"

The backyard gate opened and Jared's muscle walked out, yanking Ada along with him. She was clutching onto her sweatshirt and started screaming as soon as she saw me. "I don't want to go! I want to stay with you! Please, let me stay with you!"

A muffled sound popped and Jared's bodyguard went down. And all hell broke loose.

Ada started running for the backyard. Damian jumped down the front steps after her and Monica grabbed my arm. "You have to save Ada! They'll kill her, David! I know they will!"

I yanked free from Monica. Jared fired off a round at me. It whizzed past my ear. A second muffled shot sounded, Jared spun around, thrown off balance, and the revolver hurled from his Jared's hand. A third shot followed and Jared crumpled to the ground.

Lottie broke free.

I swerved left, full speed, yanked Lottie's hand, bolted left again, and kept running over thick, soggy grass. "The gate," I said with Lottie keeping desperate stride beside me. "Run for the front gate and the SUV."

Nat hustled in and grabbed Lottie's other arm. The front

gate was fifty feet away.

My chest was burning. My legs throbbing. "Where's Ada?"

Nat huffed out the words. "Damian has her."

I skidded to a halt, broke loose, and called, "Get Lottie to safety and don't let her out of your sight. We don't know who else is here." I spun around, charging for the house and hustling up the hill toward the back fence, determined to get to Ada before I lost her, too.

Damian was dragging Ada with him. She was yelling and kicking, digging her heels in the ground, churning up grass and mud. Galen stood firm, aiming for Damian and trying to take him out, too, but Ada's movements were too unpredictable to allow it.

Monica converged with me. "Let her go, Damian!"

I was closing in, hot on Damian's heels. I reached for Ada, swiped her shirt—

Damian darted left, bolting through the rear gate.

Galen's fourth shot fired. Monica shrieked, stumbled forward, and collapsed. Ada tripped over her feet and disappeared with Damian into the backyard. Heavy clouds rumbled overhead, blanketing the yard in eerie darkness.

I blew through the gate after him, my feet sucked in by beachfront and wet sand, and saw a chopper on a small helipad. Its rotors thwumped a slow beat then the deep rumbling became a high-pitched whine. Sand kicked up by the squall pelted my body like needles. I shielded my face against the wind and grit, trying to get a bead on Damian's direction.

Galen moved in beside me, raised his gun, and steadied his aim.

I took off for Damian.

Ada shrieked and Damian shoved her inside. The skies opened and rain pelted down, hard and fast. The chopper inched up, sand and rain whipped at my face and chest, and I jumped for the landing skid. I grabbed on—

And lost my grip.

The chopper took off.

I plunged to the beach, landing hard and wheezing for air. The last thing I saw through the hammering rain was Damian disappearing inside the chopper as it ascended into the turbulent sky.

I thought I heard Ada cry out my name. And something inside me died.

Chapter 30

Galen reached out a hand and helped me to my feet. I stood in the pouring rain and watched the chopper fade away into the dark, blustery horizon. Thunder cracked and foamy, violent waves barreled to shore. Behind us, Damian's large mansion stood in quiet sentry.

"We have to call MD," Galen said. His clothing was soaked and plastered to him. Rain streamed down his face and off his chin.

I brought my arm up to brace myself against a gust of wind. "We have to put a tail on that helicopter."

Galen moved in front of me, blocking my view. "We have to call MD. We have collateral damage."

My heart slowed to a dull thud. Another gust pummeled through. "You shot Monica." I shook my head, still unable to comprehend what he'd done. "Why?"

Galen made to leave.

I grabbed him, insistent he answer me. "Why?"

Lightning flashed, illuminating the hardness in Galen's eyes. "It was an accident."

"Bullshit."

Galen shrugged out of my hold.

"Answer the fucking question or I swear I'll make life even more difficult for you, Galen."

Thunder clapped and the ground rumbled beneath us.

He stopped and shook his head. "I said it was an accident."

I stepped in closer. Shoved my face in his. "You risked my daughter's life."

Galen held my gaze, refusing to back down. "Ada was never an issue."

My jaw clenched. "If she wasn't an issue, then Monica shouldn't have been one either. Snipers don't have accidents."

Galen said nothing for a while. Lightning streaked through the clouds behind him. "Did you ever stop to think why Monica reappeared in Lottie's life?" he asked. "Or yours? Did you really think it was all just a coincidence?"

I stared at him, wondering if I was watching a madman, a liar, or a comrade. For once, my gut couldn't get a read. I remembered watching a similar expression a very long time ago. Ayak was standing at my side when we found Lassia, dead inside the cave. His features were hard with vengeance, the determination in his voice clear as he vowed that he'd find Cilla and seek enough vengeance for the both of us.

Words Lottie had once told me after she started her first regression surfaced in my mind. "Reincarnations offer second chances, David. We're here to learn from the mistakes we made before. It's how we grow and move on. Sometimes situations occur that don't make sense to us on the surface, but with wisdom and open eyes, eventually their significance is made known."

Galen took advantage of my uncertainty, dug out his cell from his pocket, and started dialing. I looked past his shoulder to Monica, lying face down beyond the backyard gate, and wondered what sense could possibly be made out of this.

I released the gun and walked toward her, crouched down, and pressed a hand to her back. I became vaguely aware of Galen following on his phone, informing MD of three deaths and Ada's disappearance.

After he disconnected, he said, "We have to leave. The cleaners are on their way and this is officially out of our hands."

But something kept me there at Monica's side. Some puzzle piece still yet to be found.

"Bellotti. We have to go. The longer we stay here, the more exposed we become."

I hoped to the gods that my next move was the right one. I'd put a lot on the line to get here, and decided to put my trust in a man I hadn't trusted since the day I met him. Why, I wasn't sure.

I stood and walked with Galen back to the SUV.

Galen opened the front passenger door and took shotgun. I slid into the backseat next to Lottie, pulled her in tight, and kissed her. She smiled, and it was the weariest but most beautiful smile I'd ever seen.

"I love you," she whispered, snuggling in and not caring that I was soaked.

I whispered that I loved her, too. And I held onto her with no intent of ever letting go. "Do you need a doctor? Are you okay?"

"I'm fine, David. A little shaky from sedatives, but okay."

I kissed the top of her head. Pulled her in even closer.

Nat cranked the heat up to high. "What happened back there?"

I let Galen fill him in.

"I don't get it," Nat said, catching my reflection in the rear view mirror. "If Jared kidnapped Ada, why did Damian end up taking her instead?"

I had no idea.

The rain hammered at the SUV like gunshots. Galen turned in his seat to look at me. "I *am* sorry about Monica," he said. We stared at each other until his attention slid to Lottie. His expression softened and, for a few heartbeats, vulnerability and another deeper, more profound emotion surfaced. Lottie went still in my arms and I knew she was watching him as he watched her. Then Galen's softness vanished and his focus returned to me.

"I am glad that you found Lottie and that she is once again safe, as she should be." He faced front and stared out at the driving rain.

An SUV pulled into the long driveway and four men emerged. The cleaning crew. We pulled away from the house, and despite the heat inside my own SUV I shuddered as a sharp, clammy chill took hold.

A different memory surfaced. I was near the fire, swinging my daughter around by her arms. Her hair was wild and kinky and she was squealing and giggling, demanding I do it again. But I'd grown tired because I had just returned from a hunt, and put her down. I knelt so we were eye to eye and rubbed my nose against hers. She hugged me and kept hugging, and told me that I was the best *foar* a young could ever have and that she never wanted to be without me.

"Hey David?"

I focused on Nat's voice and let the memory slip away.

"That girl of yours has a lot of *cojones*. She's a tough little thing." He smiled at me through the mirror.

I nodded.

Lottie brushed her lips against my ear. "I'm so sorry, David."

I knew she was, because finding Lottie had come with a hefty price.

Nat navigated us out of the long driveway and onto the road. I stared out the window, my arm wrapped around the woman I loved. It felt good to have her there, beside me, where she belonged.

I was determined to get Ada back where she belonged, too.

Chapter 31

Lottie pulled away from David and cupped his face in her hands. He was cold and drenched, and the anguish in his eyes made her heart twist with guilt.

It was because of her that Ada was gone. Maybe Monica and the others, too.

"I'm so very, very sorry," she repeated, and the tears came and kept coming, and there was nothing she could do to stop them.

"It's not your fault," David whispered, wiping them away. "You're here and you're safe and that's all that matters."

"But Ada. And Monica."

David shook his head. "Don't do this, Lottie." He looked quickly at Galen and then at her. "It is what it is."

The weight of the moment, of what happened, finally hit her. David, she realized, saw death often. He lived it every time he commanded men, and she had known this about him ever since the day they came together in his hut so long ago. Only she'd chosen to ignore it.

"How do you live with this? With your job? With…today?" she asked, recognizing that such emotional baggage would eventually take its toll. It always did. "How?"

David drew in a long, shaky breath and pulled her back to him, holding her tight. "You make it bearable." When he whispered again that he loved her, Galen darted a glance in their direction.

Lottie felt another emotion then. A sharp, piercing reaction that lanced through her body and that she could only identify as pure, uncontrollable jealousy. Only it didn't belong to her. But it filled the SUV, the air she breathed, the blood pulsing through her veins, crushing her until she felt numb from it.

She scanned David's strong, angular profile and then Galen's softer, slightly darker one, wondering. Then the threads of another mood wove itself in, this one simple curiosity mixed with some discomfort. For some reason, the sensation compelled Lottie to look at Nat...

Until her attention was pulled away by the noxious tendrils of something hateful and spiteful. And then it all disappeared, like a curtain being lifted, and it was only Lottie, the three men, and the pounding rain outside the SUV. David, she realized, was now talking on his phone.

"I know, Mom," he was saying, "and yes, she's definitely okay." He went on to tell Rita that he wasn't in the mood to talk and then he handed the phone to Lottie. "She wants to speak to you."

Lottie sat up, swiped away what remained of the tears, and drew in a focused, calming breath.

"Jelly Bean. Oh my God, Jelly Bean!" came Rita's urgent response. "I was so worried. Are you okay? Are you hurt? Do you want me to come over? I can make you soup. Make sure you're warm. Do laundry or, I don't know, bring brownies."

Lottie smiled. Rita was the best mother she'd ever known. "No. I'll be okay. David and I need some time alone, that's all."

Rita sighed. Then sighed again. "And how is David, hmm? He didn't say much on the phone but then again he never does."

Lottie looked at him. He was staring out the window. "It will take time. For the both of us."

"In many ways, David is the strongest man I know. But he's also vulnerable, Jelly Bean. He will need your care and guidance, now more than ever, and not just because of Ada and Monica. Things are changing and…some people in your life aren't who you think they are. Especially—"

The cell phone beeped and the call disconnected from lost service. Seconds later, Nat drove under a thick canopy of trees that sent the SUV into complete blackness. Lottie sat still, an irrational fear digging its way in. Something felt off. Then the SUV emerged from the trees and the odd sensation faded.

She handed the dead phone back to David.

He took it but kept his hand on hers. His skin was feeling warmer now. "What is it?"

Lottie struggled for a smile. "I just want to go home."

Chapter 32

"Well, how long is it going to take?"

An hour had passed since Nat dropped Lottie and me and the SUV at home, and since he hired a cab to take Galen and him back to theirs. I was on the phone with Nat now, pacing the kitchen and trying to understand why he couldn't get details on Damian's helicopter flight.

"Come on, D-Man. I'm trying."

"You're not trying hard enough."

Lottie walked inside wrapped in her thick yellow robe, her hair hanging wet and loose around her shoulders.

"I understand you want Ada back," Nat said, "but you gotta give me time. This isn't something I can just pull out of my ass."

"You've pulled everything else out of your ass so far."

"Everything except your head. Now let me do this and I'll get back to you when I got news."

Nat hung up and I pitched my cell phone on the kitchen desk. It skidded across papers and mail before ricocheting off the tile backsplash. Lottie came up from behind and wrapped her arms around my waist. Her body felt soft and warm, and her voice sounded even warmer.

"How are you doing?" she asked.

"I'm feeling castrated." Before I could vent any more, my

cell phone buzzed and Lottie pulled away so I could take the call. MD was on the other end.

"That was a royal fuck-up, Bellotti," MD said. "Three bodies and a missing girl? What the hell were you thinking?"

"I had to get Lottie back. And then I had to save Ada." Or try to.

"Bullshit. I know I told you that you were on your own with this one, but your ego was stuffing up your brain and I'm not going to stay quiet about it. I need men who can make decisions with a clear head. What happens next time? Ada's gone and I know you're not going to sit still. You're going to play alpha male again and when that happens I won't send in the cleaners to fix your mess."

"She's my daughter and she deserves a family. Not the crap she's been living with for eleven years."

"Eleven years you didn't know about until the other day."

"Yesterday, last week, or last year, it doesn't make a difference. I did the right thing and we both know it."

"Don't tell me what I'm thinking, Bellotti."

Lottie opened the fridge and bent down to look inside. I watched the robe tug up and expose her thigh as she reached deep inside to pull out a bottle of orange juice. But when she straightened, her hair was short, her eyes were ringed with green, and her lips curved into the kind of pout that caused all kinds of trouble.

Monica.

I gritted my teeth and tried shaking away the image, forcing myself to focus on my conversation with MD, the dark backyard, and the hammering rain outside.

"So here's the deal with where we are right now," MD

went on. "Intelligence tells us that Ada was seen with Damian Sahin at Kennedy Airport about an hour ago, boarding a private jet bound for Istanbul."

"Did anyone stop him? Did anyone get Ada?"

"We checked, but when Federal officials stopped the plane before takeoff, they didn't find either one on board."

Cabinet doors opened and closed and I heard the crunching sound of a cereal box being opened. I chanced a glance over my shoulder and saw Lucky Charms on the counter. And the image of Monica digging inside for more.

I turned away and headed for the den, putting as much distance between us as I could. Lottie would have called it avoidance and she would have been right. "Are they still in the States?"

"Not likely and here's why. Damian Sahin manages a good portion of Monica and Jared's money. He also has life insurance policies on Monica and Jared and is the sole beneficiary for both. He will make five million each off their deaths, for a total of ten million, plus another twenty million in other inheritances as a result of their passing. Ada, however, is the sole beneficiary of Damian's entire estate and that totals about sixty million. Given everything that's happened in that family, there's thinking that maybe Damian might try to take over where Zev left off or fund someone who will."

"No." Something wasn't right. "It's too straightforward. With all the money Damian has, he doesn't need more. This is about something else."

"It's nothing else," MD threw back.

"And Ada is the key. I'm sure of that now." I straightened. "I have to find Damian. I have to get my daughter back because—" I was going to say that it was because she was critical to all of this but it was more than that. A lot more. "I just want her back."

"What do you want, Bellotti? You want me to tell the DoJ that we can't man the next op in Syria because we made you a priority? Want me to tell NATO that we're backing out of Afghanistan because one little girl is more important than thousands?"

"No, but—"

"There are no buts here. Back down and let the rest of us do our jobs. Get some rest. Take your vacation. Do what you need to do to get your head back on straight. But do not interfere or intervene. This is my last warning."

MD disconnected.

I stalked the den, replaying Ada's last words over and over in my head, hearing her screaming, not wanting to get on the chopper. I rounded the sofa, thinking how to get her back. There had to be a plane manifest somewhere. Someone had to have seen her in the airport. Taking off. Landing somewhere. *Something*. Someone knew where she was.

"David?"

"What?" I stopped pacing and faced Lottie. And I was still seeing Monica. I squeezed my eyes shut and clenched my jaw, sick and tired that I couldn't get her out of my head. "Not now, Lottie. Please. I'm not in the mood for therapy."

"Hey." Her voice was soft. Comforting. I felt her hand on my arm followed by a gentle squeeze, and her perfume wrapped around me, smelling like flowers and citrus. Monica's perfume. "Hey. Look at me."

I opened my eyes but couldn't do what she wanted.

Lottie pulled me in and rested her head on my chest. "It's okay, David. I'm here. It's just you and me. I know that you're battling a lot of different emotions right now and it's normal. And it's also normal to feel them. You can do that with me."

I wanted to. But I couldn't.

"David, I can only imagine what you're going through," she said. "But you don't have to handle this alone. We've been through so much and we've always grown stronger from it. We're tougher than this. I want to help, but you have to let me. Is it Ada? Monica? What?"

I stepped out of her embrace and rubbed a hand over the back of my neck. "It's those things, yes, but it's a lot of other things, too. Like not knowing if I was going to find you. Wondering if you were alone or hurt or worse. It killed me, not having you with me. But the not knowing was the worst."

"For a while, I was scared you might not find me, too." She took my hand and held on.

I held back a sigh.

"But I'm here now, David," she whispered. "*We're* here now. Together, we can recover and move on. And I can help you find Ada just like you found me."

"I don't think I can find Ada the way I found you," I mumbled.

"Why not? You had Nat and Galen to help, and now I can help, too."

"It's not that simple."

"Why?"

I leaned against the sofa and stared down at the carpet. It needed vacuuming. "I saw you. Sensed you." I drew in a breath. "Smelled you. That's why not. You're in here." I clutched a fist to my chest. "You're *in here*."

Only I didn't smell Lottie now, and it was then that I realized I hadn't smelled her since we left Damian's house. I didn't feel her inside me either. It was like once I found her, my bond with her had been severed. As if we were two separate people instead of the soul mates we'd once been.

"Funny you should say that," Lottie said. "Lately, I've had an incredibly strong sense of you that way, too." She leaned in and inhaled long and deep. Her breath felt warm and soft on my skin. "It's so wonderful. And amazing."

Right now, it didn't feel amazing. I was trying to move forward and get on with my life with Lottie only I was spinning my wheels and getting nowhere.

Lottie settled in next to me and nudged me out of my musing. When I regarded her she smiled, looking fatigued and drawn, but it wasn't the bags under her eyes or the small stress lines at the corners of her mouth that registered. It was still Monica.

I dropped my head, disgusted.

Lottie stroked my thigh and squeezed. "Please talk to me, David."

But I had nothing I wanted to say. Not yet.

"Okay," she said with a final squeeze. "I'm going to take a stab at this myself." She moved in front of me and pressed in close. So close that I could feel her heart beating and her chest fall and rise with each breath she took. "Whether you want to accept it or not, you've started a regression, David. It explains a lot of why and how you found me. You and I are connected on an emotional level that can't be described with words. We're…one. It's as simple as that. And it hurts me to see you in so much pain."

I moved her away, went to the kitchen, and poured a glass of water. Monica's perfume followed. For a few seconds, I considered hitting the hard stuff but decided the only thing it would get me was a hangover. Monica wasn't going to be resolved through a bottle of tequila.

I put down the glass and focused on the kitchen windows. Rain splattered against the screen. I hated that I couldn't make the images of an ex-lover go away.

"David." Lottie sounded desperate now. Hurt. And it was because of me. "David, please."

She came up from behind, wrapped her arms around my waist again, and rested her head against my back. I could feel the love in her touch, the sensitivity in her embrace, the relaxation in her breathing. The only thing I had to offer in return was the hollowness in my soul.

"I want you to make love to me, David. I need to be with you. Please."

My heart dropped and I closed my eyes again, willing myself to respond to *her*. Lottie's hands slid down lower. I grabbed them, stopping them before they went too far. "Not tonight, okay?"

She coaxed me to turn around. I concentrated on the tile floor so she couldn't see the guilt in my eyes. There was no way in hell I was going to take Lottie to bed and make love to another woman.

A heavy pause moved in.

"Fine," Lottie said. "You need your space. I understand that."

But I knew that she didn't. So I stood there, doing nothing, while Lottie left the kitchen and went upstairs, in silence and alone.

A long time later, after I was done brooding, I shut the lights and went upstairs, too. I stripped and got into bed.

Lottie rolled over, far away from me.

Chapter 33

Sleep came in fits.

I finally gave up the tossing and turning when morning sun cut through the blinds and geese squawked in the backyard. I rolled onto my back and stared up at the ceiling, and Lottie curled in beside me. The bed felt warm and cozy, and if I weren't feeling so shitty I would have told her we were staying in it all day.

I risked another look at her but Monica was still there, reminding me of times long gone.

Lottie thought my glance was an invitation for something else and began teasing my chest with her fingers. "Rough night?"

The answer was easy but it still took me time to voice it. "Yeah."

She settled onto my chest and stared at me, chin resting on folded arms. "I think you had nightmares last night. You called out for Ada a lot." She waited to see if I would say something and when I didn't she added, "It also sounded like you were reliving some memories of Monica."

My eyes met hers and held. I knew better than to ask what I did.

I turned away.

"David." Lottie's voice sounded tender and I didn't

deserve it. "It's okay."

No. It wasn't. I pushed out of bed, limbs heavy with exhaustion and heart weary from the emotional roller coaster ride I'd been on, and headed for the bathroom. I felt beaten down and angry that I couldn't stop being angry with Monica. For not telling me about Ada. For trying to infiltrate back into my life. For taking over my life, and the love of my life, as intensely as she did.

But mostly I felt angry that I felt angry. Monica was dead and her memory deserved better. If anything, for my daughter who had lost her mother.

While I was inside the bathroom my cell phone rang and I ran back to the bedroom to answer, hoping someone had news about Ada.

"Hey, D-Man." It was Nat. "Am I calling at a bad time?"

"If you were, I wouldn't have picked up," I told him. "What's going on?"

Lottie watched from the bed. I sat on the mattress with my back to her, determined not to drown in more thoughts about Monica.

"I called Trendz this morning to get a lead or new insight, you know? And get this. The store's closed and the number's disconnected."

"Not surprised," I said, filling him in on the latest details MD gave me about Damian.

"Well, here's a real kicker for you," Nat said. "Did you know that he opened a college savings account for Ada when she was born? There's currently over five hundred thou in it."

I pulled up. "Seriously?"

"As serious as serious gets. He also put Monica through

rehab a few times over the years, and took Ada in when Monica was away, trying to get clean."

"I don't get it. What's his angle?"

"Dunno. Can't tell if he's the good guy or the bad guy."

"It seems like he's protecting Ada. But why?"

"Dunno that either. But I *do* know that until we met up with him yesterday, he'd been trotting the globe and trying to dig up some archaeological legend stuff."

Lottie moved in from behind, leaned her chin on my shoulder, and wrapped her arms around me. Her fingernails traced circles on my stomach.

"So, uh, hey. You okay, David? I know it's been a bad couple of days for you."

I grasped Lottie's hand and stopped her from doing anything more.

"No, I'm not." But before Nat could press me further I said, "And I don't want to talk about it."

"Okay. I got a single malt with your name on it that's busting to be opened. When you're ready, I'm ready."

"Deal."

I leaned over and put the phone back on the nightstand. Lottie held on for the ride.

She dropped a kiss on my shoulder when I settled back in. "Nat checking in on you?"

"Sort of. Had some updates on Damian." I told her what I knew and brought her up to speed. She went back to tracing circles again.

"David?"

"Hmm?"

"Look at me."

I didn't want to but I didn't have much choice. I steeled myself for what I knew I'd see and turned around. No surprise. Monica, right there.

"If you were my patient," she said, "I'd say you're in a state of internal contradiction. But you aren't my patient. You're the man I love and you're trying very hard to find every reason to run away and hide from what scares you. But no one else has to know what you're thinking or feeling. It's safe, if only you'd trust me like you've always trusted me."

I drew in a breath. Let out a sigh.

"You're fighting denial and guilt and regret," Lottie said. "And it's all normal. I can see these things in you because I felt them when I had my first regression in July. But it doesn't have to be this way."

If only it were that easy.

"Couples go through crap, David. It's expected. But if you knew what I saw in my practice…situations like this, if left untended, snowball and the relationship becomes a shadow of its former self. And by the time either partner realizes something's wrong, the only thing that's left of that relationship is resentment and, often, separation. Do you really want that to happen? Is it really that important for you to be so single-minded about this, at our expense?"

Her voice wavered and my heart ripped in two. I was hurting her and pushing her away, and I couldn't make myself stop.

But she was right. Commanding ops—*being in control*—was what I did. Ask me to pull together a team of men with ego and swagger, airdrop them into the middle of a conflict, and direct them to take down the enemy and survive and I was ready to go. But this? Totally out of my league. On top of that, I'd become my own worst enemy and I was making Lottie pay for my self-absorption.

It was time to man up.

"I feel guilty," I admitted. "Ada was taken away and Monica is dead, because of me." I got up and paced the carpeted floor, using the time to think. "I don't know what to feel because Ada's mine and yet she doesn't feel like she's mine." I picked up my jeans and flung them into the corner with the rest of yesterday's laundry. "It bothers me that I didn't have a relationship with her this time, that I didn't know her for eleven years and then, when I finally met her, she was taken."

Without thinking I glanced at Lottie, expecting a reaction, but hastily looked away. The image of Monica was still there, taunting me, and I didn't understand why. Unfinished business maybe.

Or maybe something else I didn't want to acknowledge.

I picked up the television remote from the dresser and moved it to the other side. Noticed that the imprint next to one of the buttons was starting to fade. "It bothers me that I've discovered I've lived another life even though I've been arguing all along that past lives don't exist, and even now as I say it, it doesn't feel real." I caught my reflection in the mirror. Then saw Monica's behind me. I stepped away. Opened a drawer. Dug around for clothes, keeping myself busy, buying time to make sense out of what didn't make sense. "I don't understand the point of a past life, which I'm still struggling to understand and accept, and, above all, I don't like that I almost lost you again. For all my single-mindedness, as you say, I can't imagine a life without you and hope like hell I never have to."

I sat down, drew in a ragged breath, and dropped my hands to my lap. I had a headache and was feeling tense and irritable and about as sexually strung out as a drug addict without his regular fix. And as I sat there, I realized that as much as I might have matured in the past twelve years, there was a selfish side of me that never grew up. If it had, I would have been able to push past my lingering feelings for Monica and focus on the woman that I loved and always had.

Lottie rested her hand on my thigh. Her touch was warm and firm and all I could think was, *move your hand a little higher and get to work*. I was pissed that I couldn't stop my body's reaction and that it was, once again, to Monica and not Lottie.

I shoved off the bed and stalked to the bathroom for a second time. I opened the linen closet, not exactly sure what I was looking for, then closed it when I realized I was still distancing myself from Lottie. As soon as I closed the door, I found her leaning against the wall. Naked.

I grabbed my toothbrush and toothpaste so I wouldn't be tempted to look at her.

She watched, silent, waited until I was done and said, "That was a big step for you, David." Her tone was soft. Understanding. "I know it wasn't easy for you to admit all of that."

Saying thanks seemed inappropriate—and Lottie would have seen through it anyway. I toweled off, replaced the toothbrush and toothpaste, and brushed past her, heading back to the bedroom.

Lottie followed.

I went to my nightstand and toyed with my cell phone.

"David. Stop this."

I put down the phone. Tried pretending I felt relaxed. Like nothing was wrong.

"Look at me, David."

I refused.

"Look. At me."

I turned. Didn't make eye contact.

Lottie closed in and took my face in her hands, directing my attention her way. Her fingers felt long and slim, like Monica's. Her touch was lighter, like Monica's. Her body felt fuller, like Monica's.

And it was now pressed against mine.

I didn't want Lottie, not this way, but I didn't argue as she lured me onto our bed. Her mouth closed in and her body molded over me. Her heart was beating hard against my chest, her lips were hot on my neck, and the heat between her legs drew all the blood between mine.

"I know you want this." She stroked me. Grinned when she got the response she wanted. "You can't hide what I already feel. And I want you to feel. You *need* to feel."

I closed my eyes. Shook my head. No way in hell was I having sex with Monica.

"Stop fighting this." Her whisper teased at my ear. Sent a rush over my skin. "Go for the ride with me, David." She nibbled my chin. My throat. "Just let it take you. You need to let go." Her tongue swept over my chest. My stomach. Went lower. Her teeth grazed my thigh. Her hands stroked and readied me. And then I was in her mouth—

And back in Monica's bedroom.

It was our second time together. Her husband was on a

business trip. She was incredibly good with her tongue.

I shoved Lottie away and pushed off the bed. Lottie grabbed my arm and shoved me back down. We wrestled, rolling right then left, me pinning her down, her using her legs to wrangle back on top, until she slammed my back to the mattress and forced all the air from my lungs.

"Stay." She was flushed and breathless and as hungry as I'd ever seen her.

I cursed.

"That's exactly what I had in mind," she said, and my moment of weakness became her advantage. She held my hands overhead and straddled me. I was aware of my hips locked between hers and the aching need to be inside her. "You could very easily overpower me if you wanted to and you're not really trying. And we both know why you aren't doing it."

Her mouth seized mine and I kissed back, the curve of Monica's lips and the stroke of her tongue, once forgotten, now pulled back from memory. She writhed against me, teasing, and claimed my mouth once more. She sat up, took my hands, and guided them to her breasts. They felt more ample and heavier to the touch.

"Remember our first time, David?" Her voice sounded throaty. Her hands led mine to her stomach then her rounded hips. Hips that were slightly wider and a little more curved. Hips I hadn't touched in twelve years.

She lifted. Slid me inside. A rush of heat fired through and she began moving, slowly. Tormenting. Tempting. Reminding me of what we once had.

"This is a mistake," I muttered, and I was working hard not to move. Not to say anything. Not to play this sick game and get sucked into something I would regret later.

"So you say."

She guided my hands over her thighs. Brought one between her legs. Her skin burned, and inflamed me. She leaned in, caught my lower lip with her teeth. Bit down. I smelled citrus and flowers. Tasted Monica on my tongue.

"Say my name, David," she whispered. "Come on."

Her breath swept over me like a caress and I had a hard time finding my voice. "Lottie."

She purred, satisfied. "Do you remember our first time? Hmm?"

"The hut," I breathed.

"Yes." She purred again. "You were Makra." She pressed her lips to mine. "I was Lassia."

"Yes." My brain was short-circuiting with too many memories. My body was betraying me, aching to give in. Then a sly smile curled the corners of her lips and the spark of something naughty but perceptive lit in her eyes.

"I followed you to your hut and seduced you." Her tongue traced the small scar on my shoulder. "It was your first time with a female on top. Remember?"

I did. She was full of fire and desire and everything I'd never had before.

"You still love me on top," she said. "You love to watch me. Watch me now, David."

She was drawing me in deeper, increasing the pace. I remembered the desire, growing as hot and potent as the fire inside my hut. She was urging me on, and I felt the pressure build.

"You aren't like the other females," I said.

Because she was bold enough to look me in the eyes and challenge me. "No, I'm not, David. But I can show you who I am if you just let me."

They were the same words Lassia had spoken a long time ago.

She shifted, bringing me in as deep as I could go then pulled back. Beads of sweat rolled off my chest and my body went rigid beneath her. I was close.

She brought me in deep again. "Say my name, David. Look at me and say my name."

I did, but saw only eyes ringed with green. Her name came out with frustration. "Lottie."

A familiar pulse ran through her and fired into me.

My eyes stayed fixed with hers as she renewed the slow torture, prolonging the rhythm, working me until I was insane for the finish. I was hovering in the red zone, feeling the heat, the sweat, the fire building between us, not caring that she had the control and that I'd been crazed into submission.

Her mouth crushed into mine. Her body thrust deep and hard.

I moaned.

Satisfaction appeared on her face and colored her voice. "Let yourself go, David. For once, don't fight the feelings."

I closed my eyes, enjoying her heat and hunger. She brought my hand between her legs again, this time using the both of us to get her to climax. I remembered how much she loved this. How she loved to experiment. Anywhere. In the bedroom, in the bathroom, on the floor. In the park, the car, the beach. By the fire. In the hut. Under a bearskin in the fields, not caring if anyone could see.

She had a voice like a whispering wind. A body that fit with mine. A spirit that was bold and brazen. She was courageous.

And she was mine.

I drew her to me, scraped my teeth against her bare skin, and bit down. She shuddered, and I bit again. Her scent surfaced, penetrated me, fused us together.

Warm and woodsy.

I opened my eyes and saw Lottie looking down. Not Monica. Lottie. I could smell her. Sense her. Taste her. She was inside my blood, my soul, tied to the primitive part of me that needed to take her and mark her as mine. I saw her long black hair, beautiful mouth, and loving dark eyes.

She smiled. Sighed. Kissed my lips. "Welcome back, David."

Chapter 34

Late the next afternoon, Lottie and I were sitting in my SUV in front of Monica's house, on our way to my mom's for dinner. We'd spent the entire night, morning, and afternoon in bed doing what we did best. Not once did I sense or see Monica.

She was truly gone.

I studied the purple and blue gingerbread trim, wraparound porch, and cobblestone walk and the way the late afternoon sun played up golden shadows over the Victorian. The house looked serene but the memories were there, buried behind locked doors and closed curtains.

My breath hitched as grief began to creep in.

Lottie took my hand. "You okay?"

I nodded. Though I'd never be the same.

"You loved her," she said. "In your own way and for the relationship that it was, you loved her."

My eyes burned and I closed them.

"I'm so sorry," she whispered, stroking my fingers.

I brought her hand to my mouth and kissed it. "And I love you more than anything. Always have. Always will."

She smiled, leaned in, and kissed me. "I know. I love you, too."

I went back to looking at Monica's house. Checked the mailbox, read the house number—202—and sighed. I'd never paid attention to that detail until now. I wondered what else I'd overlooked when I was with Monica. The things that seemed trivial at the time but important now. My mind flashed to the drugs I'd recently found in her closet and the so-called deliveries that arrived when we were having the affair.

"You ever wonder why we choose to see only certain things in people and not others?" I asked.

"We see what we want to see because of our need for love and belonging, David. It's a fundamental part of human nature that keeps the species procreating."

I gave her a double take.

Lottie shrugged. "It's true."

"But if you ignore something important," I said, "that can make life difficult. Or more difficult than it has to be."

"Yes, and at some point you can't ignore anymore. Even in the most extreme situations, a person will recognize that they have to open their eyes and take a good, hard look at their relationship. And that's when the most important decisions are made."

I lost interest in the house and gave Lottie all my attention. "You've made the decision to put up with a lot lately. With me."

"Yes, I have." She squeezed my hand. "And it was worth every minute of it."

"Was Makra worth it?" I asked.

She smiled again. "More than you probably realize."

"I wonder if Cilla thought Makra was worth it."

"If you ever see her—or rather, Monica—in another life again, you can ask her, David."

I laughed at the thought, one I would have scoffed at days

ago, but the laugh died when another thought moved in. "I still don't understand the point of a past life, Lottie. All it's done for me is make me feel like shit. I keep comparing what went wrong, and trying to figure out how to keep what went wrong from happening again."

"You can't compare any of your lives, David—and yes, you've had more than just the one because I remember enough for the both of us. The point is, there may be similarities but they're not the same. That's a very important lesson you'll have to learn as you continue through your regression. Just give it time. I will work with you on this."

Lottie and I sat in silence for a while until Lottie broke it with a question. "When do you expect to hear more news on Ada?"

I shook my head. "I hate that I still have no leads to go on. And why is Ada so important to Damian anyway? It's like—" I paused, trying to get the jumble of facts in my head to make sense. "It's like he wasn't interested in her until now and that doesn't add up."

Lottie shrugged. "From what Nat told you, it seems he's always been protective of her. Maybe that's what he's doing again. Protecting her."

"I don't know. Maybe."

But my gut said that wasn't the entire story.

I put the car into gear and pulled away from the curb, watching the house grow more distant in the rear view mirror as I drove. In time, maybe my memories of Monica would fade away in just the same way. Gradually and with grace.

But always there, if I chose to find them again.

By the time we got to Mom's, I was feeling a little more

settled but still not ready to go inside. Lottie unbuckled and started playing with the hair at the nape of my neck. It tickled, but it felt good.

"We never really talked about it," she said, "but I'm curious about what you remembered about Makra and Lassia."

I released my seatbelt, killed the lights, and turned to her. I liked that I was able to get my mind on other things. "It's sketchy. I see stuff in bits and pieces, only." I told her about my relationship with Cilla, how much I loved my daughter, and how I'd never noticed Lassia until she came to my hut that night. "I grew to love Lassia very much," I said, "and was devastated when she died." I paused and added, "Ayak loved Lassia very much, too."

Lottie went still and for a while I thought she was going to say something about that. But she let it go. We were still too raw over Monica and Ada, trying to deal with the aftermath and unanswered questions and bringing up Galen, through Ayak, would stir up stuff we didn't need. And that was the difference between Monica and Galen now. In this life, Monica could never return and challenge what Lottie and I shared.

But Galen would.

I shut off the engine and nodded toward the house. "We should go in."

Lottie got out and walked with me up to the front door. I opened it for her and we went inside. Mom came running down the hall, her tie-dyed dress fluttering as she moved, and covered us with hugs and kisses, most of her affection directed at Lottie.

"Jelly Bean," she said, squeezing Lottie tight. "I'm so very happy you're safe and with us again."

"So am I," Lottie said, relaxing into the embrace.

With one final kiss, Mom encouraged Lottie into the living room with the rest of the family, grabbed my arm, and dragged me into the kitchen. An unopened bottle of Copas Añejo sat on the table with two highballs. She cracked the seal, poured, said *l'cha·im*, and we both downed our drinks. In the background, Jimi Hendrix sang about Purple Haze.

"How are you, David?" she asked, refilling the glasses. "Are you keeping it together? Is everything okay?"

I sipped and smacked my lips, savoring the liquor as it warmed my mouth and throat. "It will be eventually," I said, and the heaviness I'd been feeling over Monica's death and Ada's disappearance once again rammed into me like a truck at full speed. I poured more Copas and tossed it down, wanting to dull the pain.

"That was a hell of a price for you to pay to get Lottie back," Mom said, shoving my glass out of reach. She caressed my cheek and smiled with sympathy. "Ready to talk about it?"

"Not really." I reached for the glass, thought about pouring a third, and changed my mind.

Mom pushed a painted cookie jar in front of me. "Would you prefer my brownies instead?"

I had to laugh. "No. Not today."

"Okay. More for me then." She took one out, broke it in half, and ate the piece in one bite, then walked around the table and stood by me. "You are a very brave man, David. The bravest I've ever known. But that little voice inside your head that's kicking your ass for decisions made or not made is a useless one."

"Yeah. I know." Didn't stop the voice from bitching at me,

though.

"You are a fighter, but you also must learn patience." Mom kissed my cheek. "Still, as *Einarr*, you will always battle for what you want. Always fight for what you believe in. And that's what separates you from so many other males."

The blood drained from my face and I pulled away. "What did you just say?"

"My brownies are for more than just fun, Bubbala." She waved at the air as if it held magical secrets, and pinched my cheeks. "I use them to channel my essence and past experiences." She shrugged. Tossed down more liquor. "Besides, I spoke to Lottie earlier this morning and she filled me in on what I needed to know."

"What?"

"Oh don't give me that look. We discovered that we have lots of memories to share." My face froze in shock and my mother tilted her head, regarding me. "I was there, David. I watched you grow into a strong, red-blooded male. Watched you learn to hunt and become a true warrior. I knew when you mated with Cilla and was there to help birth your daughter. I was also there when you announced that you were taking Lassia as your Primary. And, I was there to comfort you when she died."

"I don't remember—"

"Shhh." She pressed a finger to my mouth. "It will come to you when it's time and someday, when you're ready, I'll share everything you need to know." Mom straightened, went to the oven, and pulled out baked ziti with oven mitts. "Now, take this into the dining room and tell everyone that dinner's ready."

I sat on the stool, stunned into silence.

"By the gods already," she said, "get dinner in there before it gets cold."

I carefully took the mitts and the hot dish from her and numbly did as I was told. Just before I got into the dining room, Mom grabbed my arm.

"By the way, David." She looked up at me with a conspiratorial but pleased look on her face. "It's good to know you still thrill Lottie in the sack."

I grimaced, wondering what my mother knew about my sex life, and decided not to ask.

When dinner was almost done and we were on our third bottle of wine, my cell rang. Caller ID displayed MD's number. I looked at Dad and told him I was taking the call. Chris glared at me. My sisters complained about my bad manners and demanded to know why I could take a call at the table when they couldn't. Mom told them to shut up.

"I want you to know that we finished your cleanup, Bellotti," MD said. "Any evidence that might have pointed back to you about recent events has been removed."

Good.

"I'm sorry about what happened," she said, "and now that the op has been officially handed over to the government, we're ready to move on. I expect you back in two weeks, maybe earlier, focused and ready to go. You're going to lead a team in the Middle East for a couple of months. Tension is increasing and becoming more dangerous to the general population, and we've been working with the government to stem the trouble. So you're in. See you in November."

She ended the call. I shoved the phone back into my jeans and told Lottie what MD had said. I told her I had to head out again in two weeks but didn't mention anything more about the next op. This was a given. This was the arrangement we had, for good or bad, and I didn't bring to the front those times I would be away from her, and in a dangerous place and situation.

"Such a treacherous job," Mom muttered while she spooned out a second helping for herself.

I gave Lottie a long look and rolled my eyes. She gave me a pointed one in return and said, "You'd miss your family if you didn't have them, David. Always remember that." She inched in a little closer. "We don't have to go away on vacation anymore if you don't want to. I know you'll want a home base while you try to find Ada."

"No." I kissed her. "I made a promise. Besides, I'll have my phone. I can work with Nat while we're away, and if I get a lead we'll follow it. That could mean one day away for us or ten, but I can't deny you this." I sipped wine, thinking about how a vacation might play out. "So where do you want to go? No limits."

"Really?" Lottie went still, thinking. "I always wanted to go to France. I want to see the countryside and Champagne and the Riviera. I want to lose myself in all that romance."

"Even though you know we may have to drop everything to get Ada instead?"

"Yes."

I refilled my wine glass and Lottie's, and handed hers over. We clinked and I said, "To France."

"And Ada," Lottie added.

I nodded.

"You know," Mom said, "your brother Chris was

conceived in France. On a backstreet in the Latin Quarter." She went on to share the story and I chugged down more wine, hoping the liquor would dull the details I didn't want to know and the images I didn't want to see.

"Those wheels are turning in your head again, David," Lottie said. "Don't be so hard on Rita. We had our own good time in that back alley in New Orleans. Remember?"

My eyes grazed her low cut blouse and the pink bra underneath. "God, yes." It lasted five minutes. And was the hottest sex in my life. "Can we do that again?"

Lottie gave me a grin that promised a back alley and a hell of a lot more.

I started fantasizing about the things we'd do, but the fantasy got killed when I realized we'd left out one important detail. "How are we going to spend time in France if you have to go back to work?"

"Yeah. About that." Lottie toyed with her glass. "I haven't gone through my client list and cleaned it out like Stuart Hanley wants. So, I suspect I'll be out of a job come the end of the month. I guess that means I'll have the free time to vacation."

"You know you don't have to work if you don't want to," I started to say, and then I bit my tongue because I knew better than to play the protective male. Lottie loved her independence and would live by it until the day she died. "Sorry. Bad habit."

"I do have my own career, David, just like you do."

"I know. I know."

"And I've been thinking," she said, picking at a piece of bread, "of starting my own practice after all."

"Really?" This was good. She'd been talking about doing

that for a while now. "Any idea what kind of practice?"

"I'm thinking of working with past life regression and sharing what I've learned. I want to help people like me, like us, who need it. I've been making connections along the way and I think they'd be willing to offer guidance to get me started."

"I just might be first on your client list."

Lottie's hand went to my thigh. "You just can't help yourself, David. No matter how hard you fight it, you always manage to get sucked into my psychoanalysis."

I kissed her, recognizing how lucky I was to have this woman in my life. She was everything to me, and always had been. And I swore I'd protect her and keep her in my heart and blood and soul. Forever.

I drew my lips across her neck, breathed in that warm, woodsy scent I loved so much, and bit her gently.

Mine.

My phone rang again.

This time it was Galen. "We need to talk, Bellotti."

"Not now, Galen. I'm with my family." I looked around at the expectant faces at the table, eavesdropping and wanting more.

"I think you'll be interested in what I have to tell you," Galen said, and there was a hint of something in his voice that made me sit up and Lottie lean in to listen. "I'm in Australia."

"Galen, I'm not interested in this—"

"*White Rain*, Australia."

Lottie and I went silent. We both knew the name, and we both knew its significance.

"I am watching Damian and Ada walk into a hotel," Galen

added. "They're here, Bellotti, and if you want Ada back you'd better get here, too. I can't touch her or get close to her, but you as her father can."

"Galen, if this is some kind of scam to—"

"Your daughter is here, and she needs her *foar*. Now more than ever."

Galen hung up.

I lowered my cell and saw conviction and promise in Lottie's dark eyes.

A NOTE FROM THE AUTHOR

I look for any opportunity to make stuff up. I think anything that can't so easily be explained is worth an extra look and often makes a great story. I love red wine, scotch, sunrises, Ancient Egypt, the beach—and probably a host of other stuff that would take too much real estate to talk about. The youngest of five children, I live with my husband and son on Long Island. And, in my next life, if I haven't moved on to somewhere else, I want to be an astronomer. I'm fascinated with the night skies almost as much as I'm fascinated with ancient Egypt.

If you love social media, you can also find me on Facebook at https://www.facebook.com/Terri.Ponce.Author and on Twitter at https://twitter.com/TerriPonce. I'm a member of member of Sisters in Crime and Mystery Writers of America, and you can read about me at http://terriponce.com/. Come visit. I'd love to hear from you!

I truly hope you enjoyed Covet. I have a love affair going with David Bellotti's character, and this story begged to be written. And let me tell you, I had the best time doing it.

All my very best,
Terri

PS – stay on the lookout for more stories in the Past Life Series, and a few other surprises along the way!